JOURNEYING HOME

JOURNEYING HOME

a novel

EMILY SAXE NYDAM

Hildebrand Books

an imprint of W. Brand Publishing

NASHVILLE, TENNESSEE

Hildebrand Books an imprint of W. Brand Publishing
j.brand@wbrandpub.com
www.wbrandpub.com

Cover design by JuLee Brand | designchik

Journeying Home / Emily Saxe Nydam — 1st Edition

Available in Paperback, Kindle, and eBook formats.
Paperback ISBN: **979-8-89503-002-8**
eBook ISBN: **979-8-89503-003-5**
Library of Congress Control Number: 2024922006

Readers will be enthralled . . . Touching tribute to resilience and tenacity, spanning generations of women."
–*BookLife/Publishers Weekly* Review

Emily Saxe Nydam's JOURNEYING HOME is an absorbing family drama that successfully explores how the lives of two women separated by 100 years of history intertwine.
–Craig Jones for *IndieReader*

Readers of Kristin Hannah will feel at home with this novel, but the immersive historical setting, the quality of the writing, and the story's emotional sweep reminded me more of Amor Towles, Elizabeth Strout and Anthony Doerr. *Journeying Home* is a book to savor and cherish!
–Olivia Noble, *NetGalley* Review

I love historical fiction it has always been one of my favourite genres since I was a little girl and it is because of books like this. I couldn't put it down, it is well written with well developed characters that I completely and utterly became lost in. I loved it. –Kirsty Montgomery, *NetGalley* Review

A fantastic historical fiction. Loved every minute of it. Beautifully written and explored. Will definitely look for more books by Emily Saxe Nydam! –Lo Mah, *NetGalley* Review

Dual timeline, full of adversity and courage, purpose and heartbreak. A well written, compelling historical fiction novel. –Kathleen Ryder, *NetGalley* Review

A great dual time book, that delves between different generations, a great historical fiction with great characters.
–Catherine Laverick, *NetGalley* Review

I loved reading this book! All the reviews comparing the writing to Kristin Hannah are 100% right, it is a beautifully written story with two timelines perfectly woven together. I was so invested in the characters that I didn't want to put it down! I would absolutely recommend this novel to anyone looking for their next read. –Amazon Reviewer

CONTENTS

For Myra, Polly, Edith, and Lee, who always believed in me.

Especially Polly.

Houses have character. Charm. Don't they? Houses are our comfort. And we take care of them. We speak of them almost as we would a difficult child. Needs some shaping up, of course, a little straightening out here, a little tidying up there, but, well, still a member of the family. Even if not always liked, certainly always loved.

But what is a house, really? It is a carefully arranged, but thoroughly inanimate construction of concrete and plaster, framing and sheetrock, pipes and paint. It has a history, even a future, but no awareness. It can't remember, and it can't predict. It can't have an opinion as to who should never come together, and who should find one another in a shower of romance and live happily ever after. It cannot keep secrets.

Wishful thinking that it could.

PROLOGUE

"Will there be more bunnies today?" the little girl asked, snuggling further into her companion's lap.

The silver-haired woman shook her head, carefully noncommittal. It was never helpful to raise anyone's hopes baselessly. There might be bunnies, yes, but then again, there might not.

"Let's keep watching the fence. See that dark corner? Behind the bird bath? The bunnies nest there, because they think no one can see them. Sometimes a little one will pop out and its mama has to rescue it. It might be a little while, though," she added. "And we have to be very quiet," she warned.

The little girl settled in some more. "I can be quiet," she said, solemnly.

They sat together on the steps for a little while, both pairs of eyes trained on the back fence. It was, indeed, very quiet. Just the hum of the bees in the hedge, and the uneven drone of grown-up voices from inside the house. Although the older woman was fairly sure she knew what the voices were up to, she had no desire to go inside and join in. It wouldn't make any difference anyway. And it was so peaceful in the garden. There would be plenty of time later to learn her fate. She hugged the little girl in her lap. This moment might not come again. She pushed aside an intrusive feeling of resentment. Why had this little girl not been brought to visit before? It didn't matter. She was here now.

Then, suddenly, a flash of something, vivid red. It came gracefully to rest on the rim of the birdbath. They both saw it. The little girl gasped with pleasure.

And then they heard it. A clear, crystalline song, descending. The red flash paused on the edge of the stone basin, posing, just long enough for the little girl to want more. Another burst of crystalline song, and then . . . gone. As quickly as it had arrived.

The little girl turned her face up inquisitively to her companion's.

"Cardinal," the older woman said. "It's a cardinal. They visit here quite a lot. They love the birdbath. Don't they have them where you live?"

The little girl shook her head, a little sadly. "I've never seen one," she said. The older woman thought for a moment. "Come with me," she said.

The two of them walked back through the house, past the group of serious-faced grown-ups arranged around the dining room table, into the living room with the bay window and the window seat. The older woman rummaged around in one of the drawers under the seat cushions.

"Is that where you keep your treasures?" The little girl asked.

The older woman nodded and smiled. "And my secrets," she said.

"Do you have secrets?" the little girl asked, clearly quite taken aback that a grown-up with silver hair might have something she wished to keep hidden.

The older woman nodded. "Of course," she said, continuing to look through the drawer.

Rummaging finally successful, she pulled out a picture book. "Here it is," she sighed. She held it carefully.

How many years since she'd looked at it? Too many to count. But this felt right. She sat on the window seat, patted the cushion beside her. "See?" she said, showing the little girl the cover of the book–an artist's rendering of a scarlet-feathered bird framed against snow-dusted pine branches.

"That's what we saw. A cardinal. They're very special birds."

The little girl was quiet, almost reverent. Finally, a whisper. "It's beautiful," she said. "Will more come today?"

"Sometimes they come to the birdbath, and sometimes they come to the big tree right outside this window," the older woman said. "If we sit here for a while and keep watching the tree, I think we might see some coming to nest for the night. The tree is where they like to sleep." And suddenly a memory almost overtook her. Of sitting with someone years ago, just exactly this way.

"Bunnies too?" The little girl asked.

"Maybe," the older woman said. "Maybe."

CHAPTER ONE

LIZZY

> **DARK, DARKER, DARKEST**
> Darkness has degrees.
> Gradients.
> A horse's stall? Dark. Familiar.
> A barnyard? Darker, but daunting only for its unseen obstacles.
> But then.
> Darkest. Narrow stairs lead up to a void.
> A room so black that
> I cannot see to find a way out.
> Will I?
> Can I?
> Find it?
> —Elizabeth Porter, undated

Winter 1906–Wytheville, Virginia

Lizzy couldn't remember a time when she didn't dread the dark.

Every night was the same. At dusk, there was supper. They would sit around the table, all holding hands, and Mama would pray softly, thanking the Lord for his bounty. Lizzy would close her eyes and try to feel grateful, but she didn't, really. There never seemed to be very much bounty on the table, however heartfelt Mama's prayers. When she was younger, Lizzy had offered up her own silent requests as well, in the hope that, if more prayers were sent his way, they might have a better chance of reaching his ears. But nothing ever changed, and she gave up asking.

And then, of course, there was later. The nighttime. Lizzy used to pray about that too. But those prayers never seemed to reach him either.

"Lizzy!" Mama said, her soft voice no less intense for its lack of volume. She might as well have been shouting. "What have you been up to? Get that table laid. Your papa will be inside in no time at all."

"Yes, Mama," Lizzy said, getting up from her stool near the fire and carefully placing her dog-eared magazine under it. The pages had been turned and scrutinized so many times that the very paper seemed to be growing thin. And its gently disintegrating pages were becoming increasingly less effective at their secondary task: concealing the scraps of paper that Lizzy had taken to calling her journal.

She'd read about keeping a journal in a magazine just like this one. You were supposed to have a pretty lavender or pink notebook, with a special pen, to write down all your most private and special thoughts. You needed the notebook to collect your thoughts and write them down, so there would be a record of your life. Lizzy had no notebook, and the scraps of paper were ragged. But they were a record of her life to date, such as it was. And sometimes, there were a few lines that weren't really anything all. Just pieces of thoughts. She hoped all the page scraps were tucked safely inside.

"I don't know why you waste your time with those magazines," Mama said, shaking her head. "There's far too much to be done without you daydreaming, reading about things you'll never do and places you'll never see. Where do you get hold of them, anyway? You'd best not be stealing them from somewhere. I'll hear about it, you can be sure."

"I've told you, Mama," Lizzy said, patiently, as though she were addressing a child. "Mr. Johnny in the post office saves them for me. He says they're extras that don't get claimed. He doesn't want any money for them. He just says he wants them to go to a good home. I'm not stealing," she added. "I've told you."

"Well, let's have less time spent on reading things that won't do you any good, and more time spent on getting supper ready. You know how your papa is."

Lizzy certainly did. She took the plates from the sideboard and starting laying the table. There was no point in asking what was for supper. She could smell it. Some sort of stew, more water than anything else, she suspected. She hoped that at least there was some potato. She thought she'd seen a few left in the basket in the cellar. Enough for a few more meals, anyway. Lizzy didn't know how they were going to make it through the rest of the winter. She supposed they'd be relying on church charity, and not for the first time. Papa seemed to be drinking more and bringing home less with every year.

"Addie, Essie—help your sister," Mama hissed from her place at the stove. "I've told you. Papa will be inside any minute."

"Yes, Mama," came the chorus from both younger girls. They had been playing some sort of doll game, quietly murmuring to each other in the corner of the small, one-room farmhouse, but when Mama called, they snapped to attention. Addie took the water pitcher and, wrapping herself up in her shawl, ran outside to fill it at the pump.

She had been entrusted with the water pitcher only a few months ago, on her tenth birthday. Clearly, the responsibility for the water pitcher felt to Addie like a graduation of sorts—from childhood to young woman. Having recently herself turned twelve, Lizzy wasn't at all sure "young woman" was really something to aspire to. But seeing Addie so proud of herself made her smile. Essie ran to Mama to give her a hug. At six, she was the youngest, and she seemed to feel hugging was the best use of her skills. Essie was Mama's favorite, Lizzy knew. It didn't matter, though. When Papa came inside for supper, there were no favorites. It was each for herself.

The door opened, and Addie ran back inside, trying not to slosh the water from the pitcher onto the floor. A blast of cold air followed her in.

Then, Papa.

He entered the little room like an enormous hound, coming to investigate a too-small cage and finding itself, once inside, trapped. Lizzy stood ready to take his coat and gloves. It was best if she was there, waiting, not needing to be asked. His boots left giant-size footprints on the floor. Even from across the room, Lizzy could feel Mama stiffen. Supper was about to begin.

As usual, Papa didn't say much. A few grunts, as he sat down at his place at the head of the table. Mama reached out, and they all clasped hands together. It was one of the few moments of connection that Lizzy could remember or predict.

Mama ladled the meager stew into bowls, and they ate in silence. Lizzy had been looking forward to the possibility of potato, but she suddenly found the prospect of supper a little off-putting. She hadn't been feeling herself lately, and the stew just didn't smell right. She pushed her bowl discreetly toward Addie, nodding to her sister to go ahead. Addie seemed to be getting a little taller every week these days, and she'd been looking so awfully thin. It seemed silly to waste a perfectly good portion. Addie looked around furtively, and then moved her own bowl to the side, sliding Lizzy's into its place. Mama saw, shook her head almost imperceptibly. But it was too late. Papa saw too. Lizzy wasn't sure how she could be berated for sharing her meal with her sister, but she figured Papa could find a way.

He did.

"Are you not eating your supper?" Papa asked, suddenly animated and zeroing in on the transfer. "What's the matter with you, girl? You think your sister's not getting enough? You think I'm not bringing enough home to feed my family?" He grabbed the bowl, and Addie started to cry. Lizzy refused to give him the satisfaction. Essie looked confused. Mama's face was expressionless.

Papa gazed around the table, fury suffusing his face, making them wait.

Then, a quick movement, almost too fast to be really seen. Papa swept the bowl off the table, onto the floor. The bowl was small, but the shattering crash was deafening.

"If Lizzy don't want it, then no one gets it." Papa had both hands on the table, as if he were daring any one of them to move.

None of them did.

"Get me my bottle, girl," he said, turning toward Lizzy. She got up from the table and ran to his coat on the hook, praying silently that the bottle in the deep front pocket was still full. Full meant that there was some chance Papa would pass out in front of the fire, quieted for at least a little while.

The bottle gave a satisfying slosh–still at about three-quarters, she guessed. Lizzy breathed a sigh of relief. It would have been her fault somehow, she knew, had it been emptier. She brought it back to the table, along with a glass. Papa waved the glass away, retiring to his chair by the fireplace. Another good sign. The liquor seemed to go down quicker without a glass getting in the way.

Papa turned his chair toward the fire, shifted his position a little, and looked around the room, as though daring something else to catch his fury. He caught sight of Lizzy's little stool on the other side of the fireplace, the magazine, with its concealed treasure, lying underneath it. He pointed to it.

"What's that?" he asked. Lizzy knew that he knew what it was. "What else do you all have to do all day but keep this place looking neat?" he asked, almost as though he were starting a conversation about the price of corn.

"I'm sorry, Papa," Lizzy said, scrambling to fetch the magazine and get it out of Papa's line of sight.

"Give it to me," he said, still calm.

"I'll put it in the attic," Lizzy said, starting to stammer. "I'm s-s-s-orry it's downstairs."

"Give it to me," he said, again.

Lizzy handed it to him.

And he threw it into the fire. Leaned back in his chair, closed his eyes, bottle still tightly in hand. Little flames started making their way toward the edges of the pages, but they didn't seem to quite catch. Papa, already fairly well under the influence, had missed the center of the blaze.

Lizzy looked at him for a moment. *I will not cry,* she said to herself. *He will not see me cry.* She didn't dare show much emotion, because then he would know that he had pierced her carefully constructed armor of apparent indifference. He was no better than a whiskey-fueled bully, and all bullies give up and look elsewhere if they raise no response.

Anyway, it wasn't over yet. There was a good chance she might be able to rescue the magazine and the paper scraps hidden inside once Papa passed out. She'd managed that before. She just had to hope that the scraps of paper stayed tucked safely in, unconsumed by the flames. She could get more magazines from Mr. Johnny, but the scraps of paper were irreplaceable.

She motioned to Addy. Time to clean up, rinse the dishes, put them away. Mama was already in her chair, pretending to do the mending and ignoring the confrontation. There were chores to do, and it would be dark soon.

It had turned quite chilly by the time Lizzy and Addie finished clearing up. Addie sat back down with Essie and the dolls. They both knew to stay quiet. Lizzy went out to the barn to check on Ralph and the cows. There was no moon.

Lizzy picked her way across the yard. She wished she'd brought a lantern. She had to admit, though, that the scene with Papa had rattled her badly enough that she'd barely remembered to put on her shawl. And she worried about what might be waiting for her later. Sometimes a scene at dinner seemed to satisfy Papa somehow, but sometimes, well . . . *It doesn't bear thinking about*, she told herself. *And there's no sense worrying about it. It will happen or it won't, and there's nothing I can do about it.*

She could hear Ralph softly nickering for her in his stall as she carefully felt her way into the barn. *You're *hoping for an apple,* she thought, and shook her head sadly. "Just hay for you tonight," she whispered to the horse. "I'm sorry. I wouldn't mind an apple either." Ralph whinnied in mild disappointment. But he turned to the hay without further complaint.

She made sure the cows were fed and watered, and then she stood for a while stroking Ralph's neck. He seemed happy to have her there, even without treats, and his sturdy presence was a comfort. But in spite of her initial success at putting Papa out of her mind, her worry kept returning. She found herself thinking back, trying to remember. When did it begin? Not for herself. It didn't matter for her anymore. But Lizzy was starting to feel a rising panic about Addie.

Had Lizzy been nine? Ten, perhaps? She couldn't even remember the first time, really. She had only a vague memory of a searing, splitting pain, and blood on the sheets the next morning that she tried to hide. After a while, it became predictable. Lizzy would hear Papa begin to navigate the attic ladder, and she knew. She would try as hard as she could to empty her mind. There was no point in being present for this, and Lizzy had become an expert at drifting away. It was almost as though she could leave her own body for a while and just watch, floating somewhere above, a bystander. She didn't have to smell the whiskey, or feel her father's rough beard on her face, his hands on her body. And then, well. She didn't even want to put a name to it, but she knew what it was. She had grown up on a farm for goodness' sake. She always hoped Addie, in her own little bed in the other corner, might be asleep. She doubted it, though.

And Addie was now ten. Addie had been so proud, and Mama had even managed to make a cake to celebrate the occasion. Lizzy had wanted to be happy for Addie, but she couldn't be. She was too terrified on Addie's behalf. Would Papa move on?

Lizzy had bled for the first time along about Thanksgiving last, and she had a sense that Mama might have told him. Perhaps to warn him that now there could be consequences? Lizzy couldn't be sure. There had never been any real help from that quarter. Sometimes, Lizzy felt angry. Mama *must* know what Papa was doing. But when Lizzy had tried to say something, anything at all, Mama's eyes would lose focus, and she became vague. Telling Papa that Lizzy's cycles had started was a roundabout way of helping, Lizzy supposed, but she wondered that Mama hadn't thought things through. About how Lizzy's situation might affect Addie. Lizzy snorted quietly in disgust. Lizzy sensed that Mama had given up.

It was mid-January now. Papa hadn't climbed the attic ladder for her since right before Christmas. Was he thinking about moving on to Addie? Well, if he was, he hadn't done anything about it yet. Lizzy would have known. There were no secrets in the little attic room. She knew better, though, than to hope he might have changed. No. More likely, Mama's veiled warning had at last penetrated the haze of whiskey, and he had finally given some thought to consequences. What if, God forbid, he managed to leave his oldest daughter with child? That would be something difficult to hide, even on their isolated farm.

Consequences. Lizzy was suddenly struck by a thought. She hadn't bled since that first time in November. Were there consequences already? She was pretty familiar with what pregnancy looked like in a cow, but she had been too young to notice much when Mama was pregnant with Essie. She had to admit, though, that she had been a little queasy the last few weeks. And tonight. The potato. Just looking at it had made her want to turn away.

She shook her head, as though to shake off the possibility. It can't be, she told herself firmly. It just can't. She shivered, wishing yet again she had remembered the lantern as she walked back across the yard. She really hated the dark.

Back inside, it was as though the outbursts had never been. Mama was in her chair by the fire, eyes closed, having given up all pretense of sewing. There was not much light in the little house once night fell. Just the fire and the oil lamp in the corner. And although Mama never complained, Lizzy could tell that Mama was having trouble with close work lately. She paused often to squint, hold something up to the flame of the lamp, rub her eyes. Addie and Essie had moved to the table, Addie working through her sums, and Essie laboriously trying to copy out the alphabet. Papa looked to have fallen asleep in his chair, bottle still miraculously tight in his grip. It was quiet. Lizzy glanced at the fireplace. It was empty. Could Papa have poked the magazine into the flames? She didn't know, and asking was out of the question. Sometimes Papa only looked like he was asleep. She would have to wait for a safer opportunity to look for it.

Lizzy made her way over to Mama, gently took the mending out of her lap and put it back in the basket. Mama stirred, rubbed her eyes, patted Lizzy's hand.

"Good night, Mama," Lizzy whispered. She motioned to Essie, who obediently put her copybook away and went to find the pallet where she slept in Mama and

Papa's sleeping alcove. Mama would soon bank the fire. Papa, Lizzy fervently hoped, would spend the rest of the night in his chair. Addie put her sums away and rose from the table, and Lizzy took the lamp. They climbed the ladder to their attic room under the eave.

The night was chillier than usual, and Lizzy lay shivering for a while. She could sense Addie, awake as well, on the other side of the room. There were never enough blankets on cold nights like these.

"Addie," Lizzy whispered. "Come sleep with me. Bring your blanket. We'll be warmer." Addie dutifully scrambled over to Lizzy's bed. Being together helped, Lizzy thought. If she stayed close to Addie, she felt like she might almost banish the chill. And now there were two blankets, instead of one. She closed her eyes.

A few minutes passed. "Lizzy?" Addie whispered. "Are you awake?"

Lizzy answered by way of a squeeze. It wouldn't do to make too much noise.

"I saved your reading," Addie whispered again. "It's under Mama's sewing basket. It's not too burnt up."

Lizzy thought she might cry. It seemed like a simple thing, to poke the fire and carefully move something out of the flames, but with Papa, well, if you woke him up from his chair, there was no telling what the reaction would be. She hadn't known her sister was so brave. She gave Addie another squeeze.

"Thank you," she whispered.

"All those little white scraps, they weren't burnt up either," Addie said. "What are they for?"

So private! Those scraps were meant for no one but Lizzy. But Addie had taken such a chance to rescue them. She deserved an answer. "They're for my journaling," Lizzy whispered again.

"What's that?" Addie asked. "Journeying?"

Lizzy smiled and thought for a moment. Then, finally, she responded. "I write down things I think, and things I've done," she said.

Addie was quiet. So quiet that Lizzy thought she must have dropped off to sleep. But then she spoke again. "But sometimes, on some of those scraps, there's not much room—only enough for one or maybe two words. I can tell," Addie whispered proudly. "I can read almost as much as you! Anyway, you've done more than two words' worth of things, I bet," Addie said. "Don't you need more than scraps to write on?"

Lizzy thought for a moment. "Sometimes," she said, "I just put down pieces of things. Pieces of thoughts. Sometimes that's enough."

Once again, Addie fell silent. Lizzy knew she was considering what "pieces of thoughts" might be. Finally, Addie seemed to come to a conclusion. "Well, I thought you'd be sad to lose all that. I'm glad I could save it," she said, softly.

Lizzy hugged her. "I would have been very sad," she said. "Now hush. We don't want to wake Papa. Go to sleep."

A little later? An hour? More? Lizzy couldn't be sure. She opened her eyes with a start, not completely sure why she was awake. But the next moment made it clear. And for once, it was nothing to do with Papa. It was another pain entirely, and it was excruciating. She drew her knees up, gritted her teeth, and groaned, all involuntarily. She turned on her side, hoping that it would pass, not wanting to wake Addie. But after a few seconds, she felt Addie's warm hand on her shoulder.

"Lizzy?" Addie whispered. "What's wrong?"

"I don't know," Lizzy whispered back, trying not to cry out in pain. "Must have been something I ate for supper." She felt Addie's soft touch on her forehead, checking to see if she was feverish. She knew she wasn't.

Addie pulled her hand away. "You hardly ate any supper," she whispered back. "It can't be that. I'm going down to get Mama."

Lizzy heard Addie climb down the attic ladder. She kept her eyes closed–it just seemed easier to prepare for the onslaught if she could shut down all her senses except those focused on the pain. But she could still hear. She could tell that Addie was being as quiet as possible, so as not to disturb Papa. It was bad enough to get in his way when he was finishing the whiskey by the fire. No one wanted to involve him in anything in the middle of the night. She didn't hear what Addie said to Mama, but thankfully there was no sound from Essie, so clearly she was still sleeping. After a few moments, she heard Addie and Mama both coming up to the little attic. She couldn't help herself. She groaned again.

Mama pulled the blankets back. Lizzy held herself tightly, trying to draw her threadbare nightdress closer. She heard a sharp intake of breath. "Addie," Mama whispered. "Can you go get the extra wash towels from down in the kitchen?" Addie must have nodded yes, because Lizzy heard her scramble back down the ladder. Mama gently lifted Lizzy's night dress.

"You're bleeding," she whispered. "Must be your time?"

Lizzy nodded. "Must be," she managed, before the next wave of pain hit. It hadn't been this way the first time, though. This wasn't like the first time at all.

Mama didn't seem surprised. She just arranged the towels when Addie brought them up, and she stroked

Lizzy's head a little. The stroking was nice. If Lizzy could concentrate on Mama's cool hand, it seemed she could block out everything else more easily.

Lizzy didn't know how long it all lasted. She could only steel herself for each wave and ride it out. Addie fell asleep back in her own bed, and Mama curled up around Lizzy, as though she might be able to siphon away some of the pain just by staying close. That helped a little. Lizzy dozed.

The light brightened, and Lizzy opened her eyes. Mama was still asleep beside her, Addie still curled up across the room on her own. She heard Papa's heavy and still unsteady footsteps. Somehow, he had slept through it all. Lizzy was thankful for that.

He was going outside, Lizzy knew. First the out-house, then the pump. That was the pattern. She heard the water run outside, heard him open the door to come back in. The footsteps paused. Something must have felt odd. He must be wondering where Mama is, she thought. Then she heard the creak of his chair. Not odd enough to investigate further, Lizzy guessed, and she was grateful. He would probably fall back asleep for a while longer, and she would have time to gather herself.

The pain had not stopped, but it had eased. Lizzy felt drained. Mama had arranged the wash towels under Lizzy when Addie brought them up, and Lizzy could feel now they were cold and wet. She was afraid to look, but she couldn't help herself. In the still-grey light, the towels looked black. She could feel they were saturated. It was blood, she knew. She hoped it had slowed.

She fell back against the pillows and slept a little more, deeper this time, and so she didn't hear Mama and Addie climb downstairs and put breakfast on the table.

She didn't hear Papa leave the house to go pretend he was working on some long-neglected task in the barn. More than likely, the task consisted of contributing to the ever-growing pile of empty bottles in the back corner, past the stalls.

When Lizzy finally opened her eyes again, it seemed that Mama had found clean towels to put under her. She was dry, at least, and the evidence of the night removed. She climbed slowly and carefully down the attic ladder. It felt surreal to see Mama, Addie and Essie sitting around the table as though nothing had happened, and it was just an ordinary morning. Lizzy knew exactly what had happened and exactly who was to blame. She was only twelve. But she knew.

Slowly, over the next few months, Lizzy healed. Her cycles started again. And most amazingly, Papa stopped coming up the attic ladder. He didn't come for her anymore, and he didn't come for Addie. She wondered if Mama had taken a stand, but she doubted it. No, she thought, Mama didn't have enough courage to confront Papa with something so awful. Maybe Papa hadn't been asleep after all. Maybe he heard some of the commotion that night, suspected what had happened, and began to worry. Not so much about his daughter, as about the possibility that what he was doing to his daughter might at last come to someone's attention. Papa must have finally realized that a pregnant twelve-year-old would be just the kind of rumor that might draw someone up from town to see what might be going on, even if town was an hour's ride away.

And that was what made Lizzy angriest. She was grateful that Papa had finally found a level of depravity that even he had to step away from. Nevertheless, if she really examined the situation, it was quite obvious that there was no one within a reasonable distance who would even have the opportunity to notice. There was no doctor, no local magistrate. Not even a church within less than an hour's ride. Lizzy and Mama and Addie had to deal with this all on their own. Lizzy could have bled to death, and it might have been spring before anyone in the area had any idea. Lizzy felt blessed to have survived, but she was also angry, so angry, at the randomness of that outcome. She could just as easily have died, with no one the wiser. She had never felt so helpless.

There was one good thing, though, to come out of all of this. Papa never moved on to Addie. Lizzy was never sure why. Had he made a conscious decision to leave his girls alone? Was it just that the liquor finally got the better of him and he no longer cared? Or maybe God had finally heard her prayers. She knew Mama would have put the change down to God. Lizzy had her money squarely on the liquor.

CHAPTER TWO

GWEN

Cardinals are a rare combination of good looks and amazing sounds . . .

Cardinals, S. Tekiela, p. 5.

Now–Wayland, Massachusetts

By the time Gwen came across the envelope again, it had sat on her desk for quite a bit longer than it should have. Given that the desk and its contents were in the process of being dismantled, the delay was, frankly, to be expected. But when Gwen noticed it again, really noticed it, late on a hot summer Saturday afternoon, it had clearly been moved from pile to pile a few too many times. The heavy cream stock had lost much of its crisp sheen. There was no question but that it was looking a little worse for the wear. Gwen picked it up gingerly and swore under her breath.

"What's the date today?" she called out to Rob. In answer, she heard only a heavy thumping from upstairs in the attic. *He can't hear me,* she thought wearily. It had been a long day of cleaning out drawers and closets, organizing, dusting, vacuuming. They shouldn't have started on the attic so late, Gwen knew. But Rob couldn't spare much more time, and Gwen wanted to take advantage of every moment of help. Cindy, friend

AND real estate agent, wanted to put the house on the market as soon as possible, so as to make the most of the few short months before the holidays. Gwen was doing her best to make that happen, even though she had chosen perhaps the hottest possible weekend of the summer to finish the task. The ceiling fan in her little den was trying its mightiest, but the room still felt as though a cake could be baked in it, with no need for an actual oven. Envelope in hand, she rose from her chair and trudged to the foot of the stairs for what felt like the ninety-fifth time that day, calling out to Rob as she went.

"Do you know the date today?" she called up again, standing at the bottom of the main staircase. "We're still in August, right?" She suddenly felt the need for confirmation.

"Mom," Rob called back to her. She could just see his head poke out from the top of the attic ladder. He looked like he wanted to be almost anywhere else. "It's questions like these that make me worry about you." He was smiling, but only half joking, Gwen could tell. He paused for effect. "Yes, Mom, still August," he continued. "If it was September, which it will be soon, I wouldn't be here."

Gwen shook off the slightly patronizing tone. She knew he was just as hot and dusty as she was.

"I'm just asking because, well, I completely forgot about this," she called again. Then, more to herself than to him, "And I'm hoping I still have time."

Rob began climbing down, first the attic ladder, then the stairs. "There's always still time, Mom," he said, his tone softening a little. She couldn't tell if he meant his answer philosophically or literally, but either option was encouraging, and she decided not to inquire further. He continued, taking the envelope out of her hands and starting to pull out the contents. "What is it exactly that's making you hope for more time?" He turned the envelope over and scrutinized the return address. "Mason-Hall School of Nursing?" he read, clearly curious. "What do you have going on with a nursing school, Mom?"

"You know what?" Gwen replied, purposefully taking the envelope back. "This feels like a great topic for dinner. We should quit for the day. The house is looking pretty good. There's just a few boxes of stuff left in the attic, right? Dad's taken what he wants, so if you don't want it and I don't want it, I think most of what's left up there can probably be tossed anyway. No sorting required. Let's think about dinner." She could almost hear him thinking, if it was all going to be tossed anyway, why did Mom and Dad keep it in the first place? But he held his tongue.

"If you could just bring down those last few boxes up there and leave them in the hall? That way I can quickly check them, and I won't forget them up there," she said, hoping he wouldn't get too annoyed about going back up. Then, optimistic that bribery might be successful, she added, "I think there's a nice bottle of wine in the fridge. Can I tempt you with a glass while I go shower, and maybe you can work some of your cooking magic with one of those pasta boxes that's still in the cupboard?"

"Flattery will NOT work, Mom," he said, shaking his head. But he was already on his way to the kitchen. "I hope there's some red!" he called out. "And I hope the corkscrew hasn't been 'de-cluttered'!" A pause, and then the sounds of a corkscrew search, drawers opening and shutting.

"I have faith," she called back to him as she went upstairs to shower and change. "You'll find it!"

Rob called out again, just to be sure she knew he was not forgetting. "And I still want to know about that nursing school thing!" She smiled as she made her way upstairs. She knew he meant it. "Don't forget the attic boxes!" she called back.

Her bedroom was cool, a welcome refuge from the August heat. Although she didn't like admitting it, she had to concede that Robert had been right about upgrading the second floor with air conditioning. Robert had proposed many upgrades and construction projects over the years they had been married, and Gwen had been skeptical about most of them. Their approaches to construction projects mirrored their personalities. Robert assumed everything would work out for the best; Gwen, more cautious, always expected the worst. But right now, she lay on the bed, enjoying the cool air, fruit of her soon-to-be ex-husband's optimism. *I guess he was right about the A/C,* she thought. *But I was right about the marriage.*

She still couldn't quite believe that it was really over. But today's project was nothing if not proof. The real estate agent contract was signed, and the house was clean, de-cluttered, and ready for sale. It was going on the market as soon as Cindy could come give it a final once-over and put up the sign.

At least she wouldn't have to deal with changing her name. Robert *Smith*. It had always seemed so, well, unimaginative. Not her at all. She'd kept her own surname all these years. Robert had been annoyed, but he had let it go, with only a comment that *O'Neil* didn't seem that much of an improvement, and also that *Smith* didn't seem to bother her so much when it was the name that belonged to their son. Gwen chose not to engage on those points. *O'Neil* was her name, and that was that. She was grateful now that she had held her ground. One less detail to manage.

Gwen sighed. She had felt for months that something was different—off, somehow. Robert had seemed at first just a little distracted. She had assumed, even as he became increasingly distant, that his affection was constant, even if not displayed. After all, neither one of them had ever been particularly demonstrative. Gwen had wondered if perhaps he was going through some sort of mid-life crisis. She knew it was a clichéd explanation, but it was all she could come up with. And she could be patient. He would snap out of it. They could rekindle the spark, if they just tried.

Until, of course, one of her friends took her aside and told her (with the very best of intentions) that Robert and his office assistant were becoming known around town as an item. Clichéd indeed. She was the last to know. *Nothing like a law office to kickstart that spark*, Gwen thought, allowing herself a little bitterness. She finally worked up the courage to confront him in May. Right after Mother's Day. It wasn't so much that she needed courage to confront him—more that she needed to be sure she had the courage to deal with the answer.

And the answer was Melissa. Funny, Gwen had always liked that name. But not anymore. Melissa was not even thirty, with the flat stomach and perky breasts of a woman whose body had never known pregnancy. Ah well. Gwen wouldn't trade her son for anything. Including a flat stomach. OR perky breasts.

Gwen roused herself off the bed, opened the closet door and decided to confront the reflection in the full-length mirror, as opposed to her usual approach of carefully avoiding any eye contact with her mirrored self. Truthfully? Not as bad as she had expected for her fifty-plus years. A shower and a change of clothes, and she felt she could easily pass for forty-five. She shook her head, a little ruefully. What did forty-five look like, anyway? Her hair was still long, never cut into a matronly bob like so many of her friends had done, and mostly brown even without the help of L'Oréal. Her eyes, her smile–the same as ever. The pink shorts and orange tank top were perhaps not the most flattering, but what the hell, she'd been working all day in the attic, and Rob hadn't told her the outfit was embarrassing. Which she was fairly sure he would have, if it was. He was not one to mince words. She decided to give herself a passing grade. Maybe even more than a pass. A good, solid B plus. That felt fair.

As she laid out some fresh clothes on the bed, she saw the envelope again, where she'd left it. She opened it carefully and checked the date. She saw with relief that she really did have time. The ceremony wasn't until Labor Day. The school was hosting a gala celebration to honor some of its more distinguished graduates. Her own great aunt among them.

She wasn't sure how the school had tracked her down. A vague memory surfaced of promising her father she'd continue his annual donation to the school when he'd gone. She'd been diligent at first about continuing the tradition, but now she couldn't remember when she'd last written a check to them. In any case, they had managed to find her, and she was now (except for Rob, of course) the only family member left. Unless she went, there would be no one to stand and nod graciously at the mention of her great aunt's name. Elizabeth Porter. Aunt Elizabeth, who had been a nurse in World War I. That was how her father always spoke of her, Gwen remembered with a smile. "You remember Aunt Elizabeth? Who was a nurse in World War I? And a writer too." She remembered with a start that he always added that. She had never given her aunt's accomplishments much thought.

Although the passage of time seemed to render the Great War almost quaint, a storybook tale, the invitation to the Mason-Hall school ceremony was real enough. Distinguished graduates, she mused. Distinguished how? She wished her father had told her more.

CHAPTER THREE

LIZZY

> **FENCES**
> *Green around me. All alive, and*
> *Blue above me. Soft.*
> *Sheltering, enveloping.*
> *An emerald patchwork.*
> *Safety.*
> *Illusory.*
> *What I know is that*
> *I cannot*
> *Will not*
> *Stay.*
> –Elizabeth Porter, 1916

Spring 1908–Wytheville, Virginia

"Anything for us today, Mr. Johnny?" Lizzy asked as she made her way up to the wooden counter. Mama had always told her that once she turned sixteen, she could ride Ralph into town by herself, to fetch what sugar and flour they might be able to afford, and to check in with Mr. Johnny at the post office for the mail. But Mama had recently relaxed the age requirement. Papa rarely came out of the barn these days, and Mama was running things at home with only her girls for help. She had no time to take a morning or afternoon to ride into town.

So the town runs fell to almost-fourteen-year-old Lizzy, and she was thrilled. Mr. Peterson at the general store would almost always have an apple for her to give to Ralph, and at least once a month, it seemed, an extra magazine appeared in General Delivery, undeliverable for one reason or another. Mr. Johnny at the post office always saved them for her. Best of all, it was an escape, if only a brief one, from the monotony awaiting her at home. Chores. Helping Mama. Watching for Papa. Keeping an eye on her sisters. It never changed. Sometimes it seemed to Lizzy that this must be what prison felt like. She tried not to, but sometimes she despaired of ever leaving. The weekly trip to town was her day of liberty.

Today was not her usual day, though. She usually rode in on Monday afternoons, because town seemed the least crowded on Mondays. People typically came toward the end of the week, especially Fridays and Saturday mornings, to finish whatever business they might have in town before Sunday, and Lizzy never liked running into lots of people. They tended to ask questions that she didn't want to answer, and she avoided those days if she could. But this week, she'd been helping Mama out in the vegetable plot, and Mama hadn't been able to spare her.

Until now. So here she was, on a Friday afternoon in March, elbowing her way past a group of men who had congregated near the railing where the horses were tied up. They stopped talking as she made her way through, but she could hear them start up again as she pushed the post office door open.

"Don't know how they keep those girls in shoes, him just drunk all the time." She heard one man say and snigger a little bit.

And then another comment, undecipherable, but apparently quite funny, because there was a burst of laughter. And then an uncomfortable silence. She knew they were talking about her family, and they knew she could hear them. She didn't see Mr. Johnny right away, and her heart started beating a little faster.

But then he popped up from behind the counter, a small parcel in hand. "Not a lot, Miss Lizzy," Mr. Johnny said. "But I've been holding this for you. I'm glad you came in today. These extras just take up space that I surely don't have."

Mr. Johnny pushed it across the counter, and Lizzy accepted it happily. It was another *Woman's Home Companion,* her favorite. Backing away from the counter and already engrossed in the first few pages, she collided solidly with a sturdily built woman of about forty who was walking purposefully in.

"Goodness gracious, child," the woman said, trying to move out of the way.

"Oh, please excuse me," Lizzy said, feeling her cheeks flush. "I do apologize."

"Well, if your excuse is you're reading, I suppose we can let that slide," the sturdily built woman said, smiling a little. "No harm done."

She turned to Mr. Johnny at the counter. "Anything come in for me?" she asked.

"Not today, Mrs. Jensen," Mr. Johnny replied. "But you know it's a long way from Chicago! Takes time to get here." Mr. Johnny and the woman shared a laugh.

It seemed to Lizzy, as she listened, that the woman and Mr. Johnny had run through this question-and-answer routine before. She watched them banter, while carefully rolling the magazine a little bit so that it would slide neatly into the pocket of her coat.

"Well, then," the woman said, clearly getting ready to leave. "Maybe next week. You take care of yourself Mr. Johnny," she called out as she made her way outside.

And then, not missing a beat, the woman walked pointedly through the group of men hanging about in front by the rail. The door hadn't swung completely shut, and Lizzy could see and hear her quite clearly.

"Seems as if there might be something worthwhile for all you loafers to be doing, instead of standing around here making jokes at the expense of young ladies," she said, quite loudly. The men, grumbling a little, but clearly embarrassed at being called out, dispersed. Lizzy ran outside after her. She had never seen anyone, much less a woman, speak with such self-assured confidence. As though she knew she was in the right and was not afraid to let anyone else know.

"My name is Elizabeth—um, Lizzy," she said, awkwardly. And she stuck out her hand.

"Mrs. Jensen," said the woman, taking Lizzy's hand in her own and apparently not finding it the least bit out of the ordinary to find herself trading introductions with a fourteen-year-old girl.

"Thank you," Lizzy said. "For, well, that . . ." she added, nodding her head toward the disappearing men.

"Well, I don't hold with gossip of any kind. Men or women engaging in it, it's all the devil's work," Mrs. Jensen said, quite matter-of-factly. And then, changing the subject.

"Why don't you tell me what's so special about that magazine Mr. Johnny found for you?" she asked. "You almost knocked me over you were so busy reading it, and you haven't had it more than a minute. What is it that's got your attention?"

"Everything," Lizzy replied, simply. "I think I love the 'Household Tips' the most, though."

Mrs. Jensen suppressed a smile at the incongruity of this too-thin girl, wearing a too-thin coat, and clearly getting set to return to a household with too-little money, being enthralled by the "Household Tips" section of a magazine meant for society matrons.

"And why is that your favorite?" Mrs. Jensen asked, genuinely curious.

"Because it tells me how to do things," Lizzy responded, as if the answer couldn't be more obvious.

Mrs. Jensen looked at her appraisingly. "Of course," she said. She thought for a moment and then seemed to come to a decision.

"I've only just arrived back here, you know. From Chicago. I lived here a long time ago, but I moved away. My parents are getting a little older now, though, and they need some help. I thought I'd come back and stay with them for a while. You probably know the place? The Withings'? It's on the main highway, just a mile or so from the church."

Lizzy didn't know the family, but she did know the farm. She was momentarily confused by the name, but then she remembered that, of course, Mrs. Jensen's name wouldn't be the same as her parents'. She nodded.

"Well, I might need some help. I couldn't pay you a lot, but I might be able to find a little something for you from time to time." Lizzy nodded as enthusiastically as she could. Even the faint promise of an occasional wage gave off the whiff of riches.

Lizzy was so excited to be asked to help—for pay!—that she didn't even ask what the help would entail. She had assumed it would be helping with the farm chores.

She was wrong. And she couldn't have been happier about it.

Mrs. Jensen needed help with her declining parents. Lizzy didn't know what kind of ailments they had, and she didn't want to pry, but it seemed to Lizzy after only a few afternoons spent there that their main complaint was old age. Mr. Withings was still able to get out into his rocker on the porch and sit for a while if the weather cooperated, and he could tend to Mother Withings in a pinch, but Mother Withings herself spent most of her time in bed. Mrs. Jensen couldn't be there twenty-four hours out of every day, and she asked Lizzy to help out some afternoons.

Lizzie thought it was the easiest wage she would ever earn. She sat with whichever one of them wasn't napping, read to them, listened to them talk about what they remembered from the past. Lizzy gave off no thinly veiled aura of disapproval of how much they might have forgotten or gotten confused, because their lives had no intersection with hers.

The first time Mrs. Jensen left her on her own, Lizzy was terrified. But she did the best she could, and fortunately that first afternoon by herself both of Mrs. Jensen's parents were mostly napping. Over time, she learned how to help someone with no strength left prop themself up in bed. How to feed someone who is losing the desire to eat. How to give someone a sponge bath. How to help someone manage a bed pan. Without realizing it, she was learning to be a nurse. And every session at Mrs. Jensen's house gave her more opportunity to put into practice one of the most important nursing skills of all: how to be a comfort to a patient.

One early afternoon, Lizzy brought Addie with her. Addie wanted to meet Mrs. Jensen, and Lizzy was glad of the company. But when Lizzy and Addie arrived, Mrs. Jensen was uncharacteristically brusque. The trap was hitched and ready to go, and Mrs. Jensen was clearly impatient.

"Is this your sister?" Mrs. Jensen called out from across her yard.

"Yes. Her name is Addie," Lizzy said, pushing Addie forward a little and hoping she'd remember her manners.

Manners or no manners, Mrs. Jensen didn't seem to care right now.

"Do you think she could mind things here if you were to come with me?" Mrs. Jensen asked.

Addie looked a little panicked, but, rising to the occasion, nodded "yes" at Lizzy. "I'll be all right," she said. "You go. I think it might be important."

And it was. Lizzy, singularly focused on doing her level best for Mrs. Jensen's parents, had been barely aware of the skill that Mrs. Jensen had honed during her time in Chicago: she was a midwife. And this afternoon, Carol Jonas was in labor. Tom Jonas had ridden down to Mrs. Jensen's to ask for help and had already left to ride back. He was pretty well terrified, as he had only ever helped birth calves. He had to believe his wife would require different skills.

"Not so very different, truth be told," Mrs. Jensen explained matter-of-factly as they turned down the dirt track to the Jonas farm. "But it's hard to tell men that. Especially when it's their wife that's in labor, and not the cow at all."

In general, Lizzy tried not to spend much time dwelling on the past. Whatever happened had, of course, happened. There was no turning back the clock on any of that, and Lizzy felt strongly that it did no one any good to dwell on things that couldn't be changed. The future would bring challenges enough. Anyway, a lot of the meanness seemed to have drained out of Papa lately, leaving behind only the craving for whiskey. He didn't even sleep at home all the time anymore. Sometimes Lizzy would find him in the barn; sometimes a neighbor brought him home. Lizzy wasn't even sure if he'd be up to the summer chores anymore, but that would be a problem for summer. If he wasn't an immediate threat or liability, Lizzy wasn't going to waste precious time worrying about him.

But when she and Mrs. Jensen drove onto the Jonas family yard, the first thing she heard was the guttural groan of Carol Jonas, fighting through a contraction. It didn't matter that the windows were shut tight against the spring chill. Lizzy had to believe the groan could be heard two farms over, and she was instantly back in the cramped attic room, bleeding and steeling herself against the next onslaught of pain. She started to shake.

Mrs. Jensen, stepping down from the trap, gave Lizzy a piercing look.

"I didn't bring you here to be another one needing looking after," she said, sharply. "You look like you need the smelling salts."

"It's nothing, I'm fine," Lizzy managed to croak out. "I'll get your bag."

Lizzy reached into the back of the trap and found Mrs. Jensen's valise with all her supplies in it. It was surprisingly heavy, and the weight steadied her somehow. Mrs. Jensen gave her another appraising look, but she didn't say any more. They went into the house together.

It was the Jonas's first child, and Lizzy could see that Tom Jonas was not going to be of much help. With every contraction and groan, he seemed to freeze in sympathetic agony. At least he was able to tell Mrs. Jensen when his wife's water had broken and when the pains had started. It was just past two o'clock in the afternoon now, and if Tom could be relied upon, his wife had been in labor since about five in the morning. Certainly nothing out of the ordinary for a first child. Lizzy sat down on a stool next to the bed, and she took Mrs. Jonas's hand.

"You're doing fine," Lizzy whispered, squeezing the hand encouragingly as Mrs. Jensen unpacked her things and arranged them on a little side table she'd moved over from near the hearth. A sudden memory overtook her–of curling up against her mother as she fought through waves of pain. Just feeling her mother's warmth had been a comfort. She hoped she was providing the same comfort to Carol. Thinking about how best to help Carol helped calm Lizzy's own shaking. *You're here to help someone,* Lizzy told herself. *Whatever happened to you was over long ago. It's gone.*

"We need to run out to the pump and wash up before we get started here," Mrs. Jensen said, matter-of-factly.

"I won't be a moment," Lizzy whispered again to Carol. She got a nod and a firm squeeze in reply. *Good sign,* Lizzy thought.

Back inside, Lizzy returned to her stool, positioned so she could hold Carol's hand. She watched in amazement as Mrs. Jensen pushed her arm all the way inside of Carol, it looked to Lizzy like almost up to the elbow. She must have gasped, because Mrs. Jensen gave a quick, short laugh.

"You've seen your Papa with a cow, haven't you?" Lizzy nodded. Yes, she had, but, well, it was a long time ago. Before the liquor took over. Whatever might have happened back then, Lizzy barely remembered it.

Mrs. Jensen pulled her arm out, apparently pleased with whatever she'd found, and told Tom to get busy boiling water. Clearly relieved to have an assigned task, he took the kettle from the hearth and practically jogged outside to the pump. Mrs. Jensen made a little sound that could have been disgust.

"I don't expect he'll be back very soon," she said, shaking her head. "I wouldn't be at all surprised if there's a little snort of something out there. Men," she continued, making no effort to hide her tone of disparagement. "They don't mind starting things, that's for sure, but when it comes to finishing, well, they're just less than useless." Lizzy had no argument with that.

"Miss Carol," Mrs. Jensen said after palpating her abdomen for a few seconds, "you're going to be just fine."

And Miss Carol was, indeed, just fine. As Mrs. Jensen had predicted, Tom Jonas did spend a little more time than was reasonably necessary pumping the kettle full, but he did at last reappear, and he didn't smell too terribly strongly of whiskey. Along about five in the afternoon, with one ray of fading sunlight doing its best to push through the dirty windowpane and into the room, Mrs. Jensen announced it was time to push. She called Lizzy over. "I'll need help," she said. "Newborns can be slippery."

Lizzy watched in amazement as the little head crowned, and then, after a superhuman effort on Miss Carol's part, as the baby emerged. Mrs. Jensen let Lizzy cut the cord. They sponged the baby together, Mrs. Jensen holding him and Lizzy cleaning him up. They wrapped him up in one of the towels Mrs. Jensen had brought with her, and they gave him to Miss Carol to hold. Whatever horrifying memories had threatened to overtake Lizzy upon their arrival, they were forgotten. Lizzy was euphoric. It was a birth. New life. And she had been part of it. She had helped.

On their way back to Mrs. Jensen's house, Mrs. Jensen was more chatty than usual. "I don't know if you noticed," she said, "but that little family didn't have much. These folk couldn't pay, but some of them can. Even with these folk, though, I wouldn't be surprised if there was a basket of something or other left by my door in the next few days. I'll make sure you get some if they leave something." Lizzy nodded. A half a basket of pretty much anything would be most welcome at Lizzy's house.

They rode along in silence for a bit, and then Mrs. Jensen asked Lizzy what she thought about what she'd seen. Lizzy told her.

"It was wonderful," she said, solemnly.

Mrs. Jensen smiled and patted her hand. "They likely wouldn't even have sent for me if it hadn't been the first one," she said. "Tom Jonas got nervous. And sometimes, I guess, they just need someone there. For reassurance. You did very well," she said. "You get a little older and handle a few more of these, and you can go out by yourself. They don't usually need me."

Lizzy could hardly believe it. She felt like she could explode with happiness. She had done well. And she wanted nothing more than to keep doing it.

They rode on, Mrs. Jensen holding the reins.

"Mrs. Jensen?" Lizzy asked, finally feeling brave enough to broach the question that had been needling at her for some time. "Where is Mr. Jensen? Is he still in Chicago? Did he have to stay on there?"

Mrs. Jensen looked at Lizzy for a moment, and then she laughed a full-throated laugh that Lizzy hadn't heard before. "That's what most folks think," she said. "Can you keep a secret?"

Lizzy nodded a solemn yes.

"I made him up," Mrs. Jensen said quite matter-of-factly. "Less bother that way."

Lizzy couldn't have agreed more.

Summer 1914–Wytheville, Virginia

Months, and then years, passed, and Mrs. Jensen made good use of her willing and apt new assistant. As Lizzy gained more experience, Mrs. Jensen sent Lizzy out to help with coughs, cuts and scrapes, and easy births, and Lizzy loved every minute of it. She loved feeling needed, and she loved feeling capable. The best moment of any given day was when Mrs. Jensen rode up onto the yard, hoping Lizzy might be able to help.

"You have a real gift for this," Mrs. Jensen said, somewhat unexpectedly, as they were riding home together late one night after having attended a birth where, Lizzy knew, they hadn't really been required. Certainly not both of them. But it had been a while since they'd attended a birth together, and this was a first child. The papa-to-be was nervous. So when he showed up on Mrs. Jensen's yard, she decided she'd stop by Lizzy's farm and see if Lizzy might be able to come too. Lizzy could. Things took a little longer than usual, but it was still not a difficult birth, and when Mrs. Jensen and Lizzy left the house, young Master Thomas Harris, Jr., and both his parents were dozing peacefully. Lizzy felt an almost palpable glow of satisfaction.

"I've loved every minute," Lizzy replied. She meant it.

They rode along for a little while longer. It was quite late, past midnight if Lizzy were to guess. She let her eyes close. So when Mrs. Jensen spoke again, she startled awake. She had to believe she hadn't quite heard right, so she politely asked Mrs. Jensen to repeat her question.

Mrs. Jensen smiled a little. Lizzy could hear it in her voice.

"I said," Mrs. Jensen repeated, "I'm wondering if you ever considered nursing school."

Lizzy didn't know quite how to respond. Of course she had considered nursing school. But she had never told a soul. Not even Mrs. Jensen. What would be the point of even dreaming about such a thing? There was barely money for food in Lizzy's household, much less for something as unheard of as higher education. Lizzy had loved school, but she had left after eighth grade. She could read, and she could write. She could do her sums well enough to know if she had enough money to buy supplies at the little general store next to the post office. These days, Papa was only good for finding someone who'd give him a bottle in exchange for some broken down piece of farm machinery he'd managed to acquire. Lizzy, her sisters, and Mama were running the farm on their own. Lizzy had had plenty of schooling. She was needed at home.

After a few moments of silence, Mrs. Jensen apparently realized that there wouldn't be an answer. She didn't need one.

"You shouldn't give up on that quite so fast," she said, matter-of-factly. "There's more and more of a demand for nurses these days, and a lot of nursing schools have programs where they pay your way. There's a big school in Washington, D.C.–Mason-Hall. I've run across some graduates from their program, and they're very impressive. I know Washington, D.C., feels like it's a long way away from here, but it's easier to get to than some other places, that's for sure." Mrs. Jensen, ever-cheerful, smiled at that last. "I don't know the matron except by reputation, but I can still write a letter recommending you as a candidate."

Mrs. Jensen continued. "At the very least, it couldn't hurt if I put in a word." A pause, while Mrs. Jensen let that sink in. "It's something you should think about, anyway," she added. "You'd have to be a little older, of course, I don't think they take girls under twenty."

Lizzy finally found her voice. "I'm twenty this August," she said, softly.

Mrs. Jensen turned on the bench to look at her. "Bless me," she said. "So you are. How the time goes." She looked appraisingly at Lizzy for a moment. And then fell silent.

They were both quiet for the remainder of the ride back. When they reached Mrs. Jensen's farmstead, Lizzy hopped off first and went to fetch their things from the back of the trap. She would stay at Mrs. Jensen's tonight. She often did if they got back past midnight.

Mrs. Jensen caught her arm as they were going inside.

"I mean it," she said, earnestly. "I've had a lot of young girls help me over the years. Some have a gift, some don't. You do. It'd be a shame to see you waste it."

Lizzy thought about her family. Mama, worn with work, and Papa, ruined with whiskey. Her sisters, with no good options except to follow in Mama's footsteps. Until this very moment, Lizzy had thought this was her lot as well. But as she lay down on Mrs. Jensen's uncomfortable davenport in the front room, Lizzy's thoughts started to race, and she let herself begin to dream. How in the world might one go about applying to something like nursing school? Would Mrs. Jensen help her? Of course she would, she'd as good as said so. And if Mrs. Jensen thought she could be a nurse, well, that was enough for Lizzy.

She felt something rise inside her. It felt a little like hope.

April 1916–Wytheville, Virginia

Lizzy would remember the fences, white and crisp against the impossibly blue spring sky. And of course, the letter.

She had been saddling up Ralph and riding into town faithfully once a week for what felt like an eternity, returning home each time empty-handed and a little more defeated. But today, Mr. Johnny smiled when he saw her come in.

"Something for you," he said, pushing the envelope across the wooden counter. "I hope it's what you've been waiting for."

She paused before picking it up, feeling as though her entire life had been leading up to this one moment. The return address was stamped in the top left corner. Mason-Hall School of Nursing. There it was. It had taken her the better part of eighteen months to put the application letter and supporting materials together, but she felt confident, at least, that she had done all that she could. She had carefully written out her answer on "Why I Wish to Obtain a Nursing Certification." She had obsessively itemized all her experience since she began helping

Mrs. Jensen. She had been brutally honest about her need for a scholarship. She had filled out the application the best she was able, and in the three months since she had sent it in (so as not to raise her hopes too high) she had each day convinced herself a tiny bit more of how unlikely it was she would be accepted.

Nevertheless. She took a deep breath, closed her eyes, and said a little prayer. *Won't help,* she thought to herself. *But maybe it can't hurt.* She didn't even care that Mr. Johnny was watching. She slit the envelope open with her fingernail.

"Dear Miss Elizabeth Porter," the letter began. It went on to inform her that the matron at the Mason-Hall Hospital School of Nursing in Washington, D.C., was most pleased to offer Miss Elizabeth Porter a place in the nursing school, beginning as soon as Miss Porter might reasonably arrive, but no later than the fifteenth of June. Lizzy didn't even read the rest. She found herself practically unable to breathe as she traced the words with her fingers. She could almost FEEL the writing scrolling down the page. It was as though the words were ready to jump out at her and dance. *I'm leaving,* she thought. *And no one can stop me. Only two more months.*

"Good news?" Mr. Johnny asked, solicitously.

"The best," Lizzy replied. "The very best."

On the way home, Lizzy could barely contain her excitement.

Would Mama and Papa let her go? She knew they would. She was twenty-one now, almost twenty-two. More than old enough. And with her gone, there would be one less mouth to feed. She knew that was the argument that would carry the day, even if no one said it out loud. She pushed aside thoughts of who she would be leaving behind. *Addie will manage, Essie will manage,* she told herself, wanting to believe it. Her sisters were safe, she felt sure. Papa hadn't climbed the attic ladder in years. Not for her, not for Addie. And for some inexplicable reason, Essie had never seemed to be a potential target. Perhaps because she was the baby? It didn't matter. As far as Lizzy could tell, Papa was interested only in his whiskey these days. No, Lizzy was going.

Lizzy felt as though all her senses were on fire. She was suddenly painfully aware of the afternoon sky, the breeze, gentle and cool, a perfect spring day. She felt Ralph's reassuring bulk under the saddle as he trotted slowly down the main road to the turnoff. Approaching the farm, she pulled Ralph to a stop at the first fence bordering their property. She took the letter out of her pocket and read it again, even though she already had most of it memorized. She smoothed it out and folded it neatly. She knew what she would do with it. It would be pressed carefully into the new notebook that Addie and Essie had given her for her last birthday.

"For your journeying," Essie had pronounced, prompted by Addie, Lizzy was fairly certain. Lizzy smiled, remembering the solemn presentation. The scrambled word had become part of their family shorthand. And Lizzy couldn't help but feel it was surprisingly appropriate. Certainly to her, anyway, "journeying" and "journaling" were two sides of the same coin. She had accepted the gift with the gravitas with which it had been presented. She still hadn't actually penned anything in it, except a brief memorialization of the gift itself on the inside front cover. The blank pages seemed so pristine, waiting for the perfect words. She did wonder how her sisters had paid for a brand-new notebook with a real leather cover. She knew what the prices of those notebooks were at the general store; Addie had probably seen her look longingly at the display. Addie was working some for Mrs. Jensen now that Lizzy was thinking about leaving, and Lizzy suspected that Addie had used some of her few (and hard-earned) coins to make the purchase. Lizzy was overcome with gratitude for the gift.

Ralph shifted his weight a little and gave a soft snort, reminding her that they should be getting along. She let him choose the pace as she took one last look at the fences in the distance, so white against the blue sky and green grass. And she knew she would always remember them. Because they were no longer going to hold her in.

Suddenly impatient, she kicked Ralph into a trot. There was news to share. And if ever there was a day in her life that was worthy of inaugurating the journal, it was today. She could practically feel the words bubbling up inside her. There might even be some of the pieces of thoughts she'd told Addie about. Addie would be proud.

CHAPTER FOUR

GWEN

> *For many, the Northern Cardinal is the most favorite back-yard bird.*
>
> *Cardinals*, S. Tekiela, p. 5.

Now–Wayland, Massachusetts

Dinner was delicious, but not lively. Gwen and Rob were both feeling the hours of work in the heat. They finished the pasta, and Gwen poured the last of the wine. Rob stretched in his chair, and Gwen could suddenly see him at the table, age five, stretching in exactly same way. She smiled at the memory. He smiled back at her quizzically, as though trying to read her mind. He usually could, she had to admit. But this time, he just shook his head and moved on.

"So, Mom, what is it with this mysterious envelope? You promised you'd tell me," he said, rising to begin cleaning up and eyeing her just slightly suspiciously. "Who do you know at a nursing school?"

"Well," Gwen replied, "no one. At least, no one now." Rob made a little "go on" motion with his hands, and she continued.

"Do you remember me ever mentioning my Aunt Elizabeth? Who was a nurse in World War I?" *And a writer,* she added to herself. "She was actually my great aunt–

my father's aunt. She lived for years with her sisters in a tiny little house in Richmond. I only met her once, when I was pretty young . . ." Gwen's voice trailed off at the memory.

"Anyway, she did her training at the Mason-Hall School of Nursing, in D.C. And Mason-Hall has chosen her as one of its 'Distinguished Alumnae' honorees. The ceremony is on Labor Day. I think I'm the last family member left with any real connection to her, and I feel kind of like I have an obligation to go," Gwen added, somewhat apologetically. "I guess I'm just not sure how I feel about it. I can't decide if I'm happier for her that she's being recognized, or more disappointed in myself that I've done nothing that would get me an honorary degree, in, well, anything." (And then, of course, she reminded herself, there was the failed marriage. Another disappointment.)

"Mom," Rob replied, consolingly. "I think you're being a little hard on yourself. It's great that you're planning to go. And don't sell yourself short. I mean, you're a lawyer, you went to law school, right? Graduated and did well? And you definitely get the award for best Mom ever." He smiled, which of course made her smile too.

"Thank you," Gwen replied, giving him a regal nod of her head. He was right, of course. She had gone to law school, and she had practiced law successfully, before joining the ranks of women who stepped off the career track for what they assumed would be a brief pause, but which turned out to be, well, forever. She couldn't feel sorry for herself, though. It had never been a passion.

"The 'Best Mom Ever' award I accept with pleasure," she said, solemnly. And then a yawn surprised her. "I think we're done for the day," she said, patting Rob's hand. "You're the best for cooking dinner. You'll still be here for breakfast, right? You don't have to leave right away?"

Rob nodded yes. "I've got to get on the road pretty early," he said, "but I'll have time for a quick cup of coffee before I go." He had a long drive ahead of him the next day, Gwen knew. He needed to be back in Charlottesville for History Department faculty meetings. Preparation for the fall semester was already beginning. Life marched on.

Gwen got up, stood on her tippy-toes and gave him a quick kiss on the forehead. "You've been an angel. I'm sure cleaning this house out wasn't first on your list of best summer holiday ideas. Thank you for coming and helping." He hugged her in acknowledgment.

"I'll finish up down here," he said. "You look like you're kind of done for the day."

Gwen started up the stairs, listening to the sounds of Rob still fussing in the kitchen, making sure everything was tidy. The muted clatter was comforting. Turning out the lights behind her and making her way down the hall to her bedroom, she navigated carefully around the remaining few boxes that she had asked Rob to bring down from the attic. She could tell he had been in kind of a hurry, because he had created something of an obstacle course.

She was just about to congratulate herself on successfully avoiding injury, only to run her shin into one last box that seemed to have been purposefully set squarely in the middle of the doorway to her bedroom. She swore, half-kicking, half-shoving the box out of the way and hoping her shin was still intact. *Why would Rob put that right here?* she wondered irritably, then mentally scolded herself for being critical.

He was tired, she was tired, and by the end of the day, things had just come to rest wherever they landed.

She turned the hallway light back on to examine her shin, and it was only then that she took a closer at the box. It wasn't very big, and she couldn't help but wonder how she'd managed to run right into it. Then, with a small start, she realized she recognized it. It was old, badly taped, and disintegrating. And she knew exactly what it was.

Gwen took the box into her bedroom and set it down next to her chair. She had completely and utterly forgotten that this box existed. It was her Aunt Elizabeth's keepsake box. And, as her hands traced the brittle tape holding the box together, she was instantly brought back to her last—in fact, her only—visit to Virginia to see her aunt. A visit that was memorable mostly for its interminable and, to a nine-year-old, mind-numbingly boring, small talk with aged and fragile family friends who seemed impossibly old. Everyone (at least it had seemed to her at the time) was too infirm even to raise themselves up off a sofa without assistance.

But her Aunt Elizabeth, who was in fact the reason for the visit, had seemed somehow to give off a spark. She had taken Gwen out to the back garden, showed her the carved stone birdbath and the place by the fence where the rabbits nested. For nine-year-old Gwen, the garden was magical. Her Aunt Elizabeth had found a picture book, and they had looked at it together. Gwen remembered a picture of a blood-red cardinal silhouetted against snow, and her aunt telling her that yes, cardinals sometimes came to visit this very house. And then more memories—of sitting on a window seat in the bay window, waiting for flashes of red. She remembered, too, that she had wanted to take the picture book home. She shook her head. *I wonder what happened to it?*

Gwen let herself sink back into the memory of that trip. It had not been a happy one, although Gwen had not known that until quite some years later. Her Aunt Elizabeth was in her late seventies and, in spite of managing to host the magical visit to the back garden, becoming increasingly frail. Gwen's parents had made the trip down to help clean some of the clutter out of the house and organize a nurse. Aunt Elizabeth was the last surviving sister of three—Elizabeth, Adelaide, and Esther. Only Granny Esther had ever married, and when Grandpa Frank died, Esther joined her sisters in their tiny row house in Richmond. But Aunt Elizabeth was alone now, in failing health, and too weak to manage things anymore.

Gwen remembered boxes of family treasures being sorted for sale or donation, with a few special items to be carefully packed into the car or shipped back home. One of the carefully saved treasures was this keepsake box, now held gingerly in her lap. "Aunt Elizabeth asked me to keep this for you," her dad told her, some years later. "She told me to give it to you when I thought the time was right."

Gwen had barely glanced at the box at the time. She was in college by then, interested much more in her own present than in someone else's past. She had riffled through the box's contents, but she had paid very little attention. She had shoved it under her bed, where it would stay, out of sight and mind, until she came back to clean out her room before she married Robert. Taped shut and unexamined, the box moved with Gwen from house to house, through decades of marriage, always stashed in a corner of a storeroom or an attic, out of sight. Silent.

Until now. Gwen carefully pulled the tape off the top and looked inside. At first glance, the contents looked to be unremarkable. There was quite a bit of what looked to be correspondence, once bundled neatly with rubber bands that had given up their function long since. Gwen took the bundles out carefully, trying to preserve the organization system, if there was one.

And then, something intriguing. Now revealed beneath the stacks of correspondence was a piece of thick cardstock much more substantial than the top stratum of flimsy personal stationery. She lifted it out.

It was a certificate. "The United States of America honors the memory of Elizabeth Porter," it proclaimed in flowery script. Signed by President Richard Nixon and dated December 1970, it was "awarded by a grateful nation in recognition of devoted and selfless dedication to the improvement of public health in our country."

Gwen gasped audibly in surprise. *Why did I not know about this?* She dug further down into the box and found another certificate, this one for her aunt's graduation from nursing school. *Mason-Hall,* Gwen thought. *I knew about that.* But there was more creamy paper stock beneath the Mason-Hall certificate. Gwen pulled it out carefully and found a yellowing diploma for a master's degree in public health, from the University of Richmond. Gwen shook her head, trying to take it all in. She had known her aunt was a nurse, and family lore had immortalized her experience in World War I, but . . . presidential recognition? Master's degree in public health? How had this never been discussed? What else did Gwen not know? Gwen rummaged carefully around the bottom. There was a layer of packing paper, and then another surprise.

A slender manila envelope already addressed and stamped, as if ready to be added to the next day's post. The address label was to a publisher in New York. Clearly, it had never been sent. Gwen opened it carefully.

It was a manuscript–of poems. There was no title page and no attribution. Was her aunt the author? It looked that way. Maybe this was what her father meant when he said that Aunt Elizabeth was a writer? Gwen looked through the pages. She considered herself no great judge of poetry, but, in her view at least, the poems had a spark of life. How did the manuscript end up in this box, she wondered? Was it really meant for her? Perhaps another copy was actually sent to the publisher, and this was a draft? Gwen sighed in frustration. The keepsake box offered up no answers.

Gwen turned her attention back to the rest of the contents. She was going to be quite sure that nothing else of interest was hiding in the bottom. And she was surprised again. Two sheets of brittle onionskin peeked out from under the last layer of packing paper. Two poems, by themselves. Were they supposed to have been part of the manuscript? Or perhaps rejected as not good enough? One in particular struck Gwen as heartbreakingly sad. It seemed to be about some sort of devastating loss. It gave off a sense of abandoned cribs, forgotten play toys. And the other, about fearing the dark, gave her a bit of a chill.

She leaned back in the chair and closed her eyes. She felt betrayed, somehow, although she couldn't quite pinpoint why. As though everyone else had known a special secret except for her. Or maybe she had been told, and she had just not paid attention.

She had to be honest with herself. If, for instance, she had just opened the box at some point during the decades it had sat, gathering dust, in a succession of attics, she could have known more. It was all waiting there to be discovered. She just hadn't taken advantage of the opportunity.

Gwen let her mind wander back. There had been that one visit, but other than that, no special connection that Gwen could remember. There were, of course, the obligatory "thank you" notes, written for Christmas and birthday presents (always just a bit too long after the fact, Gwen thought guiltily). And Gwen's dad calling on Sundays, when the rates were low, just to check in. But not much more. Gwen sighed a quiet sigh of frustration. She wished she could remember more of what her dad had told her about Elizabeth. *So self-absorbed,* she thought. *Why didn't I ask more questions? Why didn't I listen?* She sighed again. *No help for it now.* Her dad had died ten years ago, her mom a few years before that. There was no one left to ask.

It's too late to deal with this now, she finally decided. *I think this will feel less unsettling in the morning.*

She was gathering up a few of the papers that had fallen to the floor and had started putting them back in the box, when a heavier piece of paper fell out of the sheaf. It was a photograph—old, grainy, sepia-toned. *One more surprise!* Gwen thought. She peered at it in the dim light of the lamp next to her chair. *Could it be Aunt Elizabeth?* It was hard to reconcile the image of the tall, straight-backed and serious-looking young woman in the photo with the tiny, bird-like aunt that Gwen remembered. Next to her was a young man in a wheelchair, and behind them was a Red Cross tent. The picture was in black and white, so it was impossible to know whether the sun had been shining or not. Still, Gwen couldn't shake off a sense of rain and mud. Gwen turned the picture over, hoping for a clue on the back.

She was in luck. "Toul," read the script carefully inscribed at the top of the photo. "Elizabeth Porter with Joseph Flynn, January 1918." So it was her aunt. Gwen turned the photo over a few times, flipping back and forth between the image and the words on the back. Was it her imagination or did the back of the photo almost feel sticky? As though perhaps there had been something taped to it at some point? Well, whatever secrets the photo was keeping, they weren't going to be revealed tonight. It was late. Gwen carefully put the photo back.

Joseph Flynn, Gwen thought to herself. A nice name. And in the picture, he looked like a nice young man. Very serious, but of course that was the style in those days. No one smiled for the camera. Gwen wondered if he had survived the war. *Don't suppose I'll ever know*, she thought. She put the papers and the photograph back in the box, washed the day's dust off her face, and went to bed dreaming of serious young men courageously facing the camera.

CHAPTER FIVE

LIZZY

> *Never in all my life have I seen such a sight as this city! I should write more, but I am spent from the journey. Such crowds of people! Enormous buildings everywhere. I am blessed indeed to have been met at the platform by Miss R—, who, I believe, will become my best companion. Tomorrow my training begins. I shall work my hardest to be worthy of the task.*
>
> Journal of Miss Elizabeth Porter, 14 June 1916

June 1916–Wytheville to Washington, D.C.

Monday morning, the twelfth of June, began early, with a few high clouds and more than a bit of warmth in the breeze, warning of the summer to come. Lizzy woke up in the pre-dawn grey, watching the little attic room take shape around her, she hoped for the last time. She had been ready for days–she didn't have much to take with her, so packing was hardly a chore. Addie barely stirred in her cot as Lizzy quickly dressed and gathered up her last few things.

"Addie," Lizzy whispered, shaking her sister gently awake.

"Is it time?" Addie asked, groggily.

"I think Mr. Johnny is already outside," Lizzy whispered back.

"I'll miss you," Addie said, sitting up against her pillow. "But I'm happy for you. We'll manage here just fine.

You'll write to us, won't you? Tell us how you're doing. I'm sure you'll be the best nurse they have."

Lizzy had promised herself that she wouldn't cry. And Addie would be all right, she was sure. But she suddenly felt her eyes watering. Here was her sister being brave. Again. "I'll miss you too," she said. There was nothing more to say. She hugged Addie hard and climbed down the attic ladder.

Mama was still asleep, as was Essie. Lizzy didn't have the heart to wake them. And anyway, she had said her goodbyes the night before. Papa was nowhere to be seen. She took her case, opened the door carefully and quietly, and walked outside. Mr. Johnny was indeed already there and waiting.

"Good morning, Miss Porter," he said with a smile. "Best get going. Washington is quite a journey." Lizzy practically hopped up onto the seat next to him. Mr. Johnny had insisted on taking her, and practicality for once winning out over pride, Lizzy had accepted. She hadn't even thought to ask Papa to take her. The last few times that Lizzy and her sisters and Mama went to church, she could practically feel the whispering. She even heard one of the neighbors in the pew behind asking her husband if he thought Papa ever put that bottle down to poke his head out of the barn these days. It was a wonder those girls had survived, the neighbor said, clucking her tongue disapprovingly. A wonder indeed.

They sat quietly for the first few miles or so, and then Lizzy broke the silence.

"With me gone," she said, "it will be Addie riding into town. Maybe even Essie sometimes. Mama has too much to do on the farm to be spending a day visiting town. I'm hoping you can keep an eye on them?"

Mr. Johnny smiled. "I will, you can count on it," he replied, and continued. "It was always a pleasure seeing you ride in, and I knew you'd find your way. From the first day I gave you one of those magazines and saw your face light up. I knew you'd be something."

Lizzy was suddenly curious. She'd never asked. "The magazines," she said, "it seems to me there must have been an extra one almost every month." *Mama even accused me of stealing them*, she added to herself silently.

Mr. Johnny was quiet for a while, and then he nodded. "Those city post offices are pretty big," he said, seemingly apropos of nothing. "A lot of mail goes through there, and it's easy for it to get damaged when it gets sorted." He continued. "If a magazine gets to me and it's damaged, I'm supposed to mark it 'undeliverable' and destroy it. Seems for a few years, there were a lot of copies that got damaged. It would have been a shame to just throw them away. Anyway," he added, "no one had a damaged and undeliverable issue more than once a year. And those damaged issues found a good home."

Lizzy had never suspected. "You always told me they were extras," she sputtered, feeling her face turn bright red.

"So I did," Mr. Johnny replied. "So I did."

When they finally pulled into the Roanoke train station, Mr. Johnny helped her down from the seat and set her case down beside her.

"I'm sure I'll hear word of how you're doing from your sisters, Miss Lizzy," he said. "I know you're going to make your Mama and sisters proud."

He tipped his cap to her, which he had never done before. As he turned the horse around and rode out, he called out. "Maybe there'll be some extras of those magazines for Addie," he said. "I'll keep a lookout!"

As he drove off, Lizzy suddenly realized she hadn't paid him anything for the journey. "Mr. Johnny," she called out, as loud as she could. "Your fare!" But Mr. Johnny just waved, as though to say, "out of earshot, can't hear."

But then, he turned one last time and called back to her. "Good luck!" he shouted.

When Lizzy finally arrived at Union Station, after traveling for what was beginning to feel like her entire lifespan, the parting conversation with Mr. Johnny had taken on the hazy quality of a dream.

After Mr. Johnny left her at Roanoke, there was an endless series of trains, and Lizzy had plenty of time for reflection. She found herself thinking back on her last conversations with Mama. Mama had not been in favor of her decision (and Addie and Essie had spent the days leading up to her departure looking increasingly apprehensive), but in the end, they were unable to dissuade or prevent her from going. Lizzy knew that Mama was just scared of what might happen with Papa, but the gossipy neighbor lady was right—Papa pretty much stayed in the barn these days. Papa had two forces battling inside of him, Lizzy had decided. There was the devil that tempted him to climb the attic stairs, and then there was the demon whiskey. Whiskey had clearly won the war. While he might be useless, leaving Lizzy, her sisters and Mama to keep the farm going on their own, he was at least no longer a threat.

Now, even worn as she was from the journey, Lizzy could still feel anticipation and excitement rising inside her as the conductor called out, "Union Station, last stop."

She opened her purse and fished for the confirming letter from Matron Palmer, re-reading the last paragraph yet one more time, in which Matron assured her she would be met at the station and taken to the school. Lizzy had only to respond with the arrival date and the train she intended to be on, which of course she had done, detailing her proposed itinerary, weeks ago. Nevertheless, as the train pulled in and slowed to a stop, Lizzy saw no one waiting alongside the track who appeared to have the look of a Matron Palmer. Lizzy picked up her case, made her way off the train, and started following the crowd down the platform, into the station.

So many people. And it was so very hot inside the station. Lizzy realized she couldn't remember when she had last eaten, and she was beginning to feel a bit faint. She was starting to look around for somewhere to sit and just breathe for a few minutes, when a small woman appeared next to her, apparently out of nowhere.

"Miss Porter?" the small figure asked.

Lizzy almost gasped with relief. She hadn't even realized how much she was beginning to worry. "Are you Matron Palmer?" Lizzy asked.

"Goodness, no!" the tiny figure responded, laughing. Lizzy realized that the tiny figure was in fact possessed with a very sweet and smiling face, of about Lizzy's own age, that was almost hidden under her hat. "I'm Miss Rockford, Beatrice Rockford. Matron never comes to the station to meet the new nurses. She sends one of us. I don't mind–I enjoy the chance to get outside a bit." And then, noticing that Lizzy seemed to be growing paler with each passing minute, "You must be terribly tired from your journey. Did you come all the way from Wytheville? How long must that have taken? Goodness gracious! Let me carry your case."

And off they went, Lizzy gratefully accepting the help. Miss Rockford chattered away, guiding Lizzy through the crowded station and out into the city. Lizzy had almost no energy left for conversation, but Miss Rockford was happy to talk, and Lizzy let the words flow over her, taking in as much as she could. Miss Rockford's own journey had taken her uncountable hours, all the way from Brownsville, Tennessee (Miss Porter might notice the accent? Miss Rockford admitted ruefully that she had tried to soften it, with no success). Miss Rockford thought that she would never, ever, recover from her own long journey. But nevertheless, here she was, Miss Rockford, in this marvelous city and at Mason-Hall, which she loved. And Lizzy had to agree with these last assessments. The city was grander than Lizzy could ever have imagined. The streets were wide, and there were streetcars, which Lizzy had of course heard of, but could hardly believe she was seeing, much less riding. Miss Rockford kept up a running commentary on the landmarks they were passing, but Lizzy was too overwhelmed with the newness of everything to really take anything in.

And then, finally, Beatrice pointed. "There it is," she said, pointing to a somber-looking three-story edifice that seemed to stretch for an entire city block. "We can get off here," she said. "We'll walk the rest of the way to the nurses' quarters. I'll help you get settled in and then you can meet Matron Palmer."

They descended from the streetcar and walked up the street. Lizzy realized that what had initially appeared to be a quite monolithic structure was actually three separate buildings. "The top floor of that long one, that's where we live," Beatrice pointed again. The various wards comprised the other two buildings, Lizzy realized. Mason-Hall was in fact a nursing school attached to a fairly large teaching hospital. Lizzy found herself hoping that she might be allowed a nap and a meal before meeting Matron Palmer, but she suspected that was not to be.

Her suspicion proved correct. Beatrice helped Lizzy locate her dormitory bed (which, Beatrice was clearly thrilled to note, just happened to be right next to her own) and showed her the small trunk where she could put her things. She then led Lizzy off to Matron's office. As they walked down the corridor, Lizzy could feel her nervousness re-asserting itself. Beatrice seemed to sense this and took her arm. "Don't worry," she said. "Matron can be stern, but she's fair. She just wants all of us always to do our best. She's accepted you into the program, so she must already think highly of you. She only takes the very best candidates she can find." Beatrice patted Lizzy's arm reassuringly, and they walked down the hall together.

Lizzy wondered (only slightly forlornly) when she might actually have the opportunity to eat again. She had given up hope of sleep. *But I'm here,* she told herself. *I made it.*

Given that Matron was devoting her life to ministering to those in need, Lizzy was surprised to find that, in person, she was a remarkably stern and cold presence.

Beatrice knocked firmly, and the two young women waited outside Matron's door for some time until at last, Lizzy heard the command to enter. She was already inside before she realized that she had gone in alone. Beatrice clearly felt no need to be included in the meeting and had quietly pulled the door closed behind Lizzy after she went in. Lizzy took a deep breath and tried not to look nervous.

Matron's office was not large, and there was no place for Lizzy to sit, so she stood uncomfortably in front of the desk, not quite knowing what to do with her hands. After fidgeting for a few moments while Matron finished attending to the last of what had clearly been a tower of stacked papers, Lizzy settled on clasping her hands decorously in front. She hoped that was appropriate.

At last, Matron looked up. "Miss Porter," she said. It was a statement, not a question.

Lizzy was instantly tongue-tied. She could only nod, yes.

"You have just arrived." Not a question. Lizzy again nodded affirmatively.

"I trust Miss Rockford has shown you what you need to know."

"Yes, Matron," Lizzy finally managed.

Matron pulled a sheet of paper from one of the several smaller stacks still apparently needing to be addressed. Lizzy could see no apparent organizational system, but Matron seemed to know just what she was looking for.

"You come quite highly recommended," Matron said, first scrutinizing the paper she had pulled and then pushing it toward Lizzy. Lizzy hadn't seen it before, but she recognized the signature. It was the letter that Mrs. Jensen had offered to write to accompany her application.

"Your Mrs. Jensen is apparently a nurse herself, is she not?" Matron asked. "Trained?"

"I, well . . . not formally trained," Lizzy managed to sputter. "But yes, she's tended to our community for some years now. She taught me a lot. Everything, really."

Matron raised an eyebrow. "Everything?" she repeated quizzically. "I suspect there is still quite a fair amount that you do not know."

Lizzy was quiet. That wasn't what she meant, but she had the distinct sense that now was not the best time to offer clarification. Once again, it didn't seem that Matron Palmer wished for a response.

Matron searched through the papers for a pair of spectacles that finally revealed themselves to be hiding under a pile of journals. She put the spectacles on and peered first at Mrs. Jensen's letter, and then over the rims at Lizzy.

"Much is expected of our nurses," Matron said at last, "particularly those who are here on scholarship. This Mrs. Jensen says you are more than up to the task and worthy of your place here. I trust you will not let us down."

Then after a pause that left Lizzy wondering if she had been dismissed, Matron spoke again. "How do you feel about the war?" Matron asked.

Lizzy didn't know what to say. She knew, of course, about the war in Europe. Everyone knew. But how did she *feel*? She'd never really thought about it as having any potential to affect her personally. She looked blankly at Matron. She tried to formulate a response but was evidently taking too long. Matron shook her head in annoyance.

"You will need to have an opinion," she said, sternly. "We may all be called upon."

Lizzy nodded. She wasn't sure what she was nodding to, but it was clear she needed to make it her business to find out.

Matron directed her attention to her desk once again. Lizzy wasn't sure if that was the end of the audience, but then Matron looked up briefly from her papers as if to ask, why are you still here? Lizzy took that as her cue to exit as gracefully as she could.

Beatrice was waiting outside. "How did it go?" she asked, taking Lizzy's arm as they walked together down the hallway.

Lizzy thought for a moment. "I'm not sure," she said, finally.

Beatrice squeezed her arm encouragingly. "I'm sure it went very well," she said. "Sometimes the new girls come out crying. So you must have done just fine."

Bea was happy to share with Lizzy the rest of the rules. Lizzy would be provided two uniforms, a bed and two meals a day, plus a small stipend for personal expenses, in return for the opportunity to work what Lizzy was beginning to suspect might be twenty-five hours out of each day. Friday afternoons she was off duty from 1:00 p.m. to 6:00 p.m. Other than those ever-so-brief Friday respites, the only time Lizzy was not either working on the wards or attending a lecture was Sunday morning, when she was expected to be at chapel.

The very first Saturday after Lizzy's arrival, Lizzy could sense a little buzz of excitement among the nurses. Lizzy was still learning who was who, but she could tell that even some of the more senior nurses (the few she recognized from her dormitory) were more talkative than usual. The little buzz seemed to increase as the day went on, and after dinner several of the nurses excused themselves early. Leaning in to Bea while they were still at dinner, Lizzy asked if there was something special going on that she needed to prepare for. Bea just smiled mysteriously. "You'll see," she said. "After lights out. But don't worry. There's nothing you need to do."

Lizzy was even more confused. There were penalties for violating the lights-out policy. Extra shifts, notations in one's record. It didn't seem like something to be risked.

But after lights out, things became a little clearer. The minute the on-duty proctor left the room, several of the young nurses quietly made their way to Lizzy's cot, which Bea had already managed to push closer to her own. The two cots together made a kind of table. It seemed that the nurses who disappeared from dinner early had managed to round up quite a few small glasses from the glass rack in the cafeteria, and they were set out invitingly, almost as though they'd been placed for a formal dinner. Lizzy found herself quite puzzled.

One of the nurses nudged Bea. "We don't have a lot of time," she whispered. "There's an extra proctor tonight, and there might be extra rounds."

Bea nodded, reached under her bed, and pulled out a bottle. Lizzy could hardly believe her eyes. It was whiskey. Not what Papa drank, but whiskey, nonetheless.

Giggling a little, Bea poured some into one of the glasses. "It's for you," she said. "Your welcome party. You get the first glass. Go ahead," she said, encouragingly.

Lizzy didn't know what to do. Her only experience with whiskey was watching Papa drink it. But she didn't want to offend her new companions. She closed her eyes, took a sip, and swallowed. All at once. It burned going down. But even before the burn subsided, she could feel a warm glow beginning. *Perhaps that's why Papa likes it so much,* she thought.

The other nurses patted the beds, as though clapping, and Lizzy felt a little swell of belonging, whether from the whiskey or the welcome, she wasn't quite sure. It didn't matter. Bea poured a little for each of the nurses who had gathered around the makeshift table. "To Lizzy," she said. And they all raised their glasses. "To my new best friend," Bea added, quietly, for Lizzy's ears only.

Lizzy could not even begin to guess how Bea had smuggled in her contraband. And, over the next months, she had no idea how Bea managed to replenish her supply. She had asked, but Bea just said she wouldn't rightfully be a girl from Tennessee if she didn't have some Tennessee whiskey on hand. Care packages from her papa, perhaps? Whatever the source, it seemed that there was always enough for a small celebration—another new nursing student, an important exam passed.

Lizzy had never had a real friend. Just Mrs. Jensen, and she was more of a teacher. That Saturday night at Mason-Hall was the first time ever that Lizzy felt she belonged somewhere, with someone. The nurses scrambled back to their own cots, and Bea stashed the bottle back in its hiding place. Lizzy could feel tears starting as she closed her eyes to sleep. Tears of happiness.

Summer 1916–Mason-Hall School

As the weeks passed, Lizzy found that she loved her training. She would never have had the courage to try had it not been for Mrs. Jensen's faith in her. And now? She wouldn't trade her current position for any other, anywhere. Besides the occasional evening lecture, there was little actual instruction, but this did not intimidate her. Bea, a bottomless resource, was happy to answer any question she could, even though she hadn't been at Mason-Hall much longer than Lizzy. And Lizzy found that she loved the clinical approach, following the more experienced nurses along the wards, watching carefully and then putting any newly observed skill into practice herself. Several of the teaching nurses commented on Lizzy's aptitude, and Lizzy could feel herself swelling just a tiny bit with pride at each compliment. Any time she thought about her fate had she stayed in Wytheville, she found herself suppressing a shudder. She would much rather be emptying bed pans, sponge-bathing patients, monitoring fevers, changing linens, and even scrubbing floors, than passively waiting for what she feared would inevitably find her back home. Every now and again an image of Papa would flash across her consciousness, re-inforcing her determination that she would rather starve than return to Virginia.

Although, thoughts of home brought thoughts of Addie and Essie, and she felt increasingly frequent pangs of guilt. *I need to write them a letter*, she chided herself. *I promised I would. It's been weeks since I've been here, and I've only managed a few lines to tell them that I arrived safely.* Her "journeying" was suffering as well. Journeying indeed. It felt like she had left one edge of the world and managed to sail herself all the way to the other. She promised herself that her next Friday afternoon would be dedicated to writing–catching up on her journal entries and writing a real letter home.

And soon, Lizzy reminded herself, there might be some significant excitement to report. Notices were going up around the hospital that someone from the Red Cross was coming on Thursday evening to talk about the war effort. Lizzy couldn't stop thinking about what Matron had said to her in her entrance interview. How did Lizzy feel about the war? Lizzy was starting to suspect that what Matron had really meant was, how did Lizzy feel about *going to* the war?

Lizzy knew that several hospitals around the country had been mobilized to become base hospitals, with staff to be ready to sail for Europe should the call come. Lizzy wondered if this meeting might be to announce Mason-Hall as next on the list. Lizzy realized she was definitely starting to develop feelings about the war, and those feelings could be summed up in one word. Excitement.

Thursday, when it came, was oppressively warm. Although cumulus clouds could be seen from the windows trying to gather themselves, as yet there had been no rain, and the evening looked to bring little relief. Lizzy and Bea walked briskly down the hallway to the hospital canteen, joining the growing stream of nurses and doctors headed the same way. By the time Lizzy and Bea made it to the room, a little after 8 p.m., there were no seats left. They stood together along the back wall, near a window that had been opened to let in what little breeze there was. Lizzy found herself shifting her weight, uncomfortable. Right foot to left, left foot to right. She had been standing all day, and she was vaguely aware that her back was stiff.

Although full beyond capacity, the room was surprisingly quiet. Doctors talked with other doctors, nurses to other nurses, but only in murmurs. The import of the evening seemed to have been internalized by those in attendance, even before the speaker rose to begin.

Matron Palmer finally stood up from her seat in the front row of chairs to open the meeting, as it was becoming clear that no more attendees would be able to fit into the room. They might as well start.

"Good evening to all of you and thank you for making time to listen to tonight's speaker." Matron gestured to a gentleman seated next to her, dressed in a suit that looked to be far too warm for the sweltering room. "He has graciously offered to update us as to the current state of affairs at the Red Cross. Please give him your full attention."

Wiping his brow as unobtrusively as possible, the gentleman rose to earnest applause. There was no preamble. "You have all heard, of course, of the catastrophic shortage of medical personnel in Europe. The Red Cross is an organization dedicated to providing medical care to all. Since the war began, we have been dispatching doctors, nurses and other medical staff to the European theater—to France, to Belgium, anywhere there is a need."

He continued, "You may also have heard that some hospitals throughout the U.S. have agreed to become 'base hospitals.'" There were some nods through the audience at this, some murmurs of assent, a few quizzical looks. "For those who have *not* heard, a base hospital is a hospital that has chosen to ready some portion of its medical personnel to be mobilized for transport to the battlefield, should circumstances so require." It escaped no one that no mention was made of the American status, at least currently, as bystander to the war, and not participant.

"I am most pleased to announce that Matron and the other administrators of this hospital have agreed that Mason-Hall will be added to the growing network of base hospitals in the U.S. As for individual doctors and nurses at Mason-Hall, participation is not mandatory. If you wish to volunteer to be among the doctors and nurses who agree to be mobilized in the event, please give your name to Matron. I hope that many of you will consider adding your names to the list of those who wish to be part of this effort. But we all understand that this posting will be difficult, as well as potentially dangerous. No one shall be compelled to go."

The rumors were true! Lizzy could hardly believe her ears! The opportunity to go to Europe, to help with the war effort–this would put her as far away from what she had left behind in Wytheville as she could possibly be. "Can you imagine?" Lizzy whispered excitedly to Bea. "I'm putting my name in as soon as I can! What about you?"

"*Shhh*," Bea whispered back. "Maybe we can talk about this tonight? We shouldn't be talking now." And indeed, the two nurses sitting on either side of them were pursing their lips in exaggerated disapproval of the volume of their conversation.

Lizzy sensed reticence in her friend's reaction, and she was a little surprised. The moment that Matron had made her announcement, it felt to Lizzy as though the whole room came alive. Nevertheless, Lizzy respected her friend and held her tongue. *We'll talk tonight*, Lizzy told herself. *Bea is just overwhelmed with the opportunity that we're going to have.*

That night, lying in their narrow cots pushed together at the end of the row of nurses trying to sleep, Lizzy tried again.

"Bea," Lizzy whispered. Silence.

"You can't be sleeping," Lizzy whispered a little louder. "I know you're awake. I don't think anyone's sleeping. It's too hot to sleep." And there's too much going on, Lizzy wanted to add, but she was starting to sense that perhaps Bea wasn't quite as excited about this as she was.

"Oh, Lizzy," Bea said, turning in her cot to face her friend across the tiny space that separated them. "I know you're happy about this. But I don't know if going to Europe is something I can do."

"Of course it is!" Lizzy responded, surprised. "You're a wonderful nurse! You've taught me so much, and you're so kind, and all the staff nurses here think the world of you. Why wouldn't you go? You could do so much good."

There was a little light coming in the dormitory windows from the streetlamps outside, but not enough for Lizzy to be able to see her friend's expression. She imagined it, though. She could almost hear Bea smiling.

"I'm not like you," Bea said at last, quietly. "I don't think I'd be able to write a letter to my parents telling them I was leaving to go to war. They would be so worried. I couldn't bear that. And then what about Teddy? What would I tell him? We're supposed to be married when I finish . . ."

Lizzy didn't have a response for that. She knew about Bea's sweetheart, of course. But there was no one waiting for Lizzy back at home, and she was glad of that. All that came of those sorts of entanglements was a life like Mama had—hopeless and hard. Addie and Essie knew she had no intention of returning. Mama probably did too.

They were both silent for a few minutes. Then Bea whispered again. "Do you think it will really come to this? Do you think we'll really enter the war?"

Lizzy didn't know. Nobody knew, as far as she could tell. But she realized she was hoping, yes. It didn't seem that Bea expected a response though.

After a few more minutes, Lizzy thought that Bea might really have managed to go to sleep. But then she heard Bea say, quietly, "You're braver than I am."

Lizzy thought for a few moments before responding. Was she brave? *Addie* was brave. Lizzy had never forgotten Addie risking a beating just to rescue one of Lizzy's magazines from the fire. Lizzy didn't feel brave, not like that. Just focused. Longing for something, maybe. Something that would continue to take her as far away from Wytheville as she could get.

"I don't think I'm brave. Not really," Lizzy finally offered in reply. "I mean, I don't want to sign up by myself. And that's not very brave, is it? Please, just think about it. If we go together, it won't be nearly so scary. You can always take your name off the list if you change your mind. And who knows . . . it might never come to anything. You're absolutely right to ask if it's really going to happen. No one knows. We might just continue to be a whole country of bystanders. We might never enter. The call might never come."

Lizzy sensed more than saw Bea's outstretched hand. She took it and gave it an encouraging squeeze. "It will all work out," Lizzy said, reassuringly. "I know it will." Bea squeezed back. Lizzy hoped that meant Bea was coming around.

Bea was quiet, and Lizzy was fairly sure she had gone to sleep. But Lizzy lay awake for a while, long enough to hear the thunder finally usher in the rain and feel the hint of a cooler breeze from the open dormitory windows. As she drifted off to sleep, Lizzy decided she would sign up the next morning. And surely her friend was just suffering a momentary bout of nerves. Bea would sign up too, Lizzy knew she would. Just the thought of being part of the war effort sent Lizzy's heart racing with excitement. She found herself hoping quite fervently that her words of reassurance to Bea were wrong.

Spring 1917–Washington, D.C.

There were rumors upon rumors over the following months, of course, but no real news materialized until early April of 1917. And by then, the tension in the air at the school was practically palpable. Teaching nurses striding down the corridors seemed even more authoritative than usual. And the whispering in the dormitory after lights out was so loud that the dormitory proctors grumbled they might as well all be in the canteen at noon meal for all the sleep anyone was getting. But they all still felt compelled to compare any snippets of news any of them might have heard individually, in hopes that comparing fragments might somehow crystallize the rumors into hard kernels of truth.

"Matron says it won't be long now," Bea whispered across the cots after lights out one early spring night. "I heard her talking with one of the surgeons. We're almost sure to enter the war, and if that happens, well . . ." She didn't finish her sentence.

"That's it, then," Lizzy said, trying not to raise her voice. "So many of the base hospitals have already shipped off to Europe—we must be one of the next in line. Can you believe it? We could be in France by summer!"

Bea didn't respond.

"Aren't you excited?" Lizzy whispered, suddenly suspicious of her friend's lack of reaction. "You're not sounding very excited."

"I'm excited," Bea whispered back, a little reluctantly, Lizzy thought. "But Lizzy, aren't you scared? It's not just soldiers who get injured, you know."

"Don't be silly," Lizzy said, trying to sound as encouraging as she could. "The base hospitals are well behind the front lines, and I'm sure that's where we'll be posted. They couldn't put us in a field hospital. Only the most experienced nurses are posted there. We've barely been here at Mason-Hall long enough to qualify to go, much less be put on staff anywhere. In fact, if there wasn't a war on, we probably wouldn't be allowed to be nursing anywhere at all. We're not even due to graduate for another year! They're relaxing the rules to allow us to go, because there's just such an enormous need. There's nothing to worry about, Bea, I'm sure of it. It will be an adventure, but it won't be dangerous. They won't let us close enough to the front lines for that!" And, as she had done so many times over the last months, Lizzy reached her hand out across her bed to give her friend's hand an encouraging squeeze.

And as she always did, Bea squeezed back in return, but she didn't say anything. Lizzy took that to mean that perhaps Bea was too sleepy to continue the conversation. In the darkness of the dorm, Lizzy couldn't see her friend's shoulders shaking just little. She had no idea Bea was crying.

On April 6, 1917, the rumors finally hardened into fact, and the United States entered the war. The doctors and nurses who had signed up to be considered for the base hospital were told they would soon be mobilized. And as the weeks went by, Lizzy was forced to admit that maybe, just maybe, her friend really was not quite as enthusiastic as Lizzy wanted her to be. Bea's eyes often appeared to be a little swollen and a little red, almost as though she'd been crying. When Lizzy confronted her, Bea blamed the tiny print in the textbooks they'd been given. Fair enough, Lizzy thought. But Lizzy also surprised Bea several times as she was writing letters in the dormitory, letters that were quickly (and, she thought, a little furtively) slid into the covers of text-books when Lizzy approached.

On the first of June, Matron Palmer called a meeting of all the medical staff. Once again, it was a warm day, and all those attending were crowded into the uncom-fortably stuffy canteen. And once again, the room was surprisingly quiet.

Matron Palmer rose to speak. "You all know, of course, that we have joined the war effort in Europe," she stated, then paused for effect before continuing.

"We have heard just recently from the Red Cross that we are to be mobilized. We will be going to France, to the base hospital at Toul. We leave on the U.S.S. Olympia on the twentieth of June. I am not cer-tain how long your stints will be, but I should think at least a year, perhaps longer. You will want to alert your families, of course. When I have any additional information, I will pass it along, but details are in short supply at the moment."

Lizzy looked around for Bea, who had been sitting right next to her but who now seemed to have disap-peared into the crush of people all milling about and talking loudly over each other. She pushed her way out of the canteen and made her way back to the dormitory. The room was empty, except for Bea, who was lying on her cot, sobbing.

"Bea, whatever is the matter?" Lizzy ran over to her friend and sat down on the edge of her bed. "It's happening! We're going!"

"Oh, Lizzy," Bea replied, trying not to hiccup. "I haven't wanted to tell you, but I never did put my name on the list. I can't go. My family, well, they want me to come back to Brownsville. I just got this a few days ago from Father." And with that, Bea took a crumpled page out from under her pillow. "It's a letter," Bea said, a little unnecessarily and giving in to the hiccup. "They want me back home, and they're telling me I can be a private nurse back there. My brothers are already called up and getting ready to go fight, and, well, I guess Mother and Father don't want me over there risking myself too."

Lizzy was silent for a few minutes. "You don't have to do what they say, you know," Lizzy said. "I wouldn't."

Bea smiled through her tears. "I told you, I'm not like you, Lizzy," she said. "I couldn't bear it if I thought I was going against what Mother and Father want for me. And, anyway, you know there's Teddy. He's already enlisted, and he's finished with training, but I'm hoping maybe the war will be almost over before he gets near the front. I need to go home so I'm there for him when he gets back."

As Lizzy thought about that conversation in the ensuing days, she had time to wonder about something that looked almost as though it might have been another crumpled piece of paper, stuffed under Bea's pillow along with the letter from Bea's father. Lizzy didn't ask about it, and she would have thought little of it, save for some odd behavior on Bea's part. There were several calls for Bea on the house telephone, which struck

Lizzy as unusual, since calls were difficult to arrange, and since Bea's parents communicated almost solely by letter (the only other telephone call Bea had received from them was a brief and staticky congratulatory phone call on her birthday).

And then, there was the night that Bea never slept in her bed. Bea was there at lights out, Lizzy was certain of it. She hadn't actually been in bed, but she'd been fussing with something in her trunk, and Lizzy had assumed she was just straightening something out and would be in bed shortly. No good could come from attracting the attention of the dormitory proctors.

But when Lizzy woke up the next morning, it was clear that Bea's bed hadn't been slept in. Bea returned to the dorm a little before 6 a.m. She told Lizzy that she had been unexpectedly asked to work an extra overnight shift, but she was wearing street clothes, not her uniform. Lizzy didn't ask questions. She felt as though their relationship was already a little strained, and she felt guilty about having pressed Bea to sign up for the base hospital. A couple of the other nurses asked where Bea had been, and Lizzy repeated Bea's explanation as convincingly as she could.

Lizzy didn't believe it, though. And as she thought back on that night, she was pretty sure she knew both where Bea had been and with whom. That not-so-well-hidden piece of crumpled paper was most likely a letter from Teddy, Lizzy concluded, meant to arrange a tryst. Bea had, more likely than not, slipped out to see him. Bea had told Lizzy that Teddy was shipping out, and he must have had some leave on his way up to New York to board the troop ship.

Lizzy was a little surprised that Bea would risk her reputation and quite possibly her place at the school—

there were strict rules about leaving the premises for any reason, much less to meet a young man–but, well, it was wartime, wasn't it? People were increasingly inclined to look the other way on any number of issues.

She began to credit Bea with more bravery than Bea seemed to credit herself. Her suspicions were confirmed when a new bottle of Tennessee whiskey magically appeared in Bea's trunk. A gift from her Tennessee sweetheart–it had to be. There was no other explanation. Bea hadn't received a care package from her family in weeks. Lizzy decided not to ask any questions. Bea's business was Bea's business.

In spite of the bravado evidenced by Bea's overnight adventure, Lizzy could tell that there would be no changing Bea's mind about going to war. Lizzy thought briefly about her own family, and about what they would think when they found out she was in France. Although she had written to her sisters about the base hospital sign-up, she had conveniently failed to give details on whether or not she herself had put her name on the list. *If they don't know, they can't try to stop me,* she told herself. *I'll write them when I've made it to France.* Lizzy felt her shoulders stiffen with resolve. She was going, with or without Bea, and nothing was getting in her way. The twentieth of June was not far off at all.

CHAPTER SIX

GWEN

Originally a southern bird . . .

Cardinals, S. Tekiela, p. 9.

Now–Wayland, Massachusetts & I-95

Morning proved Gwen prophetic. She did feel better. She smelled coffee and remembered Rob's promise to stay at least long enough for a quick breakfast before he left. Hurrying downstairs, she reached the kitchen just in time to see Rob finishing both the morning crossword and his last bite of toast. And she was suddenly struck with an image of high-school-age Rob, procrastinating over the puzzle at breakfast, almost certain to be late for class. "We can finish it, Mom," he'd say. "Just another five minutes. Please?"

Since he'd left home, she'd picked up the crossword habit herself, and they would sometimes consult by phone on a particularly opaque clue. It made her feel close to him, even though they were five states apart.

But there would clearly be no leisurely crossword solving this morning. "You should have woken me up," she said, a little sad to see him so close to out the door. "You're already leaving?"

"Early bird, Mom. Gotta get on the road." He saw her face fall, though, and appeared to relent on his timing.

"But I still have time to have a quick cup of coffee with you before I go," he added, sitting back down.

Gwen hated herself for being manipulative, but she also had made it a personal rule that if she didn't MEAN to be manipulative, it didn't count. And that was the case this morning. She was just asking, not manipulating. Her "Mom Behavior" slate thus still clean, she poured herself a cup of coffee and brought the pot over to refill Rob's. She sat down, smiling at her son. "Thanks for staying a little longer," she said, and took his hand, patting it. "Busy day tomorrow, when you get back?" she asked companionably.

He nodded. "Always lots to do the week before classes begin," he said. "Just gotta make sure I've got everything set; all my materials prepped for lectures. You know how it is."

Gwen didn't, but she was happy to agree nevertheless. She sipped her coffee slowly, considered making herself a piece of toast. Rob interrupted her breakfast reverie.

"So, are you really going to this thing for your great aunt?" he asked. "It's an awfully long drive for an awfully distant relative."

Gwen thought about it for a few seconds, and then nodded in the affirmative. "You know, I wasn't sure at first if I wanted to make the effort," she said. "But I found some of her stuff last night in one of those boxes you brought down from the attic, and now, well–I guess I'm just curious about her. I had no idea, and my dad never told me much, but there was a commendation in there from President Nixon for her contributions to the improvement of public health. I knew she'd been a nurse in World War I, but no one ever told me anything about what she did afterwards. She must have been pretty impressive to get a presidential commendation."

And she wrote poetry, Gwen added quietly to herself. *What DIDN'T she do?*

"Anyway, you've been wonderful. I couldn't have finished up without your help. But I think at this point Cindy can have the house on the market pretty much as soon as she can get the sign up," Gwen continued. "Going to the ceremony will take my mind off things. Definitely less time to sit here and feel sorry for myself. And it's no fun at all trying to stay out of the way of potential buyers tramping through your house."

Rob looked at her somewhat askance. It was amazing how she could still read his mind, just from the angle of a subtly lifted eyebrow.

"I know what you're thinking," she said. "Yes, I'll be fine after the divorce. Your dad and I have figured out how to divide what we get from the house. I promise you, there will be minimal drama. It's pretty much all settled."

And then she remembered that, in fact, it wasn't. Not quite. There was still that thick manila envelope that had arrived a few weeks back–from Robert's lawyer. The envelope that Gwen just couldn't quite deal with, and which was still sitting on her desk, full of documents she somehow just hadn't found the time to read. Well, she'd get to it in time.

"And yes, of course I'll miss the house. It's been part of my life for a long time. But I have to let go of that now. It's not going to help me to stay here and wallow around in memories." Rob still looked unconvinced. She continued.

"Anyway, it's just a trip to Washington. I'll drive down for the ceremony and then I'll come back here. Maybe Cindy will have sold the house by then, and I won't have to keep it looking perfect and vacuum three times a day anymore. How long is the drive, anyway, from here to D.C.–maybe a day?"

"A long day," Rob replied, with emphasis on the *long*. "But you sound like you've thought this through, and it's always cool to learn more family history," he added, clearly trying to sound encouraging.

My son, the historian, Gwen thought to herself. *At least I'll have support from that quarter.*

"Let me know what you find out," he said as he got up from the table and cleared his dishes. "Who knows what interesting stuff may have been going on back then!"

Gwen could tell from his tone that he was quite skeptical that ANYTHING interesting could have been going on in their family close to a hundred years ago. And before going through the box of her aunt's memorabilia, Gwen would have been just as skeptical as he was. Now, though, she felt a tingle of excitement. Maybe there were some family secrets to be unearthed, she thought to herself. The trip suddenly looked less like an obligation and more like an adventure. She shivered a little in anticipation.

Today was Sunday. Labor Day would be a week from tomorrow. Maybe she could drive down next Saturday? That would give her a day to rest and regroup before the ceremony. She wondered if there would be anything to discover. Who knew? Maybe.

"So, you're really, truly, absolutely sure you're going to pull the trigger on this?" Cindy asked. "Because I'm not trying to rush you. You know that, right?" They were sitting at Gwen's kitchen table. Cindy had stopped by to do one last pre-listing inspection.

It was Tuesday, two days since Rob had left, and Gwen couldn't have been more sure. The house, now tidied and decluttered to the point of *House & Garden* photoshoot readiness, was positively deafening with memories. Gwen could hardly wait to leave.

Cindy still seemed concerned. "What about after it sells?" she asked. "Do you know where you're going to go?"

Gwen smiled, resisting the urge to pat her friend's hand. She suddenly realized she was being uncharacteristically devil-may-care.

"I appreciate the concern, Cin, I do. I promise, I'm going to be fine. The house will be easier for you to show if you don't have to work around me, right?" Cindy nodded. "And even if by some huge stroke of luck it sells right away," Gwen continued, "I'll still have some time to figure out where I want to go before the sale closes. I mean, if all else fails, I'm sure I can find an Airbnb somewhere until I figure out what I want to do."

Even as she spoke, Gwen felt a huge weight lifted off her shoulders, replaced by an intoxicating feeling of freedom. There was nothing she needed to do, nowhere she needed to be, no one she needed to take care of. The whole world was before her. She could live in a shack on a beach in Belize if she wanted. She could go where she pleased.

And where she pleased, for the moment, was Washington, D.C. The Mason-Hall School of Nursing.

Gwen gave herself a pat on the back for accuracy in estimating her day of departure. Saturday of Labor Day weekend saw her pull out of her driveway, on her way to D.C. It was a beautiful day, one of those perfect gifts when the sky is a deep, deep blue, and the air is so crisp it feels it might shatter. *I can see fall from here,* Gwen found herself thinking. The "For Sale" sign Cindy had put up late the previous afternoon gleamed shiny and white in the sun. Surprising herself a little, Gwen realized she hardly felt a leaving pang. It didn't feel so much like the end of a chapter as it did a beginning. She'd always loved driving. It gave her a sense of freedom, of infinite possibility. Exactly what she needed right now.

She sent a silent "thank you" heavenward to her dad, who had left her his prized, bright red Mustang. A love of fast cars—it was one of the things they'd had in common. The Mustang was old, but its power undiminished. *Just like me,* she thought, and smiled. She considered taking the top down, then thought better of it. It was a long drive to D.C. The first hour or two of wind in her hair might be fun, the remaining five, not so much.

Her phone pinged, and she took her eyes off the road for a split second to see who was calling. Robert. *Hmmm.* Not worth drawing her attention from the road to answer it. He was undoubtedly calling to remind her of something to do with the house that she had already taken care of, or perhaps to ask some convoluted question which was just a front for something Melissa wanted. Gwen hit "decline."

She wasn't avoiding anything, she told herself. In fact, she had taken the manila envelope with her, throwing it in the back seat (and hoping it might disappear under it). She just hadn't looked at it yet. There was no need to darken the skies with Robert, at least not today. She was no longer responsible for soothing his every anxiety. And if for some reason he was actually calling about something house-related, he was just as able to dial Cindy's number as she was. If it was Melissa-related, well, she didn't really care.

Inching along the Eastern Seaboard on I-95, Gwen was surprised to find herself–somewhat joyfully, she had to admit–singing along to the radio. It was one of those satellite stations, playing hits from the '70s, and Gwen could feel Rita Coolidge's love lifting her higher and higher with each passing mile. Or maybe it wasn't Rita's love. Someone else's maybe? *Who cares?* thought Gwen. Her house was on the market, she had left Cindy in charge, and she was doing something totally impulsive–indeed, almost irresponsible–for the first time since, well, ever.

She had actually packed for longer than just the few days book-ending the ceremony. Because, how long had it been, anyway, since she'd been away, a trip just for herself? She couldn't remember. And there were all those museums in D.C.; she'd never seen any of them. Indulging her new-found freedom, she had made a hotel reservation until the end of the week. Just in case she decided she wanted to stay on for a bit.

So, in the backseat was her new suitcase, purchased especially for this trip. And also, carefully stowed on the floor, the old, poorly taped and disintegrating box that she had literally stumbled over after Rob rescued it from the attic. It felt to her like a good luck talisman.

She had, of course, gone through the contents of the box more carefully since the evening she had rediscovered it, but she hadn't learned much more. The correspondence was entirely personal–"thank you" notes from friends for luncheons (Gwen wondered, idly, if anyone hosted luncheons anymore. Almost certainly not . . .), newsy letters from random people who had clearly long since moved away, birthday greeting cards, and holiday wishes. Gwen found herself wondering how all the personal correspondence had ended up in the box meant for her, to be honest. But none of it shed any light on the thin little manuscript that Gwen had discovered in the manila envelope or the two poems all by themselves at the bottom of the box.

There were, however, several intriguing letters from Aunt Adelaide. Gwen had shaken her head in frustration when she tried to read through them. The handwriting was almost impossible to decipher. Spidery and ornate to begin with, it had faded over time, so that it resembled nothing more than some crazily drawn black and white abstract by one of those post-Picasso artists that Gwen had never much cared for. Nevertheless, Gwen was able to make out that Adelaide was pleading for Elizabeth to return home as soon as she possibly could.

Most of the letters from Adelaide were dated sometime during the fall of 1917. Gwen wondered when Aunt Elizabeth might have actually received them, and where. Would she have still been in France? Although Aunt Elizabeth was clearly something of a saver, she had not saved the envelopes. So there was no way to learn the address to which they had been sent, or indeed whether and where they might have been forwarded. They could have followed Aunt Elizabeth halfway around the world and back, for all Gwen could tell now.

Gwen was suddenly aware that Rita Coolidge had risen so high she had quite literally floated away on the airwaves. The Eagles were now singing about the Hotel California. To her surprise, she realized she was already approaching the George Washington Bridge. Just a few hours to go, and she'd be in D.C.

It's just a stodgy old ceremony, she told herself, sternly. *I don't know what you're so excited about.* But she couldn't deny the presence of a few butterflies fluttering about in her stomach. It really did feel felt like she was going on an adventure. Would she learn more about some of the mysteries in the keepsake box? She didn't know, but right now that didn't matter. She hadn't had many adventures, and she was going to enjoy every minute of this one.

CHAPTER SEVEN

LIZZY

WAVES LIKE MOUNTAINS
Waves like mountains
Tower over me. But
Mountains stand tall, solid
Forever.
Waves crash,
Then build,
Only to fall. Then build,
And build
Again.
–Elizabeth Porter, 1917

Summer 1917–The Crossing

Whatever new experiences Lizzy encountered during her time at Mason-Hall, nothing had prepared her for the Atlantic crossing. The ship seemed to practically buzz with barely contained energy. Passengers, crew, and even the ship itself, which met each wave head-on, unafraid, all had tasks to be attended twenty-four hours a day. The sense of frenetic activity crossed over from time to time into something much more like desperation. No surprise there. They were headed to war, after all. The energy was contagious. Lizzy found it almost impossible to sleep.

Lizzy could tell the ship must have been, at some point, quite luxuriously appointed, but all traces of that luxury had been wholly erased in order to allow the ship's conversion from ocean liner to troop transport.

What previously had been snug but comfortable, double occupant staterooms were converted to hold at least six officer berths. There were rumors that some of the staterooms had bunks for even more, but Lizzy refused to believe it. Lizzy couldn't even imagine the sleeping arrangements below decks for what seemed like thousands of troops making the same crossing she was. She heard that soldiers were sleeping in shifts, head to toe, lined up in steerage like sardines in a can. She tried not to think about it. She also tried not to think about the motion of the ship, or about her bunkmates, who were completely unable to move much more than about ten feet from a lavatory (or, in a pinch, a handy bucket).

At least the weather was good. Lizzy spent as much time as she could on deck. The fresh air seemed to help keep any latent seasickness at bay, and it seemed that many of the other passengers agreed. There were often groups of soldiers on deck, walking in tight little clusters, looking quite intent and important. And handsome, Lizzy had to admit, in their crisp new uniforms. Lizzy could sense something that, if they hadn't all been headed off to an endeavor that would very possibly get them all killed, she would have said felt almost like excitement.

Excitement, whatever its genesis, often leads to parties. And no less so just because of the looming danger of Europe and the front, approaching inexorably with each slap of a wave against the ship's enormous hull. One of the ship's smaller ballrooms had escaped transformation into a dormitory–some of the officers on board had put their collective feet down and made it clear that a meeting room uncluttered with rows of bunk beds might be necessary from time to time. During the day, the officers gathered to discuss the latest battle news, but during the evenings and well into the night, the ballroom slipped easily back to its intended use. A few of the troops had apparently been unable to leave their musical instruments behind at home. Lizzy had counted at least five clarinets, and three trumpets. One young man had even brought his ukulele along. Lizzy wondered what on earth was going to become of those instruments once they all reached France, but it wasn't her problem, and she gave up worrying about it.

Not surprisingly, many of the men and some of the nurses had also realized that liquor might be hard to come by in the days ahead, and they took every opportunity to enjoy whatever liquid cheer was on hand. There was no "lights out" bugle on the ship, and it seemed that the impromptu parties went on most nights until dawn. And why not? Who would shut them down? How many more parties were there going to be on the front lines?

On the last night of the crossing, Lizzy was standing in her usual spot. To a casual observer, she might have appeared to be frowning in disapproval. Nothing could have been further from the truth. She was trying to memorize and absorb every detail, so that she would never forget. The dancing! She had never seen such dancing. In fact, she had never seen dancing at all. She watched, mesmerized, leaning against the wall by the line of chairs set up for those taking a few minutes' break from the activities.

She was so engrossed in the spectacle, in fact, that she was taken completely by surprise by the young man who came up alongside her. She didn't see him until he bowed, which, of course, she found a little funny, and also a little presumptuous. She didn't need rescuing. But she smiled, despite herself.

He smiled back, a glint of amusement in his eye. "May I have this next dance?" he asked. Not taking no for an answer, he started to lead her out onto the floor. She pulled back.

"You're terribly sweet," she said, trying to remain composed. "But I don't dance."

"Doesn't matter," the young man replied. "I can't even hear what they're playing. No one can. Hang on," he said, fishing something out of his pocket. It was a flask. "You'll dance better after a little of this."

Lizzy hesitated. She shouldn't, of course, but it was the last night of the crossing. Who was going to know or see? She took a swallow, then another. She could feel her whole body begin to relax, exactly the same way it had when Bea had shared her contraband across the cots at Mason-Hall. For all she knew, it WAS the same contraband. Didn't the young man have a bit of a drawl? Maybe he'd brought it all the way from Tennessee, just like Bea had. She tried, fruitlessly, to remember the name on the bottle that Bea had stashed in her trunk. After a third swallow, though, she didn't care anymore.

She looked, a little appraisingly, at the young man in front of her, who appeared still to believe she might join him on the dance floor. He was quite good looking, if she was being honest. Dark hair. Eyes—blue, perhaps? It was difficult to tell. A nice smile. But if there was one thing that Lizzy was NOT, it was interested in men. She had seen plenty on that score, and none of it was anything that she wanted any part of.

"You're quite chivalrous to share," she said, handing the flask back and nodding her head in thanks. "But I still don't dance."

"Everyone dances tonight," he replied. He took her arm firmly and led her out into the sea of bodies moving to the music.

He was right. Everyone was dancing. There were no complicated steps. Just a crush of limbs, moving randomly and almost entirely without regard to whatever tune it was that the few musicians were playing. The music didn't matter. She felt him put his arm around her waist, and, capitulating, she took his hand. A few steps, and they were in.

Was it just seconds later? Or hours? She was dizzy and breathless. It was so hot in the packed ballroom. "I have to sit for a moment," she almost shouted into his ear. There was no other way to make herself heard. He nodded, steering her back to the row of chairs.

"I think they have something that passes for punch at the other end of the room," he shouted back. "Would you like some?"

Lizzy nodded, yes. The young soldier-to-be plunged back into the crowded floor, and Lizzy lost sight of him almost instantly. She wondered if he'd really come back.

When he didn't, although she wouldn't admit to disappointment, she wasn't surprised. She waited a while; *longer than he deserves*, she thought. Ridiculous to be charmed by a firm hand on her waist and a mischievous glint. She knew better. And she wouldn't let it happen again. She couldn't tell how long she'd waited, but it felt longer than was appropriate. Men were not creatures to be relied upon, in her experience. No, even that assessment felt too benign. At best useless, and at worst, well, that didn't bear thinking about. He was probably just looking for some last comfort before heading off to France. It wasn't going to be her providing it.

She pushed her way out of the crowd and made her way out onto the deck. The night air felt cool, and somehow clean. She paused for a moment and looked up, amazed at the sheer number of stars. She didn't think she had ever seen that many back home. As she made her way back to her bunk, she found herself wondering what might have become of the young man.

I didn't even get his name, she thought. *He didn't get mine.* An inner voice chided her. *Silly. It doesn't matter. It was just dancing. You'll never see him again.*

CHAPTER EIGHT

GWEN

> *Northern Cardinals are reported to nest in more than 50 species of trees and shrubs . . .*
>
> *The female chooses the spot . . .*
>
> *Cardinals,* S. Tekiela, p. 13.

Now–Washington, D.C.

The Mason-Hall auditorium was surprisingly crowded on Labor Day Monday. Gwen realized, as she found a seat toward the center of the hall, that she had been mentally handicapping the attendance, subconsciously preparing herself for a somewhat depressing turnout. How many people out there would be interested in honoring nurses, however accomplished, who graduated from a little-known nursing school at the turn of the last century? Who, really, would care anymore?

It turned out, quite a few. As the lights dimmed, Gwen sneaked a quick glance over her shoulder, just out of curiosity. The auditorium was almost full. This was much more well attended than the small, informal gathering, with very little pomp or circumstance, that she had expected. She started to wonder who had been invited. Clearly not just immediate relatives of the honorees. Perhaps the school was more well known than Gwen had realized.

She turned back to look at the stage, only to see five greater-than-life-size images projected onto the backdrop. And one of them, there, right in front of her and breathtakingly vivid, was Aunt Elizabeth. Gwen was instantly grateful that she had found the photo of her aunt and Lieutenant Flynn, otherwise she might not have recognized the vibrant and proud woman on the screen. The image was so startlingly lifelike that she half expected to reach out and feel a living hand take hers.

The presenter, the current matron, spent about ten or fifteen minutes on each of the five distinguished graduates. Two of them had worked tirelessly for the Red Cross, and two had spent years working to establish modern medical care in underserved regions.

And then there was Elizabeth. She had apparently taken her public health degree and single-handedly brought decent healthcare to rural Virginia. She was continuing to establish clinics, staffing them herself when necessary, well into the early 1960s. Family members of the honorees were called out at the end of the program and asked to stand. Gwen rose when it was her turn, graciously accepting the applause, and feeling guilty about receiving accolades for having done nothing at all except have the luck to be related to someone exceptional.

Afterward, there was a luncheon reception in the school canteen. Gwen found herself next to Matron and introduced herself, complimenting Matron on the morning. Feeling a bit as though she should have done more homework on the school and the honorees, but still curious about the crowd, she tried to find a tactful way to ask Matron who precisely had been invited.

Matron was happy to oblige. "We decided to use this occasion to fundraise, of course, but also to work on raising our profile in the healthcare community," Matron explained. "Invitations were sent to school alumnae, other nursing schools, local hospital administrators. We even sent invitations to descendants of early graduates, if we could find them. I must say, we were more than pleased at the response. Our graduates and their families are very loyal to the school, and current graduates seem to be in high demand all over the country."

"Well," Gwen replied, "I was very impressed. With my aunt, as well as with the honorees."

"Your aunt had quite the reputation," Matron said, admiringly. "Is there anyone else here for her with you?"

"Except for my son, who couldn't make it today, I'm really the only family member left," Gwen replied.

"I'm so glad you were able to come," the Matron replied. "Are you going to go down to Richmond as well?"

Gwen was momentarily confused. Richmond? Why would she go to Richmond? Her confusion must have been visible, because Matron continued, almost apologetically.

"The library at the University of Richmond?" Matron asked. "We wish we had your aunt's papers here, but she felt quite loyal to the University of Richmond. I was only wondering, since you've come all this way." Matron looked at her a bit quizzically. "I had just assumed you might be wanting to go look at the collection there. We don't have much here."

Papers? A collection? Gwen had had no idea. "You're catching me just a bit off guard," Gwen admitted. "My dad was the family member who was closest to her, and he never mentioned anything about papers or a collection. This is the first I've heard."

"I'm told it's very much worth seeing," Matron said. "I haven't been able to go myself, but I know what it contains because several of my predecessors tried very hard to acquire it for our own archives here at Mason-Hall. It was a while ago, of course, but people still talk about Miss Porter. She was the most well known of our honorees, I think, because her work had such an enormous impact on our local communities." Matron went on. "It might be interesting to go see it if you have time. I think the University of Richmond has her journals, as well as some of the manuscripts for her articles. Anyway, I've heard there's quite a bit there. Especially as a family member, you might enjoy it. If you have the time, of course."

Matron trailed off a little, her attention captured by someone else. Gwen was left to ponder the implications of having a relative with collected papers in a fairly prestigious university. Gwen got the distinct sense that, even if she didn't think she had the time, Matron was of the firm opinion that she should find a way to make some. Gwen was inclined to agree.

She mingled a bit more with some of the family members of the other honorees, finally assembling a plateful of tiny sandwiches that, between holding the plate, her purse, the program and her jacket, she found she couldn't really negotiate eating. She resigned herself to just carrying it around. As the crowd thinned out, she noticed a little group surrounding Matron at the other end of the canteen. She didn't want to interrupt them to say her good-byes, but Matron suddenly excused herself from the group and made her way over to Gwen.

"I just remembered," Matron said, taking Gwen's arm. "We do still have a file on your aunt. I think the few things in it were meant to pique our interest in her collection—although truly, no enticement would have been necessary. I asked one of the office assistants to run over to the file room to check. Anyway, I thought there might be something we still had of hers, and I was right, there was. I think you should have it." Matron held out an old sepia photo. It was Aunt Elizabeth with a woman Gwen had never seen before. She turned the photo over.

"There's no inscription," Matron said. "But I can tell you who the other young lady was. Her name was Beatrice Rockford, and she was a student here at the same time as your aunt. Her family have been generous donors to the school over the years. In fact," Matron continued, turning in the direction of the little group she had just left, "I can introduce you to her daughter." Matron made as if to approach them, only to see that they were already out of sight, past the exit. Matron sighed in disappointment.

"Oh dear," she said, regretfully. "Well, I suspect Miss Jane may have been starting to tire. That's too bad. You might have had some history in common." Gwen felt inexplicably regretful at having missed the opportunity to connect with them, although she couldn't quite say why.

"If you go to Richmond," Matron said, "you must let me know what you find! I do hope to get there myself someday."

Gwen said of course she would. And as she spoke, she realized that yes, her plans had changed. She had suddenly lost all interest in touring the Smithsonian. Richmond wasn't that far away, and it would be just as easy to visit Rob from there as from D.C. There was nothing waiting for her back in Wayland, except obsessive-compulsive tidying and people parading through her house at inconvenient intervals. Cindy would have everything house related under control. There was absolutely no reason she couldn't go to Richmond.

She looked again at the photograph Matron had pressed into her hand. Although they weren't smiling (*there it is again, that silly custom*, she thought), her aunt and Miss Rockford had their arms intertwined. So clearly they had been friends. Good friends, it was easy to see. *Just one more interesting bit of history to explore*, she thought.

She was only a few hours away from Richmond, and it would be an easy enough drive. When might she have another opportunity? It was almost as though a path had been laid out. First the Mason-Hall ceremony, which led her to D.C., and now her aunt's papers were luring her to Richmond. She decided to try not to over-analyze the situation. She was going to Richmond. It was as simple as that.

Back at her hotel, she told the front desk she'd be leaving sooner than expected. They were most accommodating. She spent the evening researching Airbnbs near the University of Richmond. As she looked at the various neighborhoods, she was suddenly struck by the realization that the University of Richmond was in the same area of Richmond as the house that her aunts had shared. She wracked her brain. Could she remember the address? Maybe it was somewhere in the letters in the box she'd brought with her. She'd left the box in her car; she'd check tomorrow morning. Maybe the house was still there too. The very thought made Gwen feel almost as though a family member had resurfaced after long being thought lost. Now there was even more to explore in Richmond–her Aunt Elizabeth's papers AND her Aunt Elizabeth's house. A path laid out. It felt a little like going home.

CHAPTER NINE

LIZZY

CAROUSEL
Why is the carousel merry?
The horses frozen, eternally—
Where is the joy in that?
Cruel, the moniker. A merry-go-
Round, and around, and around again.
No rest. Just rounds.
Meals.
Morphine.
Linens.
Bedpans.
And again,
And again.
And again.
Where is the joy
In that?

—Elizabeth Porter, 1917

Summer 1917–France

Lizzy assumed (and she didn't think it was asking too much), when she signed up to be included in the roster for the base hospital, that since the word "hospital" was used in the description, she would find an actual building, housing an actual hospital, upon her arrival. This was not the case. The base hospital at Toul was nothing more than a cluster of aging shacks, each retrofitted for whatever purpose seemed to be required—dormitory, operating theater, administrative office. Nothing was clean; everything leaked. There were no roads, just tracks in mud.

Whatever the hardships, however, Lizzy did not have much time to feel sorry for herself. There were groups of wounded soldiers arriving at the hospital every day from the makeshift emergency tents closer to the front. Some of the arriving injured could be helped; some could not. Lizzy found she much preferred shifts on the rehabilitation ward over work among the actual critical care hospital beds. The rehabilitation ward housed soldiers who actually had hope of going home. They were too injured to return to the front, or even yet to undertake the journey back to their home country, but there was a good chance of a return to some semblance of their former, uninjured, selves. They just needed a little time. The rehabilitation ward was peaceful, almost restful. Her duties there seemed not really to be work at all. She helped the men write letters, asked them about their families and sweethearts waiting for them back home, played cards or games with those who were able. Lizzy signed up for those shifts as often as possible.

The other job Lizzy loved was driving.

It started as a lark. Goodness knows Lizzy had never had the opportunity to be behind the wheel of a vehicle back in Wytheville. No one in her entire town had even owned an automobile, as far she knew. But here, it seemed there was always a patient needing to be transported, or supplies to be collected or transferred, and never anyone around able to take the time. Lizzy started hanging around the edge of the hospital grounds where the trucks and the Ford Model T ambulances were parked, and she befriended a couple of the mechanics. They thought it would be quite entertaining to put the girl from backwater Virginia behind the wheel of an ambulance that needed a crank start and a driver with the shoulders of a stevedore to turn the steering wheel.

Once she got past a couple of heart-stopping near-encounters with large poplars that seemed to spring out of nowhere, Lizzy realized that there wasn't nearly so much to it as she might have thought. In fact, it was easy, once you got the hang of it. She began to enjoy the feeling of the tires almost skidding out from under her in the muddy tracks.

Behind the wheel, she was in complete and sole control. That wasn't something she had encountered growing up, and she found it intoxicating. She also loved feeling useful as she ferried supplies and patients from one makeshift hospital camp to another. If that useful feeling came with a bit of excitement, well, so much the better.

November 1917–France

It was a Tuesday. And it was raining. Which made it absolutely no different from any other day. In fact, Lizzy had started to lose track of the days, because there was nothing to mark one as any different from any other. Only her journal, with its dated entries, kept her anchored to any perception of time.

And it was hard for her to find any opportunity even to write the entries; by the time her days ended, usually well past midnight, she was so drained she could only write a few lines before bed. Certainly, there was no time to write in the rush of early morning. Helping to prepare morning meals, feeding those unable to feed themselves, emptying bed pans, changing dressings. The rounds were never-ending. Just as she felt she might have time to take a breath after the completion of one set of tasks, she would realize she was already behind schedule on another. Nevertheless, even with only the opportunity to write a few lines, Lizzy could almost always manage to think of an incident, maybe even two, that would make the day stand out. A red-headed soldier, perhaps. There weren't many of those. A new nurse arriving. Death.

And at first, in truth, the deaths were milestones. But particularly in the last few months since fall arrived, the deaths had become routine as well. There were so many that they no longer marked the days. Lizzy could feel herself becoming numb.

But this particular day would be easy to mark.

It began uneventfully enough. She rose at dawn, gulped down a quick cup of tea, made her morning rounds. Just as she was about to take her noon break, one of the camp doctors spotted her on her way back to her barracks and grabbed her arm. Lizzy could see he was panicked. "Aren't you one of the nurses that can drive?" he asked. "Can you drive a truck?"

Lizzy nodded, yes.

"I wouldn't ask unless it was an emergency, but we've lost most of our ambulance drivers."

Lizzy's eyes widened in horror, and the doctor realized what she must be thinking.

"No, no, not injured. They've just been borrowed by one of the field hospitals closer to the front. Most of them took off a few hours ago to help bring in wounded from the front lines, and they haven't managed to make it back yet. Roads must be terrible. Anyway, we need you to start ferrying some of the wounded back here, the ones that are stable enough to travel. I think most of the ambulances are gone as well—you'll have to take a truck and a couple of other nurses to help."

Lizzy felt her heart start to race with excitement. To be able to get close to the front lines, really do some good, bring the men back to safety, well, now that was what the war effort was all about! Lizzy nodded and saluted. *Was she even supposed to salute?* She felt herself turning slightly pink, never remembering what military protocol was required.

She turned and ran off to the barracks to see which of the other nurses might be available to help her. It was only after the doctor disappeared into one of the surgery tents that she realized she'd been so excited that she hadn't asked which field hospital she was to drive to. Never mind. She'd check with him before she left. It was probably Field Hospital #5, about fifteen miles east. She'd driven there once before, and she knew the road. She felt fairly sure it was one of the ones that remained passable, more or less, even in the rain. She hoped she was right.

An hour later found her behind the wheel of one of the army surplus trucks, two quickly corralled nurses crowded into the front seat beside her, almost visibly gritting their teeth against the bumps. "It feels like you're going awfully fast," one ventured timidly. Lizzy tried not to smile. She was barely going ten miles an hour. The road she thought she knew had taken on an entirely new personality after being drowned in rainwater for weeks. The act of driving became an almost metaphysical task; it seemed she needed to propel the truck forward through the ruts by sheer force of will.

"We're almost there," she told her companions, hoping she sounded reassuring. "Just past those trees on the left." Lizzy wrestled the steering wheel into submission one more time and hoped she was right.

To Lizzy's great relief, Field Hospital #5 did, in fact, appear just beyond the small grove of trees Lizzy had recognized. But as she pulled the truck off the road and looked for the staging area where she would be picking up the injured, she realized that any semblance of order in the camp had vanished. She saw tarps raised on poles, scattered in no particular order across the site, with wounded men on stretchers crowded under the makeshift shelters in hopes of staying out of the worst of the rain. A few solitary planks were laid hopefully across the mud, but they fulfilled little actual purpose. For the most part the hospital site was just as flooded and rutted as the road.

And the noise. It was surprisingly noticeable, oddly intermittent but also constant at the same time. Explosions from artillery? Rifle shots? Each burst coming just close enough on the heels of the last so as to set anyone's nerves permanently on edge, waiting for the next. It was the noise that made Lizzy realize she must be closer to the actual front lines than she had thought. She felt as though she could almost smell gunpowder. An explosion came louder than the rest, and Lizzy felt it in her eardrums. Must be closer than the others, she realized, beginning to feel just a slight shiver of worry. She shouted at her nurse companions to stay close to the truck and started picking her way carefully across the planks to the closest tarp shelter, hoping to find a surgeon or nurse in charge.

"You there, are you here to take the wounded back?" a harried looking soldier called to her from another tent.

"Yes," Lizzy called back. "Our truck is just over there. How many are there?"

"How big is your truck?" the soldier responded.

In the end, they were able to fit only two stretchers. Lizzy watched as several soldiers helped load the men in, with the nurses squeezing themselves in between the stretchers so they could watch over them on the journey back to Toul. One of the men looked to be not too badly off, talking and even managing to joke a bit about the war, the artillery noises, the rain. One, though, seemed to sleep through the entire transfer.

"How can he manage to sleep through all this commotion?" Lizzy asked one of the soldiers loading the stretchers in.

"Oh, he's not sleeping, sweetheart," the soldier replied. "You miss the class on concussions? He hasn't come around yet. No other injuries, they don't think. The docs are hoping he'll come out of it if he has a chance to rest. No sign of anything yet, though. He's been like this for a few days."

Lizzy looked at the young man more carefully. He seemed familiar, somehow, but she couldn't quite place him. Dark hair, pale, tall, perhaps, had he been able to stand. And then an image from the crossing suddenly came to mind. Of a makeshift dance floor, swaying a little too perceptibly with the motion of the Atlantic waves. A young man, with an unmistakable glint in his eye, who had offered her punch and then never returned. She felt a moment of vindication that perhaps this was his reward for rudeness, but her better instincts won the day, and she banished that thought as thoroughly uncharitable. No one deserved this severe a punishment, however uncivil they might have been on an Atlantic crossing literally months ago. *It was, after all,* Lizzy reminded herself, *just punch. I didn't want to dance anyway.*

Trying not to be too terribly insulted by the soldier who disparaged her training in recognizing concussions, she walked back around the front of the truck and hoisted herself up into the driver's seat. The soldier who had helped load in the stretchers pounded on the back, which Lizzy took to mean all clear to start the drive back to Toul.

That night, in the last few minutes before blowing out her lantern, Lizzy wrote a few lines in her journal, to try (as she always did) to capture what might make this day different from the others, identifiable as an event in its own right. It was a bit easier tonight, though. There was the drive to the field hospital, the injured soldiers. And, in particular, the young man from the ship. She didn't like admitting it, because she was still cross, but asleep like that, he was well, beautiful. An Adonis, almost. A male Sleeping Beauty.

Her interest was purely clinical, of course. She was noting his looks only so as to remember who it was she was writing about if she came back to that entry. In fact, Lizzy noted with irritation, even remaining cross with him was more effort than he warranted. Ever since she could remember, Lizzy had made a conscious effort to avoid entanglements. Honestly, "effort" was the wrong word. "Effort" implied work, and she didn't even have to try. She had had absolutely no inclination to give a man even a second glance. Papa had surely seen to that.

As she closed her journal and got ready to turn the lantern down, she realized with annoyance that she had doodled "SB" across the page. She started erasing, thankful that this entry, at least, was in pencil. She hoped she got them all.

Drifting off to sleep, though, she did find herself wondering about the color of his eyes.

Lizzy was happy to discover that, over the next few days, her hours were almost entirely scheduled in the rehabilitation ward. And, although she worked her very hardest at giving equal time and energy to all of her charges, she found herself spending a bit more time by the bed of Sleeping Beauty than might have been completely necessary. She was able to find out his name, anyway—Joseph Flynn. He was an American, and a lieutenant. But she hadn't been able to unearth any more information about him than that.

In any case, she told herself, she had learned in her training that even unconscious men responded better if they were read to, talked to. The best chance for them to wake up was to treat them as if they already had. So Lizzy read to Joseph from anything she had on hand. Old newspapers. Some Mark Twain. A copy of *A Christmas Carol* that had mysteriously made its way into the ward. She wished there were letters for him, but none arrived.

Although still unconscious, he started taking on a life in her journals, where she faithfully chronicled every encouraging stir, every slight returned squeeze of a hand, however faint. "SB color better this evening," she would note, or "SB mumbles, speech?" She knew his name but calling him SB was so much easier to write in the precious few minutes she had before sleep. And anyway, he still looked like Sleeping Beauty, with his dark hair and pale skin. Who was going to judge her for a nickname? Her journals were private, for her alone. No one would ever know.

And so it went, until Thanksgiving morning, about a week after Lizzy had driven the truck back to Toul through the rain and mud. Rumor had it that the cook staff was planning an approximation of a Thanksgiving feast, and Lizzy found herself walking with an unexpected slight spring in her step. She wondered if there might be pie.

Still daydreaming about dessert, she found herself already in the rehabilitation ward for her first shift. She noticed immediately that Joseph Flynn's bed was empty. Her heart sank. She almost ran to the Head Nurse's desk to ask what had happened to him.

"Lieutenant Flynn? He's in the wheelchair, sitting with the other officers. Just over there." Head Nurse pointed. Lizzy couldn't believe it. He was awake. Talking. Laughing. She felt an irrational flood of happiness.

And also, now that he appeared to be quite likely to survive—yes, she had to admit it, a flood of annoyance at being abandoned for punch. One should expect such behavior from men, Lizzy knew, but still.

For the entire morning, she looked for excuses to avoid the aisle his bed was on. She busied herself with linens, bandage changing, anything she could find that would take her out of his way. Until, just after lunch, she was attending to one of the officers who had been chatting with Lieutenant Flynn that morning.

As she tidied up around him and sat him up more comfortably on his pillows, he suddenly looked at her intently, grabbed her arm, and called out across the ward. "Hey Joe! This is the nurse! She's the one that's been reading to you!" He turned to her. "Nurse Lizzy, right?" Lizzy blushed. "He's been asking who it was who kept reading to him about Marley's Ghost," the officer said, still holding on to Lizzy's arm. "I think he wants to talk to you about alternative reading selections." The officer let go and nodded in the general direction of Flynn's cot. "I promised him if I saw you, I'd send you over." The brief exchange seemed to be all he could manage, and he leaned back against his pillows and closed his eyes.

Lizzy didn't know quite what to do. She was mortified. The best course was just to do her job, she told herself firmly. She walked on down the rest of the aisle and up the next, attending to her charges. Until she came to Lieutenant Flynn's bed, where it seemed only proper, after the shouted exchange across the rows of beds, to pause.

"You know, I did tell Buddy to look for you," he said. "I'm sorry if he embarrassed you. He can be a little rough around the edges."

Lizzy smiled. A hospital ward somewhere in France struck her as the very antithesis of polite society, so what did it matter. And the lieutenant's slightly lopsided grin seemed to indicate he agreed.

"I'm so glad you're awake," Lizzy said, arranging his pillows. "We weren't sure . . ." She tried to keep her tone professional, but as she realized where her sentence was headed, she stopped and turned her attention back to the pillows.

He replied, smiling again, "What encouraged me was that I was going to have to wake up if I wanted something else from the hospital library."

"I am sorry to tell you that, well, there's not an enormous amount of choice," Lizzy responded, self-consciously serious. "It's mostly old newspapers, the Dickens . . . I tried Twain, but that seemed to make you restless, so I went back to Mr. Scrooge. There might be some Robert Louis Stevenson, I can look . . .?"

He shook his head. "I'm just teasing you," he said, smiling. "Whatever you did was great. I don't even remember most of it. In fact, pretty much the last thing I remember was a huge burst, kind of behind me. It must have been an artillery shell. I think it was Buddy who dragged me out. So I'm pretty forgiving these days about his lack of social graces. I know I was really out for a while. But it was nice to have a feeling that someone was here." He turned his gaze directly at her. "Thank you." he said.

Blue, she thought. *His eyes are blue.*

And then, after that discovery, Lizzy was suddenly conscious, for the first time in months, that her blouse was not as clean as it could have been, and in fact, might not have been changed in several days, that the hem of her skirt was filthy, and that her pinafore was stained with fluids she didn't even want to consider. "I think I need to move on, Lieutenant Flynn," she said, starting for the aisle.

"No, hang on, just a minute," he said. "Now that I've woken up, does that mean you don't read to me anymore?"

Lizzy blushed again. For the second time that morning. She felt like a schoolgirl. She was also suddenly aware that Lieutenant Flynn spoke with a pronounced—and very charming—southern drawl. In fact, they both had a drawl—Lieutenant Flynn and his quite talkative friend, Buddy. It reminded her of Bea.

"I enjoyed reading to you," she said, "and I'm glad it helped. Of course I can continue. I just need to get through my shift, and I then I can come back later in the day. Perhaps this evening. I'll look for the Stevenson."

Lieutenant Flynn smiled. "I'm looking forward to it," he said. "And no need for the Stevenson. I need a refresher on what happens to the 'ghost of Christmas yet to come.'"

She made to leave, inexplicably happy about the opportunity to return that evening, when she heard him call her back.

"You know," he said, a little quizzically. "It's the craziest thing. I feel like I know you from somewhere. I guess that's not very likely?"

Lizzy didn't know what to say. She didn't want to explain, yes, we danced on the ship that brought us to Europe, and yes, you said you'd come back, and then no, you didn't. And now, you don't even remember me. So she shook her head and went to finish her rounds.

The Thanksgiving feast prepared by the kitchen staff was not quite what might have been prepared at home, but it was a good—and welcome—effort. And, as Lizzy had hoped, there was indeed pie. Lizzy wrapped an extra piece in a napkin to bring with her back to the ward, just in case there were still food restrictions in place for Lieutenant Flynn. Contraband pie would be a minor infraction at worst, and at best? Well, what could be better than pie? Certainly, she couldn't see the harm in a small piece.

She was halfway back when she remembered that the much-maligned *Christmas Carol* was still back in her bunk. She hurried back to retrieve it. It wasn't where it should have been on the tiny table next to her bed, so she had to sit and think, for a moment, of where it might be.

Her bunkmate, Alice. Had she put it somewhere? She had. Alice was always straightening up, moving things around. The book, perhaps left on the floor or on Lizzy's bed by accident, was now part of a neat arrangement on Alice's half of their shared bureau.

Lizzy grabbed the book and caught sight of herself in the scratched mirror Alice had insisted on putting up. She couldn't remember the last time she had looked. She scrutinized her reflection. Overall, not too bad. Light brown hair, some might even say honey colored. Well, a dark honey, anyway. After months of inattention, it was quite long. She kept it coiled severely in a knot, in accordance with Head Nurse's regulations, but the occasional strand would curl out and away, looking for (and often finding) escape. *The effect is not displeasing,* Lizzy thought. Complexion? Unremarkable. But certainly not bad. Face somewhat heart-shaped. Eyelashes long and dark. Hair could do with something. *Perhaps a wash,* she thought to herself, ruefully. But yes, overall, not too bad. She couldn't see her figure in the mirror—she hoped she hadn't become too thin. *But nothing to do about it now,* she sighed to herself. She grabbed Mr. Dickens, retrieved the carefully wrapped piece of pie, and started back to the ward.

She hoped he liked pecan. There hadn't been a lot of choice when she left the canteen. The apple was entirely gone, and she had nothing against cherry, but she just couldn't bring herself to associate it with Thanksgiving. So, pecan it was. She remembered Bea going on about how much she missed it over the holidays when they were together at Mason-Hall, and Lieutenant Flynn's drawl was much the same as Bea's. *That hardly means they have same taste in pastry,* Lizzy thought, but, well, the choice was made.

She found herself walking toward the wards a little faster than she usually did, with a feeling that could almost be called excitement? Anticipation? *You're being ridiculous,* Lizzy thought to herself. *You are bringing pie and Dickens to a recovering soldier who might not like either of them and who clearly doesn't remember you. There is nothing else happening here.*

But, as it turned out, there was. First, when Lizzy delivered the pie, Lieutenant Flynn declared it was his favorite. That left Lizzy with an explicable warm glow.

Second, Lieutenant Flynn asked, a little sheepishly, if they might forgo the Dickens for the evening, and just talk for a few minutes. Lizzy nodded in agreement and pulled a chair up to his bedside. For someone who had expressed an interest in talking, Lieutenant Flynn suddenly became uncharacteristically quiet. There was silence between them for a few awkward moments, until Lieutenant Flynn started to speak, a little louder than was probably necessary. Was he embarrassed? Lizzy couldn't quite tell.

"You know I said I thought you were familiar?" he started. Lizzy nodded, not wanting to meet his eyes.

"Well, I remembered where I know you from. It was the boat, right?" But he didn't need to ask. They both knew.

Lizzy started to respond, it doesn't matter, no harm done, it was a crowded ship, I didn't need punch anyway, all the usual excuses. But Lieutenant Flynn interrupted her.

"I meant to come back. I was on my way. But Buddy, well, we grew up together, and he was having a bad night. He had managed to pick a fight with some guy, Navy, I think, and the guy was about twice Buddy's size. AND feeling that the Navy deserved more respect than he was getting from Buddy under the circumstances, given that we were all in a boat and on the ocean. Navy guy seemed to have the idea that it was *his* ocean, and probably his boat too. Anyway, it wasn't going well for Buddy. I was starting to think that he might not survive the party, much less the war. I got him back to his bunk, cleaned him up a little and put him to bed, but when I finally got back to look for you, you were gone." He added, "I'm sorry." Genuinely penitent, it seemed. "I owe you a glass of punch."

Short of cross-examining Buddy, Lizzy couldn't be sure if the story was true or only recently concocted when he realized he might have fences to mend. But she decided to accept it. The sentiment seemed heartfelt enough.

"I think punch is in fairly short supply here," she said. "But perhaps you'll share a few bites of the pie? Then I think we can call your obligation fulfilled."

He nodded and smiled, visibly relieved. And then, a touch mischievously, he whispered, "You never know about punch. It shows up in the craziest places."

"You're not talking about contraband alcohol, I trust?" Lizzy asked, in mock horror.

And again, that mischievous smile. "More pie?" he asked.

CHAPTER TEN

GWEN

> *Pairs visit several potential nest sites before starting construction.*
>
> *Cardinals,* S. Tekiela, p. 13.

Now–Richmond, Virginia

Tuesday morning found Gwen giving herself a mental pat of congratulations for thinking to bring the box of Aunt Elizabeth's papers with her. After a quick breakfast in the hotel lobby restaurant, she retrieved the box from her car and took it back up to her room.

And she was in luck. Flipping once again through crumbling letters and envelopes, she managed to find one of the few envelopes that was both intact and blessed with a still legible address. Number 24 Elm Street. Once she saw the meandering script from one of Aunt Elizabeth's correspondents, it was as though she'd known the address all along. She had an instant crystal-clear mental picture of the house, the back garden, the rough stone of the birdbath by the fence. She knew the odds were small that after close on fifty years it had retained any of the dilapidated charm she remembered, but she could hope.

An internet map search revealed that, yes, the house was only blocks away from the center of the University of Richmond's main campus. It suddenly made complete sense that Aunt Elizabeth might have felt loyalty to the institution, only blocks from her house, that gave her the degree that enabled her to make so much of her life.

Gwen felt a small pang of sympathy for all the matrons at Mason-Hall who had not managed to acquire the collection, but the pang was short lived. *Of course her papers are here,* she thought. *It's the only sensible place.*

She couldn't help but acknowledge a little buzz of curiosity. The special collections were on the third floor of the main library–hours: 10 a.m. to 6 p.m. The Airbnb she'd found was serendipitously located within walking distance of both the library and the house. Gwen figured that if she made a reasonable start Tuesday, mid-morning, she'd miss most of the post-holiday traffic and still manage to reach Richmond in fairly good time.

And so she did. She didn't know what she'd been expecting, really, but the Airbnb was charming. It had clearly originally constituted the ground floor of a rowhouse, built when rooms were stately and ceilings high. Even now, after a cookie-cutter remodel to maximize occupancy and income, the rooms felt spacious, despite there being only three of them. A living room, which led into the kitchen and dining area, which led in turn to a small but comfortable bedroom in the back. There was even a small side garden off the kitchen, with just enough room for two deck chairs, although the two resident pots of geraniums looked to be in need of some TLC. Gwen wasn't sure whose responsibility it might be to water them, and from the looks of them this had been an unresolved issue for some time. At least there was air conditioning, for which, given the heat, she was quite grateful. It would do.

Although it didn't take her long to set up house-keeping, by the time she had settled in, figured out the Wi-Fi connection and visited the grocery store, it was after 4 p.m. The library would be closing soon, and she didn't want to arrive there only to have to leave again in short order.

She considered her options. Should she call Rob? Let him know where she was? He knew she'd gone to D.C., of course, but he had no idea she was in Richmond.

Well, perhaps she should call, but she realized she was very much enjoying what was beginning to feel almost illicit. She could call Rob tomorrow. If he was worried about her for some reason, the phone worked both ways last time she checked. Right now, she was going to go for a walk. And she was fairly certain the walk was going to take her right past number 24 Elm Street.

If she was being honest with herself, Gwen wasn't sure exactly what she had expected to find. But as she started out down the sidewalk that ran past the Airbnb, she realized that whatever romantic image of the Antebellum South she had imagined, the truth, at least in this neighborhood, was quite different. There were no crumbling bricks and vines left to their own devices, no gnarled trees barely contained in tiny front plots, no stained-glass panels over tall and narrow front doors.

What confronted her instead was gentrification. Renovated house after renovated house, lot-line to lot-line, all painted in what seemed to her must be a rigidly codified color scheme, with carefully coordinated hedges delicately screening front porches that, in fact, had nothing to hide. There was eggshell with black shutters, green with black shutters, grey with black shutters.

Gwen wondered who had current custody of the design manual. She imagined each house with its stainless-steel kitchen, engineered ash flooring, edgily decorated powder room at the end of the first-floor hallway.

She hoped her aunt's old house had retained some of its soul. Perhaps the back garden was still overgrown. Perhaps there might even be some undisturbed dust in an unnoticed corner. One could hope.

Rounding the corner onto Elm, she let out a sigh of dismay. The neat rows of houses on both sides of the street were clearly following the same design protocol as the houses she had already passed. She felt herself prickling with irrational disappointment. And, she realized, she was also beginning to prickle with perspiration.

A few sharp doubts rose to the foreground of her thoughts. *What in the hell am I doing here?* she asked herself. *There will be nothing here for me. What did I think I would find?* She stopped, shook her head, lifted the hair off the back of her neck. *The trip will not be a total waste,* she told herself. *You came for the library and the papers, the family history. The house was just an afterthought. You could make a trip to the library tomorrow morning, take a quick look at the collection, then get in the car, drive to Charlottesville, surprise Rob.* She almost turned around.

But then, squinting one last time down the block into the late afternoon sun, something caught her eye. An almost ghostly silhouette of a little ugly-duckling house, practically invisible, sandwiched as it was between two recently renovated behemoths. She crossed her fingers. Number 24? In spite of the heat, and even from a block away, the house gave off a sense of being tantalizingly cool, shadowed as it was by its neighbors. She quickened her pace.

And there it was. Gwen stood quietly on the side-walk in front of number 24 for a few minutes, mentally ticking off what she remembered from that long ago visit against what was still there. She arrived fairly rap-idly at the conclusion that the house was, to the best of her memory, exactly as she remembered it, right down to the aging elm dominating the tiny front yard, the pots of leggy petunias on the sagging front porch, and the gently peeling paint that might at some point long past have been teal. Seeing the house so unexpectedly and precisely preserved, Gwen had a sudden burst of hope that the birdbath might still be in the back gar-den, playing host to a new generation of cardinals, with a new generation of bunnies nesting under the fence. She found herself holding her breath, practically will-ing a flash of red to appear in the elm in the front yard and begin singing. Some sort of sign that she was in the right place, doing the right thing. No signs appeared.

A couple of cars drove slowly by, and Gwen was jolted out of her reverie. This was most definitely the kind of neighborhood where everyone probably knew everyone else, with potential trespassers quickly iden-tified and reported. In fact, she realized that a still in-distinct figure had turned the corner at the other end of the block and was striding purposefully down the street, toward her, it appeared. Neighborhood Watch, perhaps? Come to ask her about her business?

As the figure came into focus, it looked like a man—heading her way. She squinted at him, regretting that she had forgotten her sunglasses. Resident? Policeman? Yes, definitely a man. Best at this point to just avoid any potential interaction, she decided. She turned around and started to walk back to the Airbnb. Tomorrow she would get an early start. She would be at the library when the doors opened at 10 a.m. That was, after all, the real reason she had come. Although she had to acknowledge that the fact that the house was still there, an apparently perfectly preserved time capsule, made her feel inexplicably content.

She had reached the end of Elm Street to turn the corner for her Airbnb when she turned back for one last look at the house. The man was gone. As quickly as he had come into focus, he had disappeared. She squinted again down the street–no one. *Odd*, she thought. Perhaps he had turned down one of the alleys? Perhaps one of the houses belonged to him and he had run in and locked the door, quiet as a mouse? She paused for a moment, to see if he would return, but the street remained empty. *Perhaps the street has secrets*, she told herself. The thought made her smile.

The sense of illicit adventure remained through the evening. Although neither Robert nor Rob would have called what she brought back from the grocery store a meal, she was completely and thoroughly in charge of her own dining situation. So if she wanted to call cheese and crackers, a little too much wine, and half a pint of ice cream "dinner," there was no one to tell her otherwise. She refilled her wine glass once more before wandering back to the deliciously cool bedroom. She shivered a little, as much with anticipation as from the A/C. She could hardly wait to see what she might learn at the library.

It was a tiny, sweet-looking lady with impeccably coiffed snow-white hair who greeted Gwen at the special collections desk at four minutes past ten the next morning. Gwen had a sudden rush of concern–perhaps she should have made an appointment? She realized she had no idea how easy it might or might not be to request a viewing. But the Special Collections Room was almost empty. Just one table was occupied, by a student? Or professor? Gwen couldn't tell, as the occupant was almost completely obscured by piles of papers. Gwen was momentarily worried her arrival might be an interruption, but the occupant didn't stir as she walked by to the front desk. She caught a brief glimpse of dark hair among the piles of papers as she made her way past.

The tiny, sweet-looking librarian had a name tag identifying her as Ms. Hamilton. Hopeful that her lack of appointment wouldn't matter, Gwen plunged in.

"Ms. Hamilton?" Gwen asked and proceeded to give a brief summary of her story. Great Aunt Elizabeth Porter. Mason-Hall School of Nursing. Degree from the University of Richmond. Presidential commendation. Gwen's recent discovery that her aunt's papers were here. "I don't know how much trouble it might be," Gwen finished, "but I'm wondering if it might be possible for me to view some of the material?"

Ms. Hamilton appeared to be thrilled. "Of course," the tiny librarian replied, smiling. "I'm so happy to meet someone interested in our local history! We don't get that many requests to view collections like Elizabeth Porter's. She was a fairly well-known figure to those of us here in Richmond, but outside our area, well . . . Frankly, people just don't know who she was, so they have no reason to ask for her papers. I'm glad the matron at Mason-Hall directed you down here." She whispered, a little conspiratorially, "I think they're still a bit miffed we have the collection here, but, well loyalties are loyalties, aren't they?

"Why don't you get yourself set up at one of the tables, and I'll bring out what we have," Ms. Hamilton continued. "I'm awfully glad to see that someone is still interested. Such a shame, to be forgotten."

To be forgotten. When the elegant little librarian said it, it sounded like an erasure. Which, as she thought about it, Gwen decided was even worse than death. It would be as though all traces of Aunt Elizabeth had been removed, and she had just never existed. She felt a moment of intense sadness, and then determination. *Not forgotten on my watch*, she said to herself. She sat down at one of the long tables as Miss Hamilton went back into the bowels of the library to fetch whatever Aunt Elizabeth had seen fit to preserve.

Gwen was amazed at the sheer volume of the collection. Ms. Hamilton, with help from a young male library assistant at least twice her size (who, Gwen decided, must be moonlighting from the wrestling team), wheeled a book cart over to Gwen's table. The cart was almost off balance with heavy boxes. The assistant started lining up the boxes of material on Gwen's table, and Gwen, unable to wait for organization to be accomplished, started opening them, closest box first. She couldn't believe how much her aunt had saved.

Several boxes were full of what looked to be more personal correspondence. (*How many luncheons did she attend?* Gwen wondered wearily.) Yet another box was filled with what appeared to be random copies of academic journals on nursing and social work. There were boxes filled with draft upon draft of scholarly articles concerning the state of healthcare in rural Virginia. And business correspondence associated with the drafts.

But the real treasure, Gwen realized, was the collection of personal journals. Ms. Hamilton had only brought down the very first box of journal volumes, covering the years 1916 through 1920. There was more—much more, Ms. Hamilton assured her—continuing, it seemed, into the early 1970s, just before Aunt Elizabeth's death. Gwen could barely believe how consistent her aunt had been. The journals would be a treasure trove of personal and family history, Gwen realized, to say nothing of a snapshot of life in the first half of the twentieth century.

There were no photos, though. Nothing to shed any light on the photo of Lieutenant Flynn she had found in her keepsake box. And nothing to illuminate the poems. Perhaps all this would be explained in the journals? Gwen was hopeful. She couldn't wait to start reading.

All in all, the young wrestler had brought down six boxes of material to stack on (and beside) Gwen's table. And Ms. Hamilton, apparently directing the young man to wheel the cart back toward the entrance to the stacks, seemed to be sending him back for another load. "Wait," Gwen stopped her before either Ms. Hamilton, or the assistant got too far. "I know there must still be journals in the stacks, but, well . . . how much more is there?" She was beginning to feel a little overwhelmed.

"Oh, at least four or five more boxes, I suspect," Ms. Hamilton replied. "Miss Porter was quite a prolific writer, and it seems to me she saved almost everything. We are quite fortunate to have her materials here. Her earliest papers are from when she was a nurse during World War I, and when she returned, as you know, she became active in the field of public health as well as nursing. Probably something along the lines of what we would call a social worker today. She was just adored by folks in our area. Before the clinics she helped set up, there was basically no healthcare at all in the areas west of here.

"The collection is dated from 1916 to 1976, so there is quite a bit. Shall I have the rest brought out?"

"Perhaps it's best I begin with these that you've already retrieved," Gwen said. The scholarly articles and back-and-forths with publishers would certainly take some time to get a feel for. And she couldn't read through more than one box of journals at a time. No need to bring out more right away. Trying to piece together the puzzle of a life from old correspondence and journals seemed Sisyphean at best. But Gwen had an overwhelming urge to try. It felt to her as though there was a reason she had been directed to Richmond on this journey, as if something was waiting for her here, if she could just find a way in. She decided to start at the beginning. She set herself the goal of getting through one box of article drafts and associated correspondence, and then, energy permitting, moving on to the first journal volume, dated 1916.

A few hours later, Gwen was rubbing her eyes with fatigue. She was beginning to think that she herself needed a background in public health to make any headway into the scholarly articles and correspondence with the various editors. One thing she WAS able to discern, anyway, was that several of the articles were basically "how-tos" for other states looking to replicate what Aunt Elizabeth had created in Virginia.

About halfway through the box of articles, and tired of reading about the rate of influenza infection over time in Wythe County, Gwen decided to cheat a little on her goal. She moved on to the first volume of the journals. Flipping carefully through the first few pages, she was happy to read that the first entry was for a good day. Aunt Elizabeth had just received her letter informing her she had been accepted into Mason-Hall School. And just underneath the entry was a poem! No title, but it looked to be an early version of one of the poems in the manuscript she'd found in the manila envelope. The poem about blue sky and fences. It might even have been the first poem in the collection. Gwen would have to check when she got back to the Airbnb.

Although the elegant cursive handwriting was still giving Gwen a headache, she was thrilled to see the connection between the journal and the poems she had found in the keepsake box. She hoped there would be more. Art illuminating life, or vice versa, it didn't matter. Gwen was just hoping to learn more about who her aunt really was.

Gwen looked up, stretched, and glanced at the clock over the main circulation desk. Surprised at how much energy all this reading and thinking could take, she realized she was hungry. She saw Ms. Hamilton at her post at the special collections desk and wondered if she might have a recommendation for a quick lunch. She made her way over to the desk to ask.

CHAPTER ELEVEN

LIZZY

RESECTION
Surgical steel, sharp-edged,
Cuts clean incisions
Bright red with blood.
The decayed, damaged, revealed, gone.
Life pinks up again, if there is enough left.
Like December, into January,
The old year is cut away.
The patient new year awaits its fate.

–Elizabeth Porter, undated

Christmas & Winter 1917-1918–France

After Thanksgiving, in the limbo leading up to Christmas, Lizzy found herself thinking about time. How unpredictable it was. Even cruel. It could tick by so slowly when you desperately wanted to be done with something, almost as if it were enjoying your pain. But then, when something was actually right, really right, it could seem as though time was already bored with happiness and just racing to be done and back to misery. She realized this was hardly an original observation. But since time's uneven march forward had begun to affect her personally, she found herself forced to reckon with it.

It was certainly this way with Lieutenant Flynn. The days that she spent in the rehabilitation ward passed so quickly that, on any given day, the fifteen or twenty minutes she might have spent at Lieutenant Flynn's bedside could have been a dream. She knew she had been there, though, because she could look at her journal entries at the end of the week and see that she had carved out those little blocks of happiness.

"Read aloud, three pages," she had written. "SB preferred to listen. Says eyes are tired." There was nothing particularly earth shattering about tired eyes. Just a mundane journal entry. But when Lizzy re-read it, she could feel her heartbeat race just a little. Because it was a record. Proof of their time together.

Her bunkmate, Alice, had been gently teasing her for days now about how so many of her shifts were ending at Lieutenant Flynn's bedside, and how she was making a spectacle of herself. Lizzy's usual response to any such gossipy nonsense was to just ignore it and get on with her work. But now whenever Lieutenant Flynn was mentioned, she found herself blushing. Which would then prompt a mini-lecture from Alice about the dangers of wartime romance. Lizzy had no good response. They had all been warned about such entanglements at Mason-Hall. Alice was right.

Was her crush returned? Lizzy wasn't sure. Nevertheless, she found herself daydreaming that perhaps there was a future for them, after the war. She had no idea how this future might look, or how it might come to pass. But she could hope. And she did. Maybe time wouldn't slow back down.

November slogged its way into December. Lizzy visited Lieutenant Flynn whenever her shift schedule would allow. They had finished *A Christmas Carol*, made another half-hearted stab at Twain (doomed to failure from the start, Lizzy had to admit), and were now engrossed together in *Twenty Thousand Leagues Under the*

Sea. Sweeping up one morning, Lizzy had found a dog-eared copy under a briefly vacant cot. It looked like it had seen hard use, but the pages were, for the most part, intact, and anything was better than rereading months-old newspapers.

Indeed, for weeks there had been no news, and no mail. The men asked every day whether a letter might have arrived, even though, had there been any news at all, they knew that its distribution would have been the staff's first task. But they couldn't help themselves. Lizzy hated disappointing them day after day. But she had to admit that another part of her welcomed the silence. She felt as though their small slice of the world, the base hospital at Toul, had become a little bubble. As long as no news came from the outside, nothing inside would change. A precarious equilibrium. A delicately closed system.

And in this little bubble, Lieutenant Flynn was gaining strength. Lizzy was happy about this, even though as he continued to grow stronger, she started to feel more and more excluded from his world.

To be honest, although they were typically the least popular among the nurses, she found herself starting to prefer the overnight shifts. For those, at least, she could be sure of where he was—in his cot, sleeping.

During the day, as the weeks went on, he might be anywhere. She would catch a glimpse of him smoking outside the hospital tent, or perhaps chatting with his officer companions in a makeshift clubhouse they had made their own in an unused corner of one of the hospital tents. It was just a few purloined camp chairs arranged behind a torn curtain, but it seemed to create a much-appreciated atmosphere of clubby normalcy for the men. She was fairly certain she had even seen a flask of something that looked like it could be whiskey being passed around, but from a distance, of course, she couldn't be sure. So, nothing to report.

Anyway, she knew she should be relieved and happy that he was improving, and she was. She was just afraid they were going to send him away. Either back to the front or home. She tried to reassure herself that the odds of him returning to battle were low. He still had headaches, she knew. And double vision. Lizzy tried not to think about how double vision might affect someone trying to sight a rifle shot. *No,* she thought. *More likely home than—elsewhere. They couldn't send him back to the front.* She hoped she was right.

And then, as it does every year, pretty much without fail and even in wartime, Christmas came.

At first, it was almost difficult to tell. There was no shopping arriving in overstuffed shopping bags from Macy's or Marshall Field's, no furtive wrapping of gifts, no enticing aromas emanating from the hospital kitchen. But as the day approached, it seemed to bring with it a kind of anticipatory glow, infusing everything with hope and good cheer even in the dismal circumstances. Moods lifted. Recoveries in the wards sparked at an inexplicably increased rate, nurses smiled even at the end of double shifts, surgeons held their usually sharp tongues. Snippets of familiar harmonies could even be heard from time to time, breaking out among the men in the wards. All it took was a few of the men recollecting a long-ago youth spent in a long-forgotten boys' choir, and lo! A Christmas quartet was born. It was magical.

The day itself found Lizzy with truly the best Christmas present of all: a short shift. She began in the morning at nine and was done by three. She could hardly believe her good luck. With the extra time, she was able to make her way to the shower tent and actually wash her hair. It was almost dry when she started back to the ward after a quick supper to visit Lieutenant Flynn and wish him a merry Christmas.

Given the celebratory nature of the day, the ward was unexpectedly quiet. A small group of men at the end of the far aisle were singing "Silent Night," and Lizzy was taken aback at how sharply beautiful it was. One of the men—a tenor, perhaps? The one on the melody, anyway—had a haunting, clear voice. Lizzy paused for a few moments, just to listen. The singing faded away at "Jesus, Lord at thy birth." Lizzy couldn't quite be sure if that was the end of the carol, or perhaps the men had simply run out of what they remembered. Whatever the reason, she was grateful for the quiet after the carol ended. It felt respectful, somehow. Almost reverent.

Lizzy could soon see, as she walked down the aisle toward Lieutenant Flynn's cot, that it was empty. She could hear laughter coming from the makeshift officers' clubhouse behind the torn tarp, and she knew where he'd be.

Sure enough, even as she watched, a couple of the men started making their way out. If Lizzy didn't know better, she might almost have thought they were weaving a bit. As though they had managed to refill one or two of those whiskey flasks she had been faithfully ignoring. *Well,* she smiled to herself. *It is Christmas, after all.* She decided she would just pass by, to see if Lieutenant Flynn was still there.

He was. She peeked in, not wanting to disturb the men inside, only to find that Lieutenant Flynn was now sitting alone. She quickly turned to go, feeling awkward at being seen trespassing in what had essentially been transformed into an officers' lounge, even if it was only a disused alcove in the hospital tent.

But then she heard him say, quietly, "Don't go. Please. It's Christmas. Don't they let you have a little time to yourself today? Here," he said, patting the seat next to him with one hand and raising a still fairly full flask with the other. "I have a little Christmas cheer left."

"I shouldn't, you know," Lizzy said, quietly, although despite herself, she was beginning to feel a little conspiratorial. "Mixing with the officers . . . it's . . . discouraged."

Nevertheless, she pushed in through the tarp. It was surprisingly cozy inside. A few chairs arranged around an upended crate, a lantern casting a flickering light. Lizzy could see the remains of several bottles that had clearly fulfilled their cheering purpose and been tossed aside.

"You'll have to hide these, you know," she said, smiling and trying to push at least one of the empties to a less visible spot under the crate. "Head Nurse is strictly opposed."

He nodded. "I know," he said. "Keep it between us?"

"Partners in crime," Lizzy said, nodding solemnly and offering her hand as her word.

"Partners," he replied, equally serious. "Would you like some? I think I might even be able to find a glass somewhere . . ." He started rummaging around behind one of the chairs.

Lizzy smiled and sat down next to him. She couldn't think of anything she could do that would be more in violation of just about every regulation there was than to share contraband whiskey with one of the officers.

Well, she thought. *It's Christmas.* As she took the glass, his hand touched hers just a split second longer than was necessary. Surprising herself, she didn't pull back.

"Where did your friends go?" Lizzy asked. Two sips, and she could already feel the warmth. She had had it before. Courtesy of Bea, of course. The bite of the whiskey brought back memories of surreptitious celebrations, post-lights-out in the Mason-Hall dormitory. Bea seemed to think no occasion was complete without a Tennessee toast. Lizzy still wondered how Bea had managed to replenish her supply just before Lizzy left for France, although she had her suspicions. Nevertheless, she hadn't asked how Bea came by it, and Bea never volunteered an explanation. Lizzy had felt it quickly then, and she felt it quickly now.

"Well, I don't know if you noticed, but their Christmas celebrations were pretty well winding down," Lieutenant Flynn said. He sat back in his chair, stretched his legs out a bit.

Lizzy nodded. "It's just possible that I saw one or two of them wobbling a little. But you can be sure that secret is also safe with me." She took another sip. "Do you know yet what they're planning for you?" she asked. "How much longer you'll be here?" She was glad it was dark enough so that he couldn't see her face. She was afraid it would reveal that she had more than just a clinical interest in his future.

"I'm not completely sure," he replied, shaking his head. "But I think I might have heard one of the docs say they weren't going to recommend me going back to the fighting. So, I guess, that means . . . home?"

"Forgive me," Lizzy said, but the whiskey was making her bold. "You don't sound as though you're very excited about that."

"I'm not sure that I am." He touched her arm, and she was immediately aware that she was sitting so close she could feel his warmth. Any pretext of a proper, distanced, clinical relationship evaporated. He pulled her closer, and his lips were on hers. Lizzy was too shocked to move. Nor, she suddenly realized, did she want to.

"I'm so sorry," he said, pulling away. "I shouldn't have done that. Christmas. The whiskey. Those are my excuses, anyway."

"Lieutenant Flynn," Lizzy began to stammer out. "Apologies are not–"

"I think I'd prefer it if, tonight, anyway, we dispensed with rank," he said, his hand still on her arm. "I'm hoping military protocol can be suspended, at least for Christmas."

"That should be possible," Lizzy replied, a little breathlessly.

He leaned in to kiss her again, and this time she kissed him back, amazed at how much she wanted this to happen, in spite of the untold number of reasons that it shouldn't. She whispered his name, to herself more than anyone else.

He kissed her again and said softly, "Only my Mother calls me Joseph. Most people call me Joe."

The whiskey? The day itself? Lizzy wasn't sure exactly what combination of circumstances had worked together to lead her to this point. And now, she couldn't tell if she was afraid to continue, or afraid to stop.

Then a sudden image from long ago, impossible to ignore, flashed across her consciousness. The dark attic room. Pain. Blood. She pushed it aside, fiercely. This was not that. This was on *her* terms. Papa was not going to take this from her. *You haven't thought of Papa in months, years. You're not starting now.*

Joe pulled her gently onto his lap, and his hands found their way to the buttons of her blouse. There were so many, it seemed. She helped him. Underneath was her shift, and she felt his touch on her breasts through the thin cotton. She almost fainted with pleasure. He kissed her again, and her mouth opened against his. He bent his head and put his mouth on her breasts, first one, then the other. She moaned, softly.

"*Shhh*," he whispered.

She complied, not wanting to risk even the remotest possibility of discovery. She was gradually conscious of him fumbling with the buttons of his trousers, and what seemed to be a mountain of her skirts. And then, she felt him hard against her.

"We can stop," he whispered again. "We don't have to do this."

And then it was her turn to say, so quietly, "*Shhh*."

She moved a little, felt him inside her. It was everything she had ever imagined it should be. She moved again, a little more, the exquisite sensation heightening. He kissed her, and his tongue found hers. His hands found her breasts, moving lightly against her nipples. And, just as she felt herself reaching her own climax, she felt him shudder.

She leaned in against him, praying that, for just a few more minutes, they might be lucky enough to remain undisturbed.

Luck was with them. The ward was still.

For a little while, maybe almost two weeks, Lizzy was as happy as she could ever remember being. Happier, even, than she'd been when she received the letter from Matron Palmer, admitting her to the program at Mason-Hall. Happier than when the mechanics put her alone behind the wheel of a truck for the first time. She made it a point to try to visit Joe as often as she could after her shifts ended. She didn't care about the consequences, about who might see her. Head Nurse, Alice, or the commander of the entire base hospital could have all taken her aside, one by one, and lectured her on rules of behavior and the dangers of fraternizing with officers, to say nothing of the particular perils of unprotected sex, and she would have nodded and ignored every one of them.

He was all she could think about. Doing her rounds, attending to other injured young men, chatting in the mess hall with Alice and the other nurses, Lizzy felt herself an automaton. A body, simply obeying commands with no thought. Because all thought was for Joe. She felt guilty, as though she had failed in her "journeying" promise to Essie and Addie, but her journal entries had grown more and more sporadic. She couldn't put a name to the storm of emotions she was experiencing, and she decided she wasn't going to try.

After seven calendar days of blank pages, though, on the first of January, she returned to her room with her lips chafed and tender from another interlude with Joe in the makeshift officer's club behind the tarp. Fully aware of how trite the words might seem to any future reader, herself included, she wrote, "I think I am in love." No name. To name him might be a jinx. And the entry had its very own page. It seemed deserving of the space.

But perhaps just that simple admission, reduced to a single, six-word journal entry, was enough to trigger the caprice of the gods. Sometime in mid-January 1918, a postal floodgate was lifted. At mail call, the second Saturday of the month, there were five letters waiting for Lizzy. Two were from Bea, and Lizzy wondered if

Bea had finally had news of Teddy, whether he had in fact managed to avoid the front. She put those aside, looking forward to happy chatter from her friend. But the remaining three were from Addie, postmarked two to three weeks apart. Lizzy could almost see her sister's handwriting become increasingly frantic on the address lines. She hurried back to her bunk, something telling her she might want some privacy as she opened them. She started with the most recently postmarked, and she was glad she did, because Addie, who had a tendency to ramble in her letters, was clearly sufficiently frustrated by what she perceived as Lizzy's deliberate failure to respond that she got right to the point.

> *Dearest Lizzy,*
>
> *I hope that this letter finds you well; indeed, that it finds you at all, for I confess I am puzzled by your silence. Perhaps my prior letters have not reached you. I fervently pray that this one does.*
>
> *I shall say again what I have written before—I implore you to consider returning home. Essie has eloped, as I told you I suspected she would, and I am left here by myself to help Mama and Papa as best I can. I am not sufficient to this task.*
>
> *Addie*

The letter was short, but devastating nonetheless. Lizzy knew exactly what Addie had left unsaid. To leave Mama and Addie alone with Father was, well, Lizzy might as well admit it to herself—impossible. Yes, his volcanic temper and vicious cruelty had been dulled by years of whiskey. So, by the time Lizzy had left for Mason-Hall, with Addie and Essie there to stand united with Mama against him, Papa was not as terrifying a foe as he had once been. And of course there was still safety in numbers. With Addie, Essie, and Mama presenting a combined front, the force of Papa's anger could be deflected. But if Essie had truly decided she had had enough and left (with whom? Lizzy wondered idly, knowing that it made absolutely no difference), then there remained only Mama and Addie to work the farm. As Lizzy had known after finishing the second short paragraph, that was simply an untenable situation.

Lizzy had taken her chance and left, and now Essie was taking hers. Lizzy had always felt that her mother had made her own choices, and if one of the poorer ones had been to marry an alcoholic with a sadistic temper, well, so be it. But Addie . . . none of this was her fault, and Lizzy couldn't leave her to try to survive the situation on her own. Essie's bid for independence meant the end of Lizzy's.

Lizzy left the earlier letters unopened. There was no need to read them—she knew what they would say. She wrote a few lines in her journal, just so she'd remember that all this had happened today. Despair. Defeat. Departure. Sad words beginning with the letter D. She didn't have the heart to write anything more, nor could she face cheery news from Bea.

She stashed all the letters, Bea's included, and her journal under her pillow, and went to find Head Nurse. New nurses arrived every day, and Lizzy knew that she wouldn't be missed for long. But Joe. She didn't know what to tell him. She didn't even have the heart to pass by his cot that evening. Best to sleep on it. Perhaps a solution would present itself by the morning. Lizzy hoped so.

It was instantly apparent, when Lizzy arrived on duty the next morning, that she was not the only one to receive news from home. Many of the soldiers seemed to have received delayed correspondence, and a number of them, in bed after bed and up and down the wards, were engrossed, reading voraciously through sturdy stacks of letters. Lizzy couldn't quite bring herself to share her own news with Lieutenant Flynn, but she saw that he, too, had his own small mountain of letters to peruse. He looked to Lizzy to be quite distracted. Lizzy decided it might be best to move on, save her news for later. Now seemed not to be a good idea.

Until the lieutenant's friend, Buddy, noticed she was making her rounds. And then, just as he had when Lieutenant Flynn first regained consciousness, Buddy called out across the wards.

"Joe," he shouted! "Here's that Marley's Ghost gal again!" And, turning to Lizzy, he stage-whispered, conspiratorially, "He's been looking for you."

Lizzy wanted to respond tartly that there was no need to whisper, he had made that fairly clear to the entire population of the base, but she held her tongue. In the interest of heading off another outburst from Buddy, she zig-zagged through the rows of cots to reach Joe. He looked, she had to admit to herself, a bit hollow. She felt suddenly uneasy, although she couldn't say why.

"Lizzy," he said. "I've had some news."

Lizzy nodded, trying to appear solicitous while also not alarmed. It was difficult.

He went on. "There's someone back home . . ."

Lizzy couldn't believe what she was hearing. She thought she might turn to stone. And then, no. She wasn't stone. She was furious. Whatever he had to say, she didn't want to hear it. She turned to leave.

"No," Lieutenant Flynn said, a little too loudly, grabbing her arm.

"Do not touch me," she hissed. She tried to wriggle out of his grip but couldn't. Would it leave a bruise? *Just like Papa*, she found herself thinking. *They're all the same. I should have known.*

"It's not what you're thinking. Well, not exactly, anyway," he finished, a little lamely. "Yes, there is someone waiting for me back home." He gestured at the neat pile of letters on the bed. "But we weren't promised to each other. At least, I didn't think we were. I guess it looks like there might have been a misunderstanding." And with that last, he looked so miserable that Lizzy decided she would at least stay to hear what he had to say.

It wasn't a long tale. He and Trish had been friends for as long as they could remember, so long it almost felt to Joe like they were brother and sister. They lived on neighboring properties; they were the same age. They had gone to grade school together. Sunday school. Square dances. The parents were secretly plotting, hoping that Joe and Trish would marry and unite the two farms. But then the war intervened.

Joe wanted to enlist. It seemed more of an adventure than anything else. He announced he was going to Fort Washington to sign up, train, and ship out. Trish, more adventurous than he had thought she would be, announced that she wanted to do her part too. She would apply to nursing school in Washington, D.C.

"I didn't realize how she felt about me, I honestly didn't," he said sadly. "We talked about the war, sure, and I was proud of her for taking on nursing, but I had no idea . . ." he shook his head.

Lizzy started to feel a tightening sensation in her core. As though she was preparing for someone to punch her. "There aren't a lot of nursing schools in Washington," she said softly. *And no one I knew who came from Tennessee, with that charming southern drawl, except of course . . .*

"Was Trish at Mason-Hall?"

Joe nodded yes, clearly miserable.

"I wonder if I might have known her," Lizzy said, her voice flat. "When was she there?"

"Spring 1916 through the summer of 1917," Joe replied. "She went back home to Brownsville right after I shipped out."

The tightening intensified into a vice. Lizzy could hardly breathe. "Trish . . . for Patricia?" she said. "I knew most of the nurses there, but no one named Trish."

Joe shook his head. "That's what I called her," he said. "I couldn't say her whole name when we were little, it was too hard. Her real name is Beatrice, but Trish is what I've only ever called her. It was easier to say."

Lizzy couldn't breathe. This was the young man that Bea had sneaked out to see. It had to be. The young man Bea had hoped against hope would not be posted to the front. He had finished his training and was being sent to New York before embarking on the crossing to Europe. The same crossing Lizzy had been on.

"Most of these letters are from her," Joe continued, gesturing toward the neat pile. "I think she's been writing a lot of letters, looking for me. She told me she's written to one of her friends from school to keep a lookout." And then he looked closely at Lizzy. "Bea wrote that she asked her friend Elizabeth Porter for news, hadn't received any. You wouldn't by any chance know an Elizabeth Porter?"

Almost as a reflex, Lizzy started fiddling with the pin that attached her name tag to her uniform. The tag read very simply, **Nurse Lizzy P.** "These name tags don't have much information," she said, as expressionless as she could manage. "I don't know why they don't leave room for our family names. But yes, my family name is Porter. My family always called me Lizzy. Elizabeth was too big a mouthful, especially for my little sister Essie. I'm just . . . Lizzy. I got letters from her today too. I haven't had a chance to read them yet. But I'd guess she's asking me to look for you."

They sat together in silence for a few minutes, Lieutenant Flynn propped up by pillows, Lizzy in the chair next to his cot, both of them at a loss for words. Lizzy realized she had a question.

"Why in the world does Bea call you Teddy, but you're Joe to everyone else?" she asked, finally.

Joe closed his eyes, as though in pain. Perhaps he was. "Childhood nickname," he said, clearly not wanting to pursue the subject any further.

"Well, what is the news, anyway, from home?" she asked, a little numbly, gesturing to the letters on the bed. She couldn't think of anything else to say.

Lieutenant Flynn shook his head. "My pa," he said. "And Trish's ma. Looks like they both had that flu that's going around, and they're not recovering as quick as everyone would like. Someone's got to help run the farms. I know I can't fight anymore; some days I can hardly see. They've been talking to me about a discharge anyway. Looks like I'm going home."

"And Bea? Trish?" Lizzy asked, correcting herself.

A pause. "I never promised anything," he said.

"But I know she went to visit you, right before you went up to New York. I covered for her. She had to spend the night."

He shook his head. "I never promised anything," he said again. "It wasn't like that."

I bet Bea thought it was, Lizzy thought to herself.

After her shift, Lizzy made her way back to her bunk in a fog. She supposed she had best open the letters from Bea. It was no longer any mystery what they might contain, and ignoring them would not make the situation any better. She still couldn't reconcile why Bea knew him as Teddy when he was Joe to everyone else, but, well, that didn't matter now. He was who he was. Although knowing his name was Teddy might have put her more on her guard. Maybe it did matter. She almost felt herself getting a little angry. Why, she asked herself again, was he Teddy to Bea, but Joe to her?

She skipped the first two letters and went right to the most recently postmarked. It was clear that Bea had been on something of a scavenger hunt, jumping from clue to clue about Teddy's whereabouts. She had finally tracked him down to France, but (and Lizzy could almost hear Bea's southern drawl lazing across the page as she read), she wondered if Lizzy might be able to find out anything more? Might Lizzy have run across him? Had he been injured? If he was injured, could Lizzy search out any news? Lizzy knew that Bea was really just asking if Teddy was still alive. She just didn't want to put it in words, because seeing the question in ink, on paper, created the possibility of a "no." Lizzy could hardly blame her.

Lizzy leaned back against her thin pillow and wrapped the blanket tightly around herself. She had stopped for a brief dinner before returning to her bunk, but it wasn't agreeing with her. And even though it was only a little after eight, she felt done in. She was in no mood to begin writing a reply tonight. In fact, the more she thought about it, the more she decided that perhaps the best course was to simply pretend she never received the letters. Lieutenant Flynn would be going home soon anyway. Lizzy didn't have the heart for it, and who would ever know whether she had actually received them or not? Hoping her dinner would stop doing somersaults, she closed her eyes, not even changing out of her uniform. The morning shift would be here soon enough. What was the point?

As has ever been the case with the military bureaucracy, Lieutenant Flynn's discharge orders took several weeks to come through. *And a good thing, too,* Lizzy thought. Whatever her romantic feelings might be, to her clinical eye, he was still not strong enough to undertake the journey back all the way to Tennessee. Although improved, his balance was not yet reliable, and he had admitted that his vision was often so bad that reading was like trying to focus through the bottom of a canning jar. Lizzy had noticed that he had begun asking some of the other nurses to read to him. She couldn't decide if his turning away from her made things easier, or just sadder. In any case, these were not auspicious signs for an uneventful ocean voyage back. Another few weeks of delay could only improve matters.

And Lizzy had her own situation to deal with. Head Nurse had not been best pleased to hear Lizzy's request to return home. Lizzy had been treated to a quite wide-ranging lecture on personal responsibility, patriotic duty, and the fact that the Red Cross did not consider itself to be a hotel, with nurses coming and going on a whim, etc., etc. (Lizzy wanted to say that she hoped

ANY hotel would have better accommodations than what she had endured in Toul, but she held her tongue.)

However, after filling out what felt like an infinity of forms, and after ultimately making her case to the officer in charge of the base camp, her request was granted. She would be able to begin her journey home sometime after the first of March. She was reminded at every turn that there were no travel guarantees. She would have to take whatever transport might have space for her. But that was enough for her to write Addie and let her know that she would soon be on her way. She very much hoped the letter would reach Addie before she herself did.

Sometime in mid-February, a photographer from *The New York Tribune* arrived at the camp. He had been assigned to take photos to accompany an article on field hospitals, the war effort, how the troops were coping. He was supposed to make things personal, find a story that readers could identify with. Most of the medical staff found him more of an annoyance than anything else. Head Nurse recommended cooperating with him as much as possible, in the hope that if he got what he wanted, he might go away quickly.

Lizzy's first shift of the new week, Monday morning, found her in the rehabilitation ward, trying not to lose her temper. Ever since she had found out about Bea and Lieutenant Flynn, she had felt a bit, well, the best word she could think of was "off." Nothing in the canteen seemed to agree with her anymore, and she was always feeling just slightly under the weather. She had decided this was just her body reminding her of her broken heart, but whatever it was, it wasn't making her mornings any easier.

And today found the photographer already there, bright and early, setting up his flash, adjusting his camera focus, and asking several of the men to pose together for him outside, in the sun. This, of course, necessitated them getting out of bed, which was not always in the best interests of their recovery. Even more out of sorts than usual because of all the commotion, she started making her way over to the young man with the camera, moving through the cots, attempting to look reasonable while still firm, when she heard Buddy call out. Her heart sank, because she knew what was coming.

"If you want a good photograph," he shouted out, "here's your nurse! Joe!" he shouted again. "You two can be in the funny pages!"

Lizzy was fairly certain that the only way to silence the commotion was to make her way over to Lieutenant Flynn's cot. She did so, as quickly as she could.

"Please?" Lieutenant Flynn said to her quietly. "I might be able to get a print. I'd like that. So I have a picture when I write to you."

Lizzy shook her head in quiet resignation. She was not expecting any letters from him. But she quickly calculated that giving in to the photograph would be a better strategy than risking the scene that might ensue if she said no. She helped him out of bed, and they made their way out to the one patch of grass outside the tent walls that had not disintegrated into mud. As they were getting into position, she realized there was something she needed to know.

"How are you called Joe?" she asked. "I mean, Bea always called you Teddy. I don't understand. What kind of childhood nickname gets you from Teddy to Joe?"

"It's a little silly," he said, sheepishly. She just looked at him. He cleared his throat and then continued. "Joseph is my middle name. My given name is Theodore–Teddy. Folks called me Teddy when I was little. But then that whole Teddy Bear craze came on. You remember? A while back?"

Lizzy nodded. She remembered.

"Well, Buddy wouldn't let it go. He called me 'Teddy Bear' until I almost clocked him. We were about seven. After that, no one called me 'Teddy' anymore. Everyone seemed to think 'Joe' was a safer bet," he added, almost as an afterthought.

Except Bea, Lizzy thought. *Bea still calls you Teddy. Would you have put it together*, she asked herself? *If you'd known he was actually Theodore Joseph?* Maybe. She was honestly not sure. Although . . . the accent. The whiskey. But it didn't matter anymore. Joe and Bea were supposed to be childhood sweethearts. Promised to each other for as long as they could remember. She couldn't compete with that. Lieutenant Flynn was going home to Trish, and she was going home to the place she thought she had escaped.

The photographer had not forgotten his subjects, even though they had almost forgotten him, covered as he was by the black curtains on either side of his camera. He emerged, suddenly, taking them a bit by surprise but apparently ready. "Can you stand a little closer together?" he asked.

As Lizzy moved closer to Lieutenant Flynn to try to comply, she was suddenly aware he was shaking. From the cold, damp February air? The exertion of standing for an unexpected length of time? It didn't matter. "May we have a wheelchair, before you proceed?" Lizzy called out. "I think the lieutenant has developed a chill."

Looking more than a little put out, one of the or-
derlies brought one. It was clear he was not in favor of
this newspaper photography nonsense. Once again, the
photographer dove under his black cloth, fiddling with
the focus, and once again he popped out, ready. With
Lieutenant Flynn in the wheelchair, it was easier for
Lizzy to comply with the photographer's request and
stand close.

"Ready?" he called out.

They were. Lizzy stood rigid, holding the wheelchair
handles. As was the custom at the time, neither of them
smiled.

CHAPTER TWELVE

GWEN

> *A courting male will occasionally sing a song and perform a flight display.*
>
> *Cardinals,* S. Tekiela, p. 18.

Now–Richmond, Virginia

Ms. Hamilton did indeed have a suggestion for lunch. In fact, Gwen thought, she seemed fairly insistent.

"Arnaud's," she said. "It's a little too expensive for the students, so it's usually not so terribly crowded. But the sandwiches are lovely." Ms. Hamilton drew a little map on a piece of scrap paper so that Gwen wouldn't get lost.

Gwen didn't have the heart to tell her that her phone could have helped her just as well. *Analog lives on,* Gwen thought, smiling to herself. She made her way out the double doors and felt the full blast of the late summer Richmond heat. Thankfully, it wasn't a very long walk.

Arnaud's was just as convenient as Ms. Hamilton had promised it would be. In addition to the counter that greeted her when she walked in, there were some small tables in the back. Since Gwen's lunch companion was going to be her cell phone, she decided sitting unobtrusively at one of the tables would be her best bet. She ordered, then noticed not only was there a text from Cindy about the house, but while she had had her phone silenced in the library, apparently Robert had called. Several times. She remembered with a brief stab of guilt that he had also called her a few days back, while she was driving down. And now his name was right there again, on her screen. No text. But a voicemail. She wasn't sure she wanted to hear it.

Waiting for her sandwich, she scrolled through her emails. Nothing important there. The message from Cindy was just a progress report on how many potential buyers had come through. She dashed off a response, thanking her for the update.

Then she texted Rob. Guess where I am? she wrote. That would probably both annoy him and get his attention at the same time. And then, taking a deep breath, she dialed into her voicemail to see what Robert had to say.

She could have predicted it. There was an end table and a couple of vases that it turned out he and Melissa (mostly Melissa, she was pretty sure) had decided they wanted after all. Would Gwen mind if those went to him?

Her first reaction was to dig in and text him back instantly that yes, she would mind. She was fairly certain, in fact, that one of those vases had been an expensive gift TO HER, intended to hold the two dozen roses he brought her on the Valentine's Day not long before she found out about Melissa. A guilt offering.

The memory hit her harder than she would have expected, and she sat at her little table for a minute or two, her head in her hands. And then took a deep breath, sat up straight. *For heaven's sake,* she scolded herself. *They're not worth it.* She was leaving that life behind. Robert and his perky-breasted girlfriend could have whatever they wanted. Whatever new place she ended up in, she'd want new stuff to put in it anyway.

Her sandwich came, and she put the phone down. No need to respond right away. She'd let him stew a little.

Just as she was gathering up her things to go pay the bill at the cash register in front, her phone rang. It was Rob, not texting, but actually calling. A once-in-a-blue-moon occurrence indeed. She must have really gotten his attention. She made her way to the front of the restaurant, trying to juggle her purse, the bill, and her credit card, while simultaneously answering her phone and fishing some cash out of her purse for the tip. She managed to pay at the register, but she missed the call.

Outside in the heat once again, she swore. Her phone screen now showed Rob as a missed call. Even if she called him right back, she knew he probably wouldn't answer. His track record of answering his phone, even only seconds after he himself had initiated a call, was terrible. Her best bet was to wait and try him again tonight. She started walking back to the library, only to become aware after a block or so that there was someone behind her, calling her name. That was something of a surprise, since she knew precisely no one in Richmond.

She stopped and turned, only to see that the voice calling her name belonged to a figure half-walking, half-running down the street in her pursuit and in spite of the oppressive heat. Something about him looked inexplicably familiar, although she couldn't quite think why. Since it was broad daylight though, and they were on a busy street, she figured the chances of him being a serial killer were slim. If he was that intent on catching up with her, she was willing to wait.

When he finally did catch up to her, it took him a few seconds to catch his breath (frankly, given the heat, she was surprised he had managed any kind of pace at all). And then, "Ms. O'Neil?" he managed, panting. "Gwen O'Neil?"

She nodded, a bit taken aback. How did he know her name? And then he held up a credit card, her name in all caps at the bottom. It was hers.

He wasn't a serial killer at all. In fact, he was trying to catch up with her to return the credit card she had apparently left at the lunch counter. Not scary, just endearing in a puppy-ish sort of way. She looked at him more closely, realizing that yes, he did seem just slightly familiar. Was he the owner of the dark hair almost buried in paper at the other occupied table in the library? He might be. He must have also been at Arnaud's. She hadn't noticed him. But she had to admit, she had been pretty engrossed in her phone. Seeing Robert's name light up on her phone screen had distracted her perhaps a little more than she would have liked to admit.

"I can't believe you ran after me to give this back," she said, smiling. "The heat alone must have nearly flattened you."

"I'm used to it," he replied. "I come from a long line of Southerners. We don't even take off our parkas unless the thermometer is about to explode."

Gwen laughed.

"Do you mind if I walk with you?" he asked, falling in step beside her. "I think I saw you in the Special Collections Room this morning, didn't I? I'm headed back there too."

Gwen nodded in surprise. So it *was* him. The dark hair just peeking out over the towering piles of paper at the other occupied table. They walked together in silence for a few paces, as he continued to catch his breath.

"Have you been here before?" he inquired, still breathing hard. "It's just that, I spend a fair amount of time in that room, and I don't think I've seen you there." Then he added, explaining, "It's usually empty. New faces stand out."

"No, actually, this is my first visit." Even as she spoke, Gwen was surprised to hear herself say "first visit" as if there might be more visits in her future. "As it happens, my great Aunt Elizabeth's papers are here. I only just found out about the collection, and I wanted to learn more."

He nodded, as if it was the most natural thing in the world to have a family member with papers in the Special Collections Room. "I tend to set up there because it's quiet. A great place to grade papers in peace. The students don't seem to have figured out yet that I hang out there, so less risk of awkward chance meetings with students who'd like to persuade me they're doing better than they are in my class. I'm a professor here–History. Jack Sommerall." And he stopped for moment and held out his hand.

"Gwen. Gwen O'Neil." *Silly,* she thought. *He already knows that.* She took his hand in return. He had an easy handshake. Definitely not a serial killer, she was sure.

"What did your great aunt do to get her papers accepted here?" Jack asked, and Gwen explained as best she could. Nursing school, World War I, rural clinics, presidential commendation. Jack seemed suitably impressed.

"That's actually my area," he said, as they walked back into the library. "First half of the twentieth century, 1900 to about 1940. The 'War to End All Wars,' and then the run up to the next one." He held the door for her, which she found sweet, in an old-fashioned kind of way. She wondered for a moment if he had actually followed her from the library to Arnaud's. She couldn't decide if she found the possibility intriguing or creepy. Then she remembered Robert's voicemail message from the morning. Thoughts of Robert brought her to thoughts of Melissa, which brought her to depressing thoughts of age and invisibility. She decided to be flattered by the attention and stick with intriguing.

"It was nice to meet you, Jack," she said. "I think this is me." She gestured to her table, so completely covered with papers and journals that the surface was barely visible.

Jack looked at it for a second, shook his head. "Well," he said, "if you ever need any help with . . . any of it. Like I said, it's my area. I'm pretty easy to find. I'm here at least a couple of days a week."

He made his way back to his own table, with its own mountain of papers. Student essays. She sighed in sympathy. A thankless task, she was sure. But she had her own task to think about. She put him out of her mind and went back to the journals.

After what felt like only a few minutes, Gwen looked up and was surprised to see that the clock over the main desk was reading 5:15 p.m. She could hardly believe it–the library would be closing soon, and she felt as though she had barely scratched the surface of her aunt's papers.

She started to wonder if she might be allowed to take any of the materials back with her to the Airbnb. She suspected that it would be breaking all kinds of library rules to remove anything from the collection, but, given that she was family, perhaps protocol might be relaxed a little on her behalf?

As it turned out, it could be. Ms. Hamilton admitted that there was not an enormous amount of interest in the collection, so she thought it was unlikely that any other researchers would be inconvenienced. In fact, Gwen suspected she might have been the first to request a viewing since the papers had been donated back in, well, Gwen didn't even know. After a friendly but firm warning about coffee cups, wine glasses, and pets (*well, at least no pets,* Gwen thought with relief), Ms. Hamilton asked what part of the collection exactly did Gwen want to take home? Gwen didn't hesitate—the first box of journals, dated 1916 to 1920.

It seemed to Gwen that dinner should, perhaps, be a bit more substantial than it had been the night before. On her reconnaissance walk after she arrived, she had noticed an Italian restaurant that had customers already lining up to get in at 5 p.m. It seemed like a good bet for takeout, and she decided to walk over and pick something up. *No harm in passing by the house on Elm Street, either,* she thought. She changed out of her "legitimate researcher investigating family history" outfit of blouse, blazer and smart trousers, and into shorts and a T-shirt more suited to the oppressive heat.

As she approached the little house, almost invisible between its shiny and overstuffed neighbors, something didn't look the same. *What could have changed in the twenty-four hours since I walked by yesterday?* she wondered. And then she saw. There was a "For Sale" sign staked in the postage-stamp front yard, taking up most of the space between the aging tree and the sidewalk.

Could she have missed it yesterday? No chance. The sign was too big, the patch of grass in front too small. No, it was new. She wandered over to take a closer look.

She couldn't explain it, but she felt very proprietary. As though the house was hers, and someone was selling it out from under her. *You're being ridiculous,* she told herself.

She was examining the sign for more information about the seller when the front door opened. She looked up, and who should walk out but her credit card rescuer from lunch.

How is he here? she wondered. She must have been so engrossed in her aunt's papers that she didn't notice him leaving the library.

"I'm starting to think you're following me," she called out. She stood by the tree, hands on hips, her stance as though daring him to answer.

Turning from his struggle with the front door lock, he shaded his eyes from the late afternoon sun and shook his head. "Not a stalker, I promise," he said, smiling. "Family property. We're putting it on the market. My mom just went in to senior living a couple of months ago, and, well . . ." He gestured behind him to the deteriorating but somehow still charming house. "We can't keep it," he said. "Too much to take on. Mom doesn't need it anymore, it needs too much work for us to rent it out, and I already have a place. It's got a lot of memories, but, well, sometimes you just have to move on." She could almost have finished the sentence for him. He hopped over the little retaining wall on to the sidewalk.

"You know, this may seem a little forward. But I'm wondering, would you like to get dinner? There's a great little place just a couple of blocks over, and I'd love to learn more about your aunt. World War I is absolutely the area I've been concentrating on lately."

Gwen knew the place. It was precisely the restaurant where she had been planning to pick up takeout, and the thought of dinner with this very nice-looking professor was tempting. However, she was suddenly quite conscious that her shorts and T-shirt, while certainly suited for the heat, were perhaps a little smaller, and hence a little clingier, than she felt comfortable with. Jack's offer was tempting, but she didn't know him. At all. And she was dressed like an aging teenager wannabe. And she had to deal with Robert. And Rob still didn't know where she was. All in all, it felt best to decline.

"Sorry, I have some material to review tonight–don't tell anyone, but Ms. Hamilton let me take some of my aunt's materials home, and I promised her I'd have it all right back tomorrow morning, so . . ." Gwen shook her head. Jack looked a little deflated, but he didn't press it.

"Our secret," he replied, solemnly.

"I'll probably see you in the Special Collections Room again, though?" she said, her voice rising as though she was asking a question, even though she meant it more as a statement. Damn. She hated when she did that.

"Oh, sure," he said. "Absolutely." He looked at her for a moment as though he wanted to say something else, but then changed his mind. "See you maybe tomorrow," he called out, as he strode off down the sidewalk. Gwen was a little surprised to find herself hoping she would. The attention felt nice. It had been a long time. And, if she was being honest, he was cute. In an eager sort of way. Yes, she definitely hoped she'd see him again tomorrow.

Back at her Airbnb, Gwen started in on her phone calls. Getting the least fun out of the way first, she dialed

Robert to let him know she didn't care about the end table or the vases. He could have them. Happily, she didn't have to talk to him, because the call went straight to his voicemail. *I wonder if this is just how we'll communicate now,* she thought. *My voicemail talking to his.* The prospect was appealing.

And then she called Rob, who was satisfyingly amazed at both her sense of adventure and her uncharacteristic spontaneity. "You're where?" he asked, a little incredulous. "You mean, you went to that nursing school ceremony and then just drove to Richmond? Mom, I'm proud of you. Seizing the moment! I mean, I'm still not sure about what you're looking for in all this stuff about your aunt, but, if it's important to you, I think it's great."

A little patronizing, but Gwen had heard worse. They talked a little while longer, Gwen inquiring how the beginning of the semester was going, and Rob asking about what kinds of materials Gwen had actually found. Gwen reminded Rob that Charlottesville was not far from Richmond, and that perhaps they could get together for a visit while she was there. Rob sounded genuinely excited about the prospect, for which Gwen was grateful.

A few hours and two glasses of wine later, the takeout fettucine was congealing in its container, and Gwen realized she had lost track of how long she had been hunched over the journals. Her neck hurt, and her eyes itched. And she had questions. A lot of questions.

Gwen had brought home the first five volumes of journal notebooks, with the first volume beginning in 1916, just as Aunt Elizabeth was preparing to set off for the Mason-Hall School. She decided it needed a more careful look than just the quick scan she'd given it in the library before lunch.

The very first writing in the book, not even a real entry, was scribbled on the back of the front leather cover. It was a recap of the gift of the journal notebook itself, and Gwen wondered, just as her Aunt Elizabeth had, how Addie and Essie had ever managed to scrounge up the funds to buy it. Gwen smiled as she read Essie's pronouncement that the notebook was for Elizabeth's "journeying." *An apt malapropism if ever there was one,* Gwen thought. Gwen was also amazed when she realized that the piece of paper protruding a little from the back pages was the actual (carefully folded and pressed) acceptance letter from Mason Hall. Gwen could almost feel the joy radiating from the page.

And, to Gwen's delight, there were several draft poems scribbled in among the entries. "Fences" was the first, and Gwen recognized several others from the manuscript in her keepsake box. As she made her way further into the entries, she felt fairly sure that her initial impression was correct; some of the poems, at least, did seem to relate to near-by entries. "Fences," for instance, was quite clearly a celebration of finally discovering a path to moving on. Another poem, about an ocean voyage, was scratched in at the bottom of one of the entries concerning Elizabeth's journey to France. But there were no entries that seemed to correspond to the two poems that had been loose, on their own, in the bottom of the box. The one about a suffocating darkness, and the other giving off a sense of tragic loss.

Gwen read on. She was impressed with her aunt's consistency, given how busy she clearly was at the school. There were, of course, some gaps, followed by fervent apologies for the falling off of entries, but for the most part, the record was consistent. Gwen noted there was quite a bit mentioned about Bea, who, Gwen knew from chatting with the matron after the alumnae gathering, was her aunt's close friend, Beatrice. And there were increasingly frequent musings on whether or not the Mason-Hall nurses might be called up to go to France. If the journals were any guide, Aunt Elizabeth was quite thrilled at the possibility.

But there was also an undercurrent that Gwen couldn't quite place. There were cryptic entries about "Papa," usually included in an entry noting how ridiculous it would be to give up one's chance at a nursing career for marriage to some silly soldier. The force of Elizabeth's disdain for marriage seemed a little out of proportion to the fairly ordinary pairings she was describing. It was almost as though Aunt Elizabeth was hiding something. This would have been odd, Gwen decided, since the journals were only for Aunt Elizabeth's own eyes. Why would Aunt Elizabeth be trying to hide something from herself?

Gwen unfolded herself from the rug in front of the coffee table and wandered into the kitchen. She decided some tea might help her think, and she leaned against the kitchen counter, waiting for the water to boil. The Elizabeth emerging from the journals was brave, funny, and apparently absolutely desperate to get as far away as possible from anything to do with the family she'd grown up with. *Why, I wonder?* Gwen asked herself. She found herself wishing (not for the first time, or for the last) that she had asked her father more questions while she had the chance. She let out a small sigh of regret as she watched a few stray tea leaves swirl and darken the water in the mug.

Somewhat revived, Gwen decided she had enough energy to read through a few more entries. She felt a little guilty about not reading every word penned by a family member, but nevertheless she said a silent *mea culpa* and skipped to where she hoped things might get both clearer and more interesting.

There was a mysterious entry about Beatrice disappearing for a night on some sort of unofficial "leave," just as it seemed the school was gearing up to send staff to France, but she couldn't quite untangle the subtext. There were several entries about the journey from the school to New York, where Elizabeth was to board the ocean liner that would take her to Europe, but these entries were, for the most part, fairly dry, travel-related details. Train numbers, departure and arrival times, food purchased along the way.

As for the crossing itself, Gwen concluded that Aunt Elizabeth must have been the lone passenger who was not completely incapacitated by seasickness. Gwen skipped most of the descriptions of Elizabeth's fellow travelers confined to their bunks (still impressively clinical and nausea-inducing, even almost a century later), but she did note an intriguing entry about a dance on the last night of the crossing. *A dance,* she mused. *On a troop ship? Well, why not,* she concluded. It might be the very last bit of fun some of them would ever have.

After Elizabeth's arrival in France, there were a lot of entries about rain. And also about mud. And being cold. And gruesome injuries. And death. Gwen found herself growing inured to the horrors Elizabeth must have seen, just as she suspected Elizabeth herself had. She started paging through more quickly, trying to avoid the more horrific details, when she noticed a couple of very brief entries about an "SB."

Truth be told, it was not even instantly clear that SB was an actual person, rather than a thing or an event. Gwen only noticed the first entry because the letters appeared first by themselves, in the margin, near a somewhat unremarkable entry but not seemingly part of it. Elizabeth had driven a van to pick up some wounded soldiers, had had her pride somewhat damaged by a soldier who dared to question her nursing skills, and had driven back. One soldier, it seemed, was more seriously injured than the rest.

Then, in the margin, the two letters. SB. Gwen's curiosity was growing, but so was her fatigue. It had been a long day. The flowery script was starting to blur, and Gwen was having an increasingly difficult time deciphering it. And it was just possible that she'd had a little too much wine, and not enough tea. The morning would bring clearer insights, she decided. She closed the journals and went off to bed.

Back in the library the next day, Gwen once again noticed her credit card rescuer from the previous day's encounter. He gave a polite wave, and she gave a little half wave back, not sure of the appropriate level of wave for someone whom you'd barely met. She couldn't even be sure he'd seen it, surrounded as he was by his piles of papers. Gwen decided that to have accumulated such stacks of papers, he must be quite behind in whatever it was he was grading.

Once again, she was soon engrossed in her own canyon of paperwork. "SB" began to appear with some frequency in the entries, and it became clear that SB, no longer just marginalia, had to be a person. One of the injured soldiers from the van, perhaps? It seemed very possibly so. There were entries commenting on how his recovery was proceeding, coupled with a few mysterious quotes that Gwen was pretty sure came from *A Christmas Carol*. Then, a particularly effusive entry on Thanksgiving of 1917, when it seemed from the entry that "SB," whoever he was, must have woken up.

Gwen almost missed the most intriguing entry of all. For most of the morning, Gwen had been paging through Volume 5 of the journals, trying to determine whether she had perhaps missed something that might shed light on who "SB" might have been. As noon rolled around, though, Gwen found herself sneaking glances at her rescuer's table, to see if it looked like he was thinking about a lunch time excursion. She was slightly surprised to realize she was hoping that she might, purely coincidentally of course, happen to bump into him as she was thinking about finding lunch somewhere herself, and maybe they could go together? As she turned and rose from the table, she inadvertently nudged the journal she was working on, and the notebook, as though from long habit, fell open to the back of the very last page. It was almost as if that particular entry had been visited so many times that the page opened of its own volition, greeting the reader like an old friend.

"I think I am in love," the entry read. January 1, 1918.

There would have been no reason to turn ahead from the previous page. It looked like it was the last page of the volume, and it was yet another entry about rain. Gwen was starting to think that there was no more to say about the weather, however miserable it might have been. The sentence was written on the back side of that very last page, facing the inside back cover, and Gwen would never have seen it, had the book not opened to it as if by magic. A whole page, devoted to just one line. It seemed out of character for her aunt, who tended to scribble up and down the margins, filling every last millimeter of page space. Gwen could hardly believe her economical great aunt could have been such a literary spendthrift as to use one entire page for six words.

Now there's something, Gwen thought. *No name.* But Gwen didn't need one. It was SB. Had to be. Whatever level of mild curiosity she had had before just ratcheted up tenfold. *Who was SB? What happened to him?*

CHAPTER THIRTEEN

LIZZY

ERSATZ
The photographer presses a button,
Summons a flash.
The moment is captured
In two dimensions, no more.
No breath. No flesh.
No life.
–Elizabeth Porter, undated

Spring 1918–The Return

It was not an easy journey back from the front line in France all the way to Wytheville, Virginia, but neither had Lizzy expected it to be. She was not at all surprised by the endless series of hastily arranged rides on hospital vans, almost-missed train connections, or even by the longer delays while she filled in at some short-staffed hospital or other.

No, what surprised her was something else. Although frankly, if she was being honest with herself, she had to admit that she should have suspected this too. Expected, even. She was a nurse, after all. And a farm girl. She knew how things went. And then, of course, there was that long ago memory, not as deeply buried as she had hoped, and even harder to push out of the way these days, of how things had been with Papa. When she had miscarried. Her own father's child.

But whatever had happened so long ago, in that tiny attic room, was utterly irrelevant here in the present. She was going to have to focus on the here and now, not the past, because she was going to have to deal with it.

She was pregnant.

In retrospect, the signs had all been there. She just hadn't paid attention (or she had rationalized them away). Fatigue? Hardly out of the ordinary. Everyone was fatigued pretty much all of the time. There was a war on, after all. Nausea? Well, who even knew when the next meal might come, much less what it might consist of. Anything short of raging dysentery should be filed under "consumption of meat, unknown origin and/or age," with a cross reference to "be grateful a little mild nausea is all you have to manage." It was only when she realized that she had missed at least one cycle that she began to suspect. And when her skirts began to grow just a tiny bit tighter, even though the only food she could reliably keep down was the corner of a saltine, she knew.

She told no one, of course. Except her journal. Her journal was her only repository, her sounding board, her friend. She filled page after page, until even though she still had the urge to confide, she didn't feel she had any more to say.

It was then, when she thought she was empty, that she realized that wasn't it at all. She just needed to say it differently. She didn't need so many words. Just the "pieces of thoughts" she had confessed to Addie. The poems. To be decrypted by no one but herself. She wrote in her journals, and when she ran out of space in her notebooks, she wrote on scrap paper, train schedules, shift rosters. Anything. She'd been composing them all along, but now they became her own secret code. It was the act of writing that kept her sane.

She could figure her due date fairly well herself–it would be sometime in late summer or early fall, she guessed. And there was not much to be done, except continue her journey and hope her condition was not discovered. She briefly entertained the idea of finding someone to "take care of it," as she imagined Lieutenant Flynn might have suggested, but there was no Lieutenant Flynn to discuss it with. He was on his own journey home, back to her closest friend. Lying in bed at night, chasing sleep, she tried to push that thought away, almost always unsuccessfully.

But just the thought of trying to find an abortionist in a foreign country was overwhelming. One lonely night somewhere outside of London, as she lay, sleepless again, in a nursing dormitory, waiting for her passage back to New York, she almost entertained the idea of recruiting a discreet friend in the medical community.

The next morning, in the unforgiving light of a grey British dawn, she came to her senses. It was an untenable plan for many reasons, not least of which was that it was illegal. And what if she asked for help and was turned down? Her condition would then be public, and she would be humiliated. The thought of a home remedy was no better. She had seen firsthand, back in Wytheville with Mrs. Jensen, just how ineffective home methods could be, and the kind of tragic outcomes they could yield. She found herself praying for a miscarriage, to no effect. In spite of her prayers, she remained infuriatingly pink-cheeked and glowing.

Lizzy's one hope was that, by the time her condition could no longer be disguised, she would be back home with Addie and Mama. She could wait out the last few weeks in the isolation of the farm; no one would be the wiser. Perhaps Mrs. Jensen, if she was still there, could help her find a home for the child. And she calculated that her chances of getting home in time were fairly high.

She had managed to find a berth on a ship that would get her to New York by mid-June. There were boarding houses in New York that she knew of through the Red Cross grapevine, and she could stay in one of those while she rested a bit from the crossing. Then she would begin the trek back to Wytheville, to Mama and Addie, and whatever else awaited her back on the farm. Whatever she found, she'd deal with it as best she could. And she'd give birth when her time came. That was all she could do.

Lizzy had written Addie from New York to let Addie know her plans, but there was no way to know if Addie had received her letter. So it was a relief to see Mr. Johnny waiting for her at the Roanoke station. Addie must have received it.

"We weren't expecting to see you so soon," Mr. Johnny said as he helped her up into the trap and took her case. "I hear you made it all the way to France?"

"Indeed, I did," Lizzy replied. She did her best to respond to his questions about what France was like, what the ocean crossing was like, what the war was like, but he soon seemed to realize that the questions were tiring her.

She had some questions of her own, although she wasn't sure how to ask without giving her concern away and providing fodder for local gossip. How was Mama? Papa? Her sisters? She'd find out soon enough, she supposed. Although she was a little surprised that Mr. Johnny didn't volunteer any information.

As they cleared the last rise and the trap drew level with the house, Mr. Johnny finally spoke again. "Too bad about your mama and papa," he said, sympathetically. "I hope Miss Adelaide is doing all right." He stopped the trap, helped her down, and put her case by the fence.

Lizzy looked at him quizzically, and Mr. Johnny, seeing her face, quickly turned, as though to head off any further conversation. He tipped his hat, once again refused to take any money for the ride, and rode off. Lizzy felt a twinge of apprehension.

She stood for a few moments by the fence, taking it all in. She could see her dilapidated farmhouse up the dirt track, the only structure visible for miles. A horse was grazing in a small field to the west. Even from a quarter mile away, Lizzy could recognize the swaybacked silhouette. Ralph. That was encouraging. Perhaps there were still a couple of cows in the back, in the small pasture behind the house. She felt her heart start to beat just a little faster. Maybe things weren't so bad after all.

The cloud of dust kicked up by the horse dissolved into the sunlight as the trap disappeared from view, and after about five minutes she couldn't hear it anymore. Midday. Silent, but for the oddly piercing buzz of insects. And so, so hot. It was mid-July in Virginia, so the heat should have been no surprise, but Lizzy had forgotten just how oppressive it could be. She fished a handkerchief out of her pocket and dabbed at her forehead. Her clothing situation would need some attention. Although absolutely indispensable for the winter she had just passed in France, woolen uniforms would clearly not be appropriate here.

She left her case by the fence and started walking up the dirt path to the house. To even call it a path seemed a bit grand for the reality of the thing. It was overgrown with weeds, sprinkled liberally with rocks, and deeply rutted from rain. Lizzy had to pick her way carefully along in order to avoid turning an ankle. The state of the path–uncared for and abandoned–did not bode well for the state of the family within. Lizzy hoped she was reading too much into a quarter-mile dirt track.

As she approached the house, a small figure made its way out of the door. The sun was in Lizzy's eyes, and she couldn't quite make out who it might be. Too small to be Papa, Lizzy was sure. And Essie was gone, eloped with her young man, wasn't that what Addie had written? So then. Mama? Addie?

Lizzy called out. The figure paused. Then started running, utterly oblivious to the rocks and ruts. It was Addie. Lizzy held out her arms.

It was not the homecoming she expected.

Yes, Essie was gone. Eloped just after Thanksgiving last. "You never knew him, Lizzy," Addie said. "Essie took up with him a while after you left. You remember the O'Neil family over closer to town? It's their youngest. Frank O'Neil. He and Essie are in Richmond now. I think Frank is trying to make a go of a dry goods store. Essie's helping him. She's expecting. Sometime this fall, she says. Before Christmas."

Lizzy nodded. They were sitting at the little table in the front room of the house. Everything looked even shabbier than Lizzy remembered. There hadn't been much in the kitchen for a mid-day meal, and Addie looked awfully thin. Lizzy had been glad she had some bread and cheese to share, still in her carryall left over from the last leg of her journey. The house seemed very quiet. Essie's absence was accounted for. But Mama and Papa? Lizzy was surprised to find Mama not in evidence. And Papa, well. He could be anywhere, but most likely someplace with whiskey easily to hand. Lizzy looked around. All was still. Unnaturally quiet, she felt. She thought of Mr. Johnny, expressing his sympathy about her parents. Something was not right.

"And Mama?" Lizzy began reluctantly. She never got to the question, because Addie burst into tears.

"Oh Lizzy," she sobbed. "You can't imagine how hard it's been. Mama's gone; Papa's gone. There's just me. I've been hoping and praying you'd get home soon. I didn't know what to do."

Lizzy felt herself go numb. She felt as though perhaps if she sat very, very still, Addie's words might just float up and away, like feathers on a light breeze. As though they had never been said.

That was, of course, not what happened. After a few minutes of sobbing, Addie regained some of her composure. Lizzy found her handkerchief again and offered it to Addie, who accepted it gratefully. Interspersed with hiccups gradually decreasing in frequency, the full story came out. It wasn't a long one. Essie left just after Thanksgiving last. Lizzy knew that, of course. Essie's departure was what prompted Lizzy's journey back from France.

"After Essie left, Papa seemed to just fade away," Addie said. "One morning, a colder one, along about February, we couldn't find him anywhere."

Eventually, Addie and Mama found him in a corner of the barn. He had apparently been there for a while. A stroke, the doctor thought. Or maybe his heart. It didn't matter, because there was clearly no one to blame except himself. Years of whiskey catching up with him.

"And Mama?"

"Well, have you heard about that terrible influenza? Did it get to the front lines in France?" Addie asked.

Lizzy nodded yes. Addie didn't need to explain any further.

Lizzy wondered briefly why Mr. Johnny had not gone into more detail, but then she realized that he probably thought she knew. When it became clear that she hadn't yet received the news, he probably would not have wanted to be the first to tell her. She couldn't blame him.

"How long have you been alone?" Lizzy finally asked. "How have you been managing?"

"Well," Addie said. "First, I sold one of the cows. That lasted me for a while. I didn't want to sell them both, because then I'd lose the milk. I sold a few chickens from the hens, some eggs. Essie's been sending me a little bit of money every now and again. When she can spare it. I couldn't sell Ralph though," she finished, a little lamely. Lizzy nodded her understanding. Selling Ralph would have been like selling a member of the family. Under any circumstance, he would have been the last to go.

"Mama died on the first of June," Addie said, after a brief pause. "I wrote you lots of letters," she added. She was clearly trying not to sound accusatory.

"And I wrote you back. But if the mail from Europe to Virginia is as unreliable as the mail from Virginia to France, I'm not surprised you never received anything from me. I wrote you that I'd be on my way as fast as I could, but it was a long journey. And I never received any of the later letters you sent me. I wasn't ever in any one place for very long, and mail would have had a hard time catching up to me. I'm so sorry you've been on your own through all of this."

Lizzy reached out across the table and took Addie's hand. "But I'm here now. Maybe you can show me later where they've been laid to rest," she said. "And then, I have something to tell you as well."

The small church they had attended since either of them could remember was several miles down the road toward town. Lizzy helped Addy hitch Ralph to their dilapidated trap, and they set off.

Lizzy took her sister's hand and held it gently as they rode. "After Mama died," she asked gently, "why did you stay? Why didn't you just go to Essie?"

Addie shook her head. "It didn't seem right," she said. "I had to get Mama buried, and then there was Ralph, and the house . . . And I didn't know when you might get back, and what would happen if you came home and there was no one here? So, it just seemed best to stay."

Lizzy nodded and kept her questions to herself for the rest of the ride. She wondered why Essie hadn't put her foot down and forced Addie to come to Richmond, but maybe Essie hadn't realized how bad things were. Well, Essie as the youngest had always been good at looking after herself, and mostly just herself. Lizzy didn't blame her for it; she'd had to—otherwise she would have been swallowed up in the family sinkhole. Essie probably hadn't really wanted to know how things were going. She would have come for the funerals, looked around to see if things still looked more or less the same, and then gone right on back to Richmond to her house and her life and her expected child. There didn't seem to be any point in quizzing Addie about this now though. Addie was in no good state for a cross examination, even a friendly one.

The church was quiet and locked, which was to be expected for a random weekday afternoon. They didn't need to get into the church, though, just the neatly maintained churchyard around the back. They followed the little path that led around the side of the building, and Addie pointed to two new-looking plots side by side in the far corner. The little churchyard was almost full, so full that one of the new plots was more or less outside the manicured periphery. The dirt still looked newly disturbed, and there were no headstones, only wooden crosses marking the spot. Lizzy hadn't really expected headstones. She suspected they would have been an insurmountable expense under the circumstances.

"Which one is Mama?" Lizzy asked, softly. Addie pointed to the plot closer to inside. Lizzy nodded. That seemed right. Mama inside the churchyard, nearer to God, maybe; Papa on the outside looking in. *That's as close as he'll get to salvation*, Lizzy thought bitterly.

Lizzy took Addie's hand and started to walk back. *We need to manage headstones for them,* Lizzy vowed silently. She'd get started on that right away. But other than that last task, there was nothing for either of them left in Wytheville.

When Lizzy finally got around to telling Addie the secret she was quite literally carrying with her, Lizzy knew that Addie must have already suspected. Lizzy thought she had done an admirable job concealing her growing belly, but Addie was a farm girl too, and Lizzy had to admit that it was getting harder and harder to disguise her condition. With everything out in the open, her condition became something she could talk about, just like any other problem facing her. What to do with the house. With Ralph. With her soon-to-be-born illegitimate child.

Lizzy kept waiting for Addie to ask about the father, but the question never came. *Another irrelevant father figure,* Lizzy thought, with not a little irony. *No surprise there. They seem to run in our family.*

There wasn't much discussion in the end, because there weren't many options, save one: sell the farmstead, make their way to Essie and Frank in Richmond, and begin their lives again there. Lizzy was not sure how welcoming Essie would be, but that was not an insurmountable problem. Lizzy and Addie could stay with Essie and Frank at least until they got a little settled, Lizzy felt sure. As long as Essie could be assured the arrangement wasn't permanent, Lizzy thought she'd be amenable.

Many of the nurses Lizzy had met in France were counting on being able to work privately upon their return, and Lizzy knew of nothing preventing her from doing the same. She could make a living; she was sure of it. There were any number of veterans from any number of conflicts who were in need of home nursing care.

As for the baby, well, Lizzy was beginning to see the bones of a plan: the miracle of twins. It was just as easy to have one baby as to have two, wasn't it? And the due dates were close enough. If Lizzy's child were just a little bit late and Essie's just a little bit early, who would be the wiser? Essie and Frank hadn't lived in Richmond for very long, so it was good odds that they weren't yet well known in the community. If there was ever a heaven-sent opportunity to disguise the arrival of a baby by having it become someone else's, this was it. And Lizzy would be close by. She could play the role of adoring aunt. It was perfect. All that remained now was to write a letter to Essie, to let her know the plan. It was decided that Addie should be the one to write. Lizzy didn't trust herself to come up with the right tone.

There was, of course, one more hurdle to be crossed: the actual *having* of the baby. Lizzy had been avoiding thinking about this because, well, frankly, she was terrified. She doubted that Essie would want any association with the event, so Richmond was not an option. That left home—the tiny house with only horrifying memories and Addie for company. Lizzy had been disappointed to learn that Mrs. Jensen was no longer a resource. Her aging parents had passed away in the years since Lizzy had been gone, and Addie had heard she'd gone back to Chicago.

It didn't matter. Chicago or the moon itself, Mrs. Jensen was equally unavailable. Lizzy did have her apprenticeship with Mrs. Jensen to count on, and there had been maternity wards and midwifery lectures at Mason-Hall. So Lizzy was not without experience. But that experience had been some years ago, and with other women's deliveries. Not her own. And frankly, even if Mrs. Jensen had still been nearby, Lizzy wasn't sure she would have called for her. It would have been one more person privy to what Lizzy fervently hoped she could keep secret. No, this time, there would be only Addie to help. Not even Mama. Lizzy hoped Addie was up to the task.

The letter went out to Essie and Frank in mid-August. Addie was as matter-of-fact as she could be. She and Lizzy would be arriving in Richmond sometime in early October. They were selling the farmstead and leaving Wytheville. They would be bringing with them Essie's share of the proceeds from the farm sale, and also a newborn baby. The baby was Lizzy's. Discretion about the baby would be much appreciated, and details for the care of the baby could be discussed upon their arrival. They hoped to stay with Essie and Frank for a little while as they were settling into their new life, but they wished to impose for as short a time as possible. Addie would write again when they had a better idea of their arrival date. There. It was done.

The month of August was spent cleaning up the house and arranging the sale of the farmstead. Addie did most of the negotiating, as Lizzy was too big at this point to show herself in public. Lizzy was proud of her.

And Mr. Jonas from down the road was excited at the opportunity to add their acres to his. He was still grateful for Lizzy's help in delivering his and his wife's first child, and the sale went forward smoothly. Mr. Jonas was also perfectly happy to take Ralph and the remaining cow in the bargain. It was only after Ralph's future was secured that it came home to both sisters that they were really leaving.

In addition to all their leaving preparations, Lizzy sent Addie on a special errand back to the church to talk to Reverend Weston about headstones. They might as well know what the cost would be, she decided, even if it was out of the question right now. Reverend Weston agreed that he also did not like the look of the bare plots in back, but he assured Miss Adelaide that grass would grow there soon enough. The price of headstones was quite shocking. Did Miss Adelaide have any idea? Miss Adelaide did not and was suitably appalled to learn that each headstone would cost seven dollars and fifty cents. At fifteen dollars for the two together, it might as well have been a million.

When Addie reported this back to Lizzy, Lizzy sighed, resigned. She hadn't realized they would be quite so expensive, but she hoped that when she started working in Richmond, she would be able to manage it. She added it to her mental list of tasks to be finished once the baby arrived. Move to Richmond. Build a nursing clientele. Become an aunt. And now, headstones. She would make sure Mama had hers first.

Monday, the ninth of September, started out hazy and hot, with the temperature misery index seemingly increasing exponentially as the sun rose higher in the sky. There was a barely discernable fizz of electricity in the air, warning of possible thunderstorms to come, but that was hardly unusual. Storms were a daily risk in late summer. You never knew what the afternoon might bring. The only thing that could be counted on was that the heat would get increasingly unbearable as the day slogged on. Lizzy and Addie had some time ago begun sleeping in their parents' bed, in the futile hope that it might be cooler on the main floor. It was perhaps a little more comfortable, but not much.

Lizzy had awakened that morning feeling as though she hadn't slept at all. There was no position these days in which she felt she could get comfortable. As she looked down at her belly, it seemed just too big to be real. A vague memory of a long-ago Sunday school picture book floated across her consciousness—*Jonah and the Whale*. It had fascinated her. Particularly the engraving of the leviathan, ponderous, and grey. Awkward, it seemed, even in its own watery world. Exactly how she felt. Ponderous and grey.

And her back hurt. Throbbed, truth be told. She wiggled her toes. She hadn't been able to see them in weeks, but she could feel them. If they swelled any larger, she thought they might actually explode. Addie took one look at her and went out to the well for water. Lizzy guessed she looked like she could do with something cool. And water seemed to be just about all she could manage. Addie tried to tempt her with a bit of toast, but it didn't look appetizing, and Lizzy nodded a polite no-thank-you.

Lizzy's back continued to throb as the morning went on. Addie told her, in no uncertain terms, that there was to be no housework, no packing, no worrying about money or about the future—in fact, no work at all today. Addie was quite firm that she didn't quite like the way Lizzy looked. She fetched the low stool that usually lived by the hearth and put some pillows on it, so that Lizzy could rest on the davenport and put her feet up comfortably. Lizzy was not used to sitting still and having others at work around her, but on this morning, she accepted the help and the pampering without objection. She didn't feel herself.

At about two o'clock in the afternoon, it was suddenly very clear why she had been feeling out of sorts all day: her water broke. Grateful for the Red Cross timepiece that she asked Addie to retrieve from its place of honor still pinned to her old uniform, she started timing her contractions. They were fairly far apart, although nonetheless painful.

She remembered helping out Mrs. Jensen with births and exhorting the young mothers-to-be to be brave, grin and bear it, breathe into the pain. She knew now why a lot of those mothers seemed to ignore every word she said. She hoped this would not be one of those first-time labors that lasts for days. She didn't think she could bear it. Addie left her side only to fetch more water from the well.

"I could read to you for a bit," Addie offered, trying not to look worried. "That might take your mind off things." Lizzy was a little surprised that there was any reading material at all in the tiny house, since Papa had been basically illiterate, and Mama never sat down long enough to invest time in a book. But Addie disappeared into a corner of the sleeping alcove and rummaged around for a few minutes, only to reappear with a small stack of *Woman's Home Companion* magazines. Lizzy could hardly believe it. She smiled through her gritted teeth. They reminded her of Mr. Johnny and his many kindnesses.

"Where did you get all those?" Lizzy asked, realizing she sounded just like Mama, accusing her of stealing all those years ago.

"After you left, Mr. Johnny said since you weren't here anymore, he'd give these extras to me now," Addie replied. Lizzy could tell that Addie was just as accepting of the "extra" explanation as she herself had been.

"Read me some recipes, then," she said, through gritted teeth. And she was suddenly reminded of Lieutenant Flynn, and the hours she had spent reading to him in the field hospital in France. She was surprised to realize she'd barely thought of him the last few weeks that she'd been back in Wytheville, and here she was, giving birth to his child. She didn't know whether to feel guilty or relieved that he was out of her head, at least for the time being. Then another contraction took her, and she was neither guilty nor relieved. She was just furious at having been put in this situation by a man who was clearly just as good-for-nothing as all the rest of them.

All she could do to keep herself tethered to reality was to focus on Addie, who was reading her a recipe that seemed to be for some sort of vanilla pudding. And that was their afternoon, through the thunderstorm, through the cool front blowing through the grimy lace curtains, through the dinnertime which neither Lizzy nor Addie observed.

Along about 11 p.m., there was a shift. Lizzy suddenly started to feel the urge to push. Was it the right time? She had no idea, and no way to check. She told Addie to be ready. The baby could come quickly, and there would be no one to welcome it into the world and cut the cord but Addie. Addie nodded. She knew.

And then, with a huge and unearthly groan from Lizzy and a gasp of surprise from Addie, Lizzy's daughter was born. Addie placed her on Lizzy's chest, and Lizzy scrutinized her. She was perfect.

There was not a single flaw. All fingers and toes present and accounted for, everything exquisitely intact. Perfect eyelashes. Perfect little nose. The most perfect child ever to come into this world, Lizzy was certain. Lizzy was instantly besotted.

"Eliza," she whispered to Addie as she fell back onto the davenport pillows arranged behind her. "That's her name. Eliza." It seemed right. Eliza from Elizabeth. The name and the child, both of them parts of her.

Lizzy's hands-on experience with childbirth and its aftermath was decidedly not current, but there were a few salient commands from Mrs. Jensen still in her memory bank. Make sure the afterbirth is delivered. Get the mother up and out of bed, start her walking around. Encourage breastfeeding. And most important, watch for fever and chills. Watch for too much bleeding.

Fever and chills would be easy enough to spot, Lizzy remembered thinking, but as for bleeding, what would be too much? She had no frame of reference. Mrs. Jensen had assured her she'd know when she saw it.

Lizzy was afraid she was seeing it now.

She didn't quite know what to do. She could tell, though, that Addie was getting worried. As Lizzy drifted in and out of consciousness in the days and nights following Eliza's arrival, alternately pulling up the blankets (in spite of the late summer heat) and then throwing them off, she was vaguely aware that she wasn't hearing Eliza cry very much. In fact, hardly at all. *Have to ask Addie about that,* she told herself. All she heard was Addie's voice, reading something about pudding. And then corn. Cornbread. It made no sense, but Lizzy decided questions could wait, and she would ask about all this later. And also for details about how Addie was feeding Eliza, because Lizzy couldn't really remember. Had Eliza already been at her breast? She wasn't sure. So many questions. She needed to ask Addie right away. And she would, right after she closed her eyes, for just a second or two.

Friday morning, as the sun began to rise and gather heat, Lizzy stirred, opened her eyes, and realized she was neither shivering cold nor feverishly hot. Also, she was quite hungry. Addie was sitting across from her, in Mama's old chair. It was very quiet. Too quiet? Lizzy was suddenly wide awake.

Addie saw her move, and instantly jumped up from the rocker. "Thank God," she said. "I didn't know if you were coming back."

Lizzy could think only of the baby. "Eliza?" she almost croaked. She felt like she could drink three buckets full of water, right then, one right after the other.

"She's still with us," Addie said, bringing the bundle over to Lizzy. "But I think you need to try to feed her. I've been giving her sugar water, but I don't know if that's right. It was the only thing I could think of to do. Oh Lizzy, I hope she's all right. You haven't been yourself."

She handed Eliza off to Lizzy, and Lizzy held her as though she was holding something made of glass that might shatter at any moment. Lizzy looked into Eliza's eyes. She was startled to see that they were already a deep blue. Just like Joe's. Eliza stared right back at her. It looked to Lizzy like the gaze of someone evaluating her performance to date. Lizzy was a bit worried she was being found wanting. "We'll figure this out, won't we?" Lizzy whispered to her child. "We can do this."

And they more or less did. Lizzy's chills and fever passed. Although she continued to bleed, the flow lessened with each passing day, and her fears of catastrophic hemorrhage abated. Eliza was a quiet baby, for which Lizzy was grateful. And she was growing stronger and looking plumper each day. Lizzy had not believed she could have the capacity to fall so completely in love with any living creature.

As far as Lizzy could tell, other than the deep blue of her eyes, Eliza bore no resemblance to Lieutenant Flynn. Perhaps a resemblance would emerge in time, but for now, Eliza was just—herself. Lizzy felt as though each day held new discoveries. Didn't it seem that Eliza's nose was perkier on Tuesday, her fingers perhaps more elegant on Saturday than they had been the day before? She quizzed Addie incessantly. Addie just smiled and nodded. Yes. Of course.

Lizzy was smitten, and she knew it. She had come close in France with Lieutenant Flynn, but she had not surrendered completely. She felt as though there had been a small kernel inside of her that knew all along how things would turn out. With Eliza, though, there were no escape routes. And for once in her life, she decided, she wouldn't fight it. She would allow herself the luxury of losing herself in someone else.

Lizzy's strength continued to return.

As of the end of September, they had still not received any sort of reply from Essie, but they couldn't delay any longer. The house had been sold, and Mr. Jonas was being patient, but still, they had to be off. On the first of October, cases in hand, down by the fence on the main road, they waited for Mr. Johnny. The house was clean and swept, and all that remained was to say their good-byes to Ralph. Beyond that, the sisters felt absolutely no attachment whatsoever to the house they were leaving behind. Mr. Johnny didn't ask any questions about the baby bundled up in Lizzy's lap, and neither sister volunteered an explanation. It was still wartime, after all, and that terrible flu going around as well. For all Mr. Johnny knew, the sisters could have been looking after someone else's child, both parents having succumbed to war or pestilence. These days, people tried not to ask too many questions.

Mr. Johnny did ask if they thought they might be coming back? Or leaving for good? Lizzy told him it was their intention to live in Richmond from now on. Mr. Johnny nodded. He said he would miss them, and they trotted on.

Lizzy had a sudden thought. "Did you happen to pack those magazines?" she asked, quietly. "*The Woman's Home Companions*? Eliza seems to like them." Addie nodded, yes. Indeed, in the rare instances when Eliza fussed, reading a quick recipe for some unlikely main dish seemed to soothe her, perhaps because Addie's voice reading aloud had accompanied Eliza's entry into the world. It didn't matter why, though. Best to take anything along that might soothe the baby. And Lizzy had to admit, Addie's reading aloud had soothed her too, while she was in labor, and while she almost drifted away afterwards. Addie's voice was something to hold on to, just like she wondered if maybe her voice had been for Lieutenant Flynn, before he woke up. She hadn't confessed to anyone, but she had taken the battered copy of *A Christmas Carol* with her when she left. No one would miss it, she was sure. And it felt as though it had become hers.

As the trap cleared the rise and the farmstead grew smaller in the distance, Lizzy realized that the only thing she would miss about the place she grew up was Ralph.

CHAPTER FOURTEEN

GWEN

> *Adults sing in earnest . . . to establish territories and attract mates.*
>
> *Cardinals,* S. Tekiela, p. 11

Now–Richmond, Virginia

"In love."

Gwen had to take a moment. From everything she had read so far–all the letters, all the journal entries–Gwen had to believe her Aunt Elizabeth would not have been one to utter those words lightly. Gwen paged back through the journal, but no obvious clues emerged, and as luck would have it, the "in love" entry was the last one in that volume. It was almost as though Aunt Elizabeth had decided that last entry was, quite simply, the end of a chapter. Literal or figurative? Perhaps both.

A little frustrated, Gwen started searching through the boxes stacked on the floor at the far end of the table for the box containing the next volume, Volume 6. When she found it, she wondered if there might have been an error somewhere. A missing addendum, perhaps? A notebook lost? Because the entries in Volume 6 picked up right around December of 1918. There was almost a full year of entries missing between the end of Volume 5 and the beginning of the next.

Skimming through the first third or so of Volume 6, Gwen deduced that, by then, Elizabeth was living in Richmond with Addie, Essie, and Essie's husband, Frank. Gwen could sense an undertone of relief at escape from an untenable situation, but Aunt Elizabeth shared no details. Gwen was left with so many questions. *How did Elizabeth make her way home from Europe? What about the farmstead? How did they all find themselves together in Richmond?*

But there was more. Essie and Frank appeared to have had twins.

If Gwen had felt before as though there were things she didn't know about her father's family, this was the confirmation. Twins? That meant her father had had a sister. She had had an aunt, whom she never knew. Who was never discussed. If Gwen hadn't already been sitting down, she would have had to find a chair.

Gwen sat and thought for a few minutes. Not a single person in her family had ever mentioned this. She realized she was having trouble processing the discovery of a new family member, and she decided perhaps she needed to take a break. But as she got up to go to lunch, she decided a quick stop by Ms. Hamilton's desk was in order.

She just couldn't believe there were no journal entries noting Essie's pregnancy and the birth of twins. She had to believe that, back in the day, before fertility treatments became widely available, twins would have been a fairly noteworthy event. But not only had Aunt Elizabeth apparently made her way back to America from Europe, first to Wytheville and then on to the house in Richmond in which her sister had given birth to twins, she had done so without a single journal entry, when in previous volumes something as trivial as the lack of cream for morning coffee had merited a fairly in-depth discussion. No, there had to be something missing, something mislaid somewhere.

Ms. Hamilton was understanding, but firm. She was quite sure that no volumes were missing. The collection intake process was rigorous, Gwen was assured, and the staff were obsessively careful about cataloging any materials coming in. Ms. Hamilton was one hundred percent certain that nothing had been lost, mis-numbered, mis-dated, or mislaid. She was sorry, but there it was.

Gwen felt a bit as though she'd been reading a book, only to find a quarter of the pages in the middle had been yanked out, with no path to reconcile the beginning with the end. As though Cinderella had somehow ended up as Catwoman, and no clues as to how that transformation might have been accomplished. She walked back to her table, wondering about alternate routes to answers, only to find that Jack had made his way from his table to hers.

"That didn't look like the answer you wanted," he said, nodding his head toward the collections desk where Ms. Hamilton had resumed her collections desk tasks. A pause, and then, a little uncertainly, "I was on my way to lunch, would you like to join me? I've spent an awful lot of time here," he said, gesturing grandly around. "If it's a library problem you're dealing with, I'm your man. Maybe I can help."

"Lunch would be good," she said, smiling. "Any and all help gratefully accepted." She felt a little more hopeful as they walked out together. Plus, she felt the stirrings of a warm glow as they made their way to the restaurant, which she realized she hadn't felt in a long time. It was the glow of someone who feels a little pursued. In a good way.

Arnaud's was just as delightful as it had been the day before. Jack listened sympathetically to Gwen's frustrations, especially Gwen's astonishment at discovering that her dad appeared to have had a twin sister that Gwen had never known about, but in the end he could only confirm what Ms. Hamilton had already told her. It was very unlikely that the library staff had made any mistakes when they logged the collection in. They were scrupulously careful.

"What's more likely," Jack said, looking thoughtful, "is that whoever donated the collection–your aunt herself, or even maybe a friend–kept something back. Something that was either just not interesting, or possibly even compromising. You'd be surprised," he added, "how often that happens. Anyway, if someone did keep something back, it's pretty unlikely you'll find it. When was the collection donated again? Back in the '70s? If anything actually is missing, it's going to be long gone. Maybe you could piece things together from some of the other materials?"

Gwen shook her head. "Maybe," she said, sounding unconvinced. "It's true, I haven't looked carefully through the remainder of the journals yet. Maybe there'll be some clues buried in some of the later volumes. The journaling seems to get a lot less personal, though, beginning mid-1920s and later. I mean, there are some entries about family and holidays, things like that, but it gets a lot less interesting as time passes, at least from a family history standpoint.

"And then there are the poems. My dad always told me this, and I can see he was right–my aunt was a gifted writer. I have what looks to be a manuscript of poems she wrote—she put it aside for me years ago, and I only just discovered it in a . . . well, that doesn't matter. What *does* intrigue me is that I am recognizing some of the early versions of some of the poems in the manuscript. They've been scrawled into the journals, and they do seem to make sense based on whatever the surrounding journal entry is. There are a lot more poems in the manuscript than there are drafts penciled in among the journal entries, though. I was kind of hoping I'd find clues to some of my questions, either in the journal entries or the poems—or both, for that matter, but I'm not getting very far."

Gwen paused, then added almost as an afterthought, "I was never very clever anyway at trying to figure out what a poem is trying to say. So the poems that aren't tied to entries in the journals might be taxing my fairly rusty literature analysis skills under the best of circumstances." And, Gwen added silently to herself, nothing so far had helped her make any progress on either of the two poems that had been almost buried, by themselves, in the bottom of the box. If they were tied to some family event, it wasn't one that Gwen had uncovered in her research as of yet.

Gwen finished, a little lamely. "The rest of the materials seem to be just a lot of scholarly articles on how to set up rural health clinics. She was definitely a trail blazer for community health. It's all interesting, I'm sure, and undoubtedly historically significant, but no help at all with uncovering family secrets."

"Well," Jack said, "I guess just keep looking. You may find more than you think."

Gwen nodded. "Maybe," she said.

They walked back to the library together, chatting about nothing in particular. Jack shared a little of his family history—he had lived in Richmond all his life, was not married, never had been. Gwen felt too awkward to ask about current attachments, but she realized she was finding herself hoping there were none. She in turn shared her "almost divorced" status, her son living in Charlottesville and teaching at the university there. Jack was easy to talk to, and they were back at the library before she knew it.

After settling herself back at her table, Gwen continued looking through later journals and started in on the boxes of scholarly articles. She was impressed to find that Aunt Elizabeth was writing articles well into the late 1960s. She was absorbed, but not so much that she didn't notice Jack wave goodbye as he left around 3:30. *Leaving earlier today,* Gwen noted. *Maybe he has a class?* And then she blushed at the sheer high-schoolness of her reaction. *How long have I known this guy? About two days?* She could feel her inner chaperone working up a good scolding. *I'm just enjoying getting to know him,* she protested. *And he's helping me to research Aunt Elizabeth.* Her inner chaperone was not fooled.

The trouble with ex-husbands is that they are usually "ex" for a reason. Gwen had often heard people say that it takes two to really destroy a relationship. Nevertheless, she was still of the firm opinion that Robert was a lot more culpable than she was. And she was reminded of that as she was finishing up for the day at her table in the library.

Her phone had been on silent. It was a library, after all. So she hadn't seen the call from Robert come in. He had left another voicemail, which Gwen found as she was checking her phone, just as she was making her way out the main doors. Gwen wondered if perhaps he hadn't listened to the message she left the day before? When she graciously ceded all claim to the table and the vases? Was he becoming like Rob and his generational cohort, unable to muster the fifteen seconds or so of attention required to listen to the voicemail message? Anyway, his voicemail to her was short. Basically just "call me." Fine. She guessed they could continue for a while to communicate at a safe remove, one electronic device conveying a message to another. Very civilized. Very low risk. She tapped his number and waited for his automated greeting.

Only it wasn't his automated greeting that picked up. It was actual, non-voicemail, real-life Robert. Gwen felt flustered. She hadn't talked with him face to face since their last meeting at her lawyer's office, back in July. Hearing his voice on the phone felt like an intrusion. Like he had suddenly penetrated her world, an uninvited and, she was instantly aware, unwelcome guest.

"Hey," he said.

Is this how you open conversations with your new partner? she thought to herself. She kept silent. *No sense escalating things when we haven't even made it past the greeting.*

"So, what's up?" she asked. Might as well get right to the point. She hoped she sounded nonchalant.

"Well, just wondering how things are going with the sale of the house. I stopped by the other day, and Cindy was there. I asked how things were going, what was going on, and she told me not to worry, long distance house sales happen all the time, she was keeping you updated on everything. So, what is it that I should be not worrying about? And where are you, anyway?"

As she had suspected, it soon became apparent that he was not calling to inquire solicitously after her well-being. She hadn't thought he was. Robert usually had an agenda, but you had to wait and get a little further into the conversation to get to it. It was pointless to rush him. Gwen, accustomed to this particular dance, answered his questions as they came. The house had been on the market about a week, there had been a fair amount of activity. No, she wasn't there, but no, there was no reason to worry.

Road trip to the D.C. and Virginia area—Robert remembered her Aunt Elizabeth? (Gwen doubted he did.) Her nursing school was honoring her, and Gwen had traveled down for the ceremony, tacking it on to a trip to visit Rob in Charlottesville. As she spoke, she realized she was telling a small white lie. She did plan to visit Rob, of course, but the real reason she'd extended her stay in the area was Aunt Elizabeth. She hoped Rob would back her up on her fib should the need arise. For some reason, she didn't want to reveal the library and her venture down the rabbit hole of Aunt Elizabeth's history. It felt like part of her new life, and Robert had forfeited his right to share in those details. Robert was pretty quiet, just listening. Gwen hoped that the real reason for the call would reveal itself sooner rather than later.

Finally, it did. It came out that Robert was feeling a little frustrated, he said, by what he felt was the slow pace of activity—on the house, and particularly on the divorce. He didn't mean to put pressure on anyone, but, well, if he and Melissa—and Gwen as well, didn't she think?—were to move forward, they all needed to get this house transaction settled and behind them. And the divorce finalized as well. Basically, the call was a "what's the holdup?" inquiry.

"I mean," he added, "it's a little irresponsible of you to just up and leave the area, when the divorce papers aren't signed, and the house isn't even under contract."

Gwen felt a small pang of guilt. There was that manila envelope, probably still squished under the backseat of her car, that she had kind of let herself forget about. Robert was right. She was part of the holdup. They both needed to move on. She was so caught up in this train of thought that she almost missed his last bombshell.

"We need to get moving on this," he continued, a little petulantly. "Melissa and I are going to need to find a permanent place, especially for when the . . ." and then he caught himself.

Gwen suddenly felt as though she needed to find somewhere to sit, because she knew what he was going to say. He was going to say, "especially for when the baby comes." She hadn't been married to the man for so many years in order to miss picking up on cues like that. Most of the time she could finish his sentences for him, this one included.

Her heart was racing, and she was starting to sweat. She looked around, a little wildly. *Don't all college campuses have random stone benches just waiting for situations like this? Where people can gather themselves after life's little tragedies are revealed? A failing grade, a lost job, your ex having a baby with his new girlfriend who's young enough to be his daughter?* She couldn't find a bench. Instead, she just paced back and forth across the flagstone plaza in front of the library.

"The house is under control," she said, icily, deciding to ignore the unsaid for the time being. "It's probably better I'm not there—it's easier for Cindy to show if it's empty. You're right, she should be emailing you status reports as well, I'll make sure she does. My lawyer knows exactly where to find me, I'll check in with her now to see where we are on the documents. Is that it?"

"Yes," Robert replied, a little hesitantly; mollified, but apparently not quite sure how to take Gwen's response. "And the table and the vases, thanks for those," he added, as though trying to make up for his previous tone.

"No problem," Gwen said, now wishing a little spitefully that she had mounted more of an effort to keep them. "If that's all, I gotta go," she said. And she tapped the little red telephone icon to end the call.

As she thought back on the afternoon, she realized she wasn't sure how she made it back to the Airbnb, much less how she ended up, damp from perspiration and tears, sitting on the crumbling retaining wall of her Aunt Elizabeth's house. But there she was, in the shade of the ancient elm dominating the tiny front yard. The house, dilapidated as it was, felt comforting, somehow. Like it was giving her a giant, wood-and-shingle hug. She couldn't explain it, and she decided not to try. She just sat there, sniffling and trying to analyze exactly why Robert's news had hit her so hard. She didn't have to think long. It was jealousy, pure and simple. Not jealousy of Melissa, if she was going to really analyze things, but jealousy of the two of them together.

Robert was beginning his youth all over again, and Gwen had never felt so old. She was being discarded in favor of a new and improved model, and Robert got to have a whole second act. She was sad and furious at the same time, not least because the whole situation reeked of cliché. *He's not worth it,* she told herself, over and over. *They're not worth it.* But she couldn't stop crying.

And that was how Jack found her, still sitting there, as the afternoon cooled just the tiniest bit into evening. He wouldn't take no for an answer this time, and after a brief walk, which gave her enough time to mostly compose herself, she found herself sitting across from him at the little Italian restaurant she'd had takeout from the evening before. She didn't care anymore that she'd only known him for a couple of days. He seemed nice. And it had not escaped her notice that he was quite good looking. Dark hair, blue eyes. Hard to guess his age, but, well, it didn't matter how old he was. Forties, maybe? Old enough to be a professor, and that was good enough for the moment. Also, she'd wound up at his house all on her own, so she could hardly accuse him of stalking. No, this was just a nice gesture from an acquaintance who thought she looked in need of distraction. She was grateful to accept.

"I don't suppose you want to talk about what's going on?" he asked, a little hesitantly.

She shook her head. "Boring. Family stuff. What are families for, right? Except to reduce you to tears on a Thursday afternoon?" She smiled, trying to look ironic. She was not at all sure she'd succeeded.

"Interesting fact, though," she continued, doing her best to sound a little cheerier and also change the subject. Who wants to hear about someone else's ex-husband, really.

"Your house is part of my family too. My two great aunts lived in it for years. Elizabeth and Adelaide Porter. They never married. My grandmother—Esther, the third sister—joined them there after my grandfather died. I guess that's why you keep finding me hanging out by your front yard. The last time I visited here was sometime in the early 1970s. And I was curious to see if the house was still here." She paused for a minute. "The neighborhood has changed a lot," she went on, "but the house looks pretty much the same. Kind of a time capsule." As she spoke, she looked at Jack a little quizzically. "When did your family buy it?" she asked.

"Sometime in the seventies, I think," Jack said. "I wonder, is it possible we bought it from your family?"

Gwen tried to think back. Her visit was sometime around 1972. Aunt Elizabeth would have passed away shortly thereafter. The timing seemed to work. Weren't there databases these days, where things could be checked? Gwen made a mental note to ask Ms. Hamilton at the library. She was silent for a bit, thinking.

Dessert and coffee arrived.

"Do you want to see it? The inside, I mean?" Jack asked, a little out of the blue. "We could walk back over after dinner . . ." he trailed off, as if expecting a negative reply.

"Actually?" Gwen said, "I'd love that."

It was getting dark by the time they reached the house. Most of the properties along Elm now boasted fancy outdoor lighting, designed both to deter intruders and to highlight elegant facades. But once they reached the property line for number 24, everything seemed to go dark, and a little mysterious. There was just one very old-school naked bulb hanging from the front porch ceiling, and it looked to be doing an underwhelming job of illuminating anything other than a narrowly circumscribed circle of concrete stoop in front of the door.

"Careful," Jack said, and took her elbow as they walked up the few steps from the street to the front path. "A lot of roots from the tree. It's kind of an obstacle course."

The same as when I was here in 1972, Gwen thought. With each little detail that revealed itself to be the same as it had been decades earlier, Gwen felt a little jolt of happiness. She couldn't explain it, but there it was, nevertheless. Jack fumbled with the lock, opened the creaky front door. They went inside.

Gwen stood still at the entrance, taking it in. The front hall was almost exactly–no, PRECISELY–as she remembered. She could have sworn that even the carpet runner was the same. The hall opened on the right into what might have been termed the "front parlor" back in Aunt Elizabeth's day, with a window seat under the front bay window looking out on to the street. Gwen had to smile, because the cushions on the window seat were sufficiently tattered as to have been possibly the same vintage as the cushions that Gwen remembered from her childhood visit. And there was the cupboard below, where, she suddenly remembered, Aunt Elizabeth had told her the treasures were kept. And secrets. *Wasn't that where Aunt Elizabeth kept the book with the cardinal on the cover?* Gwen thought so. *What other treasures could there have been?* It was all so long ago. She couldn't be sure anymore.

The front room segued into the dining room, which in turn connected through a swinging door to the kitchen she knew was in the back of the house. She knew the layout of the upstairs as well, even without seeing it. A big bedroom at the back, with two smaller rooms and a bathroom arranging themselves along the upstairs hall. And, of course, a rickety, pull-down staircase just outside the big bedroom, leading to a stuffy, dusty attic. Gwen remembered her father struggling with the stairs, covered with cobwebs as he made his way back down. The prospect of the attic had seemed very spooky to nine-year-old Gwen. Now, it just seemed inconvenient. Who would go to the trouble of putting anything important up there? She couldn't imagine.

Jack switched on the lights as they walked through, downstairs first and then upstairs. "It's a perfect little house," Gwen said, a little sadly. "Are you sure you can't keep it?"

Jack just shook his head. "We just can't carry it along with the fees for my mom's care," he said. "And it's not grand enough to compete in the rental market," he added, although he didn't have to. If there was ever a real-estate version of an ugly duckling, this was it.

They came down the stairs, and Gwen walked through to the back one last time. The kitchen was dated, that was certain. Not the same appliances as her Aunt Elizabeth had had, but not many generations newer, either. Gwen made her way over to the little window set into the back door and peered out. "And the garden?" she asked.

"I'm embarrassed for you to see it," he said. "It hasn't been my top priority lately. But it's definitely all still there. We haven't paved it over. Of course, take a look. Just don't judge my gardening skills by what you see. What with moving my Mom and the start of the fall semester, I've kind of let things go."

Gwen opened the door to a blast of humidity. The evening air, which had almost started to cool down a little bit at sunset, had somehow managed to climb back up the thermometer to the misery level. Gwen didn't care. Jack was right; the postage stamp garden was definitely overgrown, making it look even more jungle-like than Gwen remembered. But she could still feel a bit of the magic she had felt when she went out exploring with Aunt Elizabeth all those years ago.

She had a sudden memory. "The birdbath?" she asked, but Jack looked at her a little blankly, and Gwen felt instantly guilty. Everything had been so perfect, right up to that moment. "Doesn't matter," she said, shaking her head. "Just something I remember from a long time ago. No big deal. Thank you for letting me see the house again. It makes me feel like some things don't change, and today especially, that's a nice feeling."

They walked out together, Jack locking up behind her. Although Gwen protested that she was perfectly capable of walking home by herself, Jack would have none of it. You never know what's prowling the streets after dark, he warned her, quite seriously. If it hadn't been such a long day and she hadn't been quite so wrung out, she would have laughed. Lions and tigers and bears, it seemed, might be on the loose patrolling the wild streets of Richmond. But regardless of the reason, it was nice to have his company for the few blocks back to the Airbnb.

"You're quite chivalrous," she said, as they reached her door.

"My pleasure," he replied, suddenly a little awkward. They stood there for just a moment, and she turned to go inside, then turned back. He had already started down the path to the street.

"I'll see you tomorrow?" she called out.

He paused for a moment, backtracked a little. "Actually, I don't think so," he said. "I have class in the morning, and I'm stopping in to visit my mom after that. At her place. Just making sure she's settling in. She hasn't been there very long," he offered, as though an explanation were needed. Which, of course, it wasn't.

"Well, I hope the visit goes well," Gwen said. "Maybe next week, then?"

"Absolutely," he called from the sidewalk. "Monday lunch?"

"I'll be there," she called back.

As she let herself in the door, she had the odd sensation that she had missed an opportunity. As though she and Jack had skirted something and pulled back. A goodnight kiss? How old-fashioned. And after only two days? How brazen. The net effect of the evening, though, was that she was no longer thinking about Robert. Or Melissa. Or any of their potential progeny. No, she found herself feeling like a teenager and thinking about Jack.

CHAPTER FIFTEEN

LIZZY

> *I was not prepared for what I found upon my return home—both Mama and Papa gone, and Addie on her own. But Addie and I remain ever thankful for Essie and Frank and their help. Theirs is a full house, to be sure. I am so grateful they have opened it to us!*
>
> Journal of Miss Elizabeth Porter, 1918

Fall 1918 into 1919—Richmond, Virginia

It was clear from the moment they arrived at their sister's house in early October that Lizzy and Addie would need to make other arrangements as soon as was practical. Essie and Frank's house was small and cramped. And its closeness was only magnified when Essie and Frank's own baby arrived, the day before Thanksgiving. Lizzy had been right—no one seemed to be any the wiser that one of Essie's "twins" was not her own, but Essie made it quite clear that she did not approve of the ruse. She reminded Lizzy several times that this would be A LIFELONG charade. And she wasn't at all sure she wanted to be part of it.

While Addie had sensed that there was no point whatsoever in discussing the identity of Eliza's father, Essie had no such reservations.

"Can he not send support?" she asked several times. "What about his family? Can they not send support?

Why are we to raise this child without help from his family?"

Wearied by all the questions, Lizzy was tempted several times to just say she had been secretly married, and that her new husband had quickly and conveniently died somewhere in France and his parents expired from the influenza, but that seemed to involve fabricating even more elaborate lies. Inventing a wedding, in-laws, multiple deaths somewhere. Imagining all the inquiries made her head spin. No, there was nothing for it.

In spite of Essie's clearly professed reluctance to be a party to Lizzy's scheme, Lizzy still felt that Essie taking Eliza was the cleanest solution. There was a child, and there was no father. Essie and Frank would take her. End of story. Essie would come around. Lizzy even kept up the pretense in her journal entries. If one must lie, she concluded, consistency is always best.

In fact, Lizzy's biggest worry now was how she might manage to successfully pretend Eliza belonged to someone else, even if that someone else was her sister, and close by at that. Each day, Eliza grew stronger, plumper, rosier. She was the very definition of the perfect baby. While they were all crammed in together at Essie's house, Lizzy could remain Eliza's mother. But when Lizzy and Addie were to eventually find a place of their own (which the cramped house and Essie's nerves ensured they would have to do soon), Lizzy honestly didn't know how she would be able to leave Eliza behind.

Nevertheless, it was clear that something needed to be done. She and Addie could not stay indefinitely with Essie and Frank. And Lizzy had a plan. Within a week of their arrival in Richmond, she had placed a tastefully worded "Situation Desired' advertisement in *The*

Richmond Times-Courier. Given the number of returning war veterans in need of care, she was able to put together a solid schedule of clients in fairly short order. Paying clients. Her Mason-Hall credentials stood her in good stead, and everyone knew that the returning Red Cross nurses were well-trained, honest, and reliable. With the income stream from her private clients and the small windfall from the sale of the Wytheville property, she had enough resources, she was fairly certain, to find a place for herself and her sister.

Lizzy did not intend to remain a private nurse forever, though. She was beginning to realize that, in most cases, "private nursing" care was more "light housekeeping" than anything else. There was not much medical knowledge required to help an aging Civil War veteran change his bedding and tidy up once or twice a week. The work at the local hospital was not much more challenging. She had imagined more when she left home for Mason-Hall and then left Mason-Hall for the war.

What she had imagined, as it happened, turned out to be just down the street at the University of Richmond.

On New Year's Day, January 1919, lying in bed next to Addie in Essie and Frank's tiny spare room, one ear ever alert for Eliza's cries, Lizzy whispered her plans to Addie. She intended to enroll in the university's public health program. Several of the nurses she had become acquainted with had mentioned it, and it seemed as though it would offer just what she was hoping for. Training in how to actually make a difference.

"From there," Lizzy said quietly, "I can apply for a job. Maybe at the Virginia Department of Public Health. It will be a steady income." *And a meaningful pursuit,* Lizzy thought quietly to herself.

The medical care in rural communities such as Wytheville was at best spotty, and at worst almost dangerous. Wytheville had been lucky to have Mrs. Jensen—she was competent, and willing to provide her services to the entire county. But Mrs. Jensen, like so many others, had come and gone. Without her, or someone like her, it was each one for him- or herself. There had been no one to help Lizzy back when she was struggling to deal with the repercussions of her father's assaults, and there had been no one to help her with Eliza's birth. That had to change. Lizzy wasn't sure how, but if there was a way to improve the services available to underserved parts of the state, she wanted to be part of it.

Addie didn't even question whether Lizzy would be able to manage the program. As far as Addie was concerned, Lizzy could do anything she set her mind to. After a few minutes, though, Addie did whisper a question. "However will you pay for it?"

Lizzy didn't answer, because she didn't quite know. There would be a way, though. There was always a way. She would visit the office of the public health program director this coming week.

It only occurred to Lizzy much later that neither she nor her sister spent even a millisecond thinking about finding a suitable man to marry and support them. Both of them seemed just to assume they were on their own. Lizzy barely even thought of her father anymore. As for Lieutenant Flynn, however much Lizzy adored Eliza and wouldn't change the fact of her birth for anything in all the world, she could not shake the conclusion that Joe had abandoned her. And Addie, well, she kept her own counsel, but young men and marriage did not seem to be a consideration. Lizzy sometimes wondered if what Addie had pretended not to see or hear in the attic had colored her view of men. It would have been understandable.

Lizzy took Addie's hand and patted it a little. Addie patted back, and the sisters drifted off to sleep.

Fall 1919

Lizzy had always loved autumn. Even in Virginia, where the change in seasons sometimes felt measured in infinitesimal increments of mercury, fall could be glorious. The air would finally lose some of that cotton-wool heaviness that seemed to blanket everything from early May into at least September, and sometimes there would be a whisper of a breeze that was almost cool. The walk from Essie and Frank's house to the University of Richmond was becoming something Lizzy found herself looking forward to.

And it was late September, on the way to her Tuesday morning class, her first semester as a student in the university's Studies in Public Health program, when Lizzy noticed some commotion at one of the houses on Elm Street. Although most of her private clients lived within walking distance of Essie and Frank's house, and she had thus spent a fair amount of time getting to know the neighborhood, this particular house was not one she had paid much attention to. It was small, even in an area known for its tiny houses pushed close together in rows, and it was showing its age. The paint was peeling in more than a few places, and the roof looked uncertain. But there was a lovely, robust sapling in the front yard, showing itself off to passersby as though daring anybody to think the property had passed its prime. Lizzy slowed her pace a little to take a better look.

Some very burly men were making their way in and out of the house, carrying what looked to be most of the furnishings out of it. It was broad daylight, ten o'clock in the morning, so Lizzy doubted this was some kind of burglary. She caught the attention of one of the men, who confirmed that the owner of the house, a Mr. Springer, had finally passed on, God rest his soul.

"Who's in charge this morning, then?" Lizzy asked. The workman pointed to a young, nicely dressed man holding an important looking sheaf of papers and standing just inside the front door. Lizzy thanked the workman and went over to talk to the young man. The house appeared to be the perfect size for two sisters looking to establish themselves on their own.

Lizzy had managed to persuade the program director at the University of Richmond that, if anyone was deserving of a scholarship, she was. She had highlighted for him her own rural upbringing, which gave her a personal knowledge of the areas she wished to serve. She paid particular attention to having been a scholarship student at Mason-Hall, whose matron clearly believed in her skills enough to allow her to go to the front in Europe without having even quite finished the program of study. The end result of all this skillful self-promotion was that Lizzy was admitted to the program, tuition free, beginning in September 1919. She would graduate in the spring of 1921. And she had not had to touch either the small inheritance from the sale of the Wytheville homestead or any of the funds from her private nursing clients. Addie had kept intact her portion of the proceeds from the sale of the farm property as well. And the house had apparently not sparked anyone else's interest in the weeks since Mr. Springer's passing. So when Lizzy and Addie made their way together to the young man's office, they were able to bid on the property without competitors and with sufficient resources so as not to be required to take out a loan.

The young man felt duty-bound to tell them it was a bit unusual to have two sisters purchasing a property, but, well, the fact that they could pay in cash prompted him to overlook the irregularity of the transaction. The house would be theirs, and only theirs. Frank didn't even need to vouch for them.

Lizzy couldn't decide if she was thrilled beyond belief at the prospect of her own space, or completely broken-hearted at the thought of leaving Eliza behind with Essie and Frank. Essie had warmed to Eliza over the months she'd been with them, and Lizzy could only wonder to herself that it had taken as long as it did. Frank Jr. was a little terror, as far as Lizzy could see, but Eliza was (Lizzy felt with absolutely 100% objectivity) the perfect child.

She loved nothing more than to sit quietly in someone's lap and be read to. Lizzy had fished the old, battered copy of *A Christmas Carol* from its home buried out of sight in her trunk, and Addie had already begun reading to her from the *Woman's Home Companion* magazines she had brought along from Wytheville. The Dickens made Lizzy think of Lieutenant Flynn, and the magazines reminded her of Mr. Johnny, but Lizzy doubted that Eliza understood a word of any of it. Story or picture books would have been better choices, most certainly, but this was what was on hand. Perhaps a birthday or Christmas might bring something more appropriate for a toddler. Lizzy continued to shake her head at how dense the Dickens was. She had remembered it as more magical. Ah well.

Perhaps the magic was attributable more to the special circumstances in which it had been pressed into service. Lizzy pushed those out of mind.

Lizzy was grateful to have convinced Essie that Eliza and Frank Jr. would share Frank Jr.'s birthdate. Essie seemed, if not excited about it, at least accepting of the idea. They'll only be a few blocks away, Lizzy told herself. She would still be a part of Eliza's life.

December 1919 arrived, and Christmas with it. Lizzy actually felt hopeful. She had a place to live. She had income from her private clients and the promise of more upon her graduation. She had Addie for companionship, and Essie and Frank were just down the street. She could see Eliza as often as she wished, and she often took Eliza for an afternoon or evening so that Essie could have a bit of time with her own child. She had promised Essie, who worried about these things, that she fully intended to contribute funds for Eliza's support as soon as she was able. It wasn't a perfect situation, but it was as close as she could make it.

Christmas Day itself was almost warm, but as Lizzy and Addie walked to Essie and Frank's house in the late afternoon, they could feel the weather beginning to turn colder, a stiff breeze working itself up and a few fat clouds scudding in. Lizzy was reminded that Richmond could get cold enough for gloves to be required. She had only her old Red Cross mittens from the war, and those were no longer fit to appear in polite society, she was afraid. Gloves for next Christmas, perhaps.

She curled her left hand through Addie's arm and tucked her hands into her sleeves. On her right arm dangled a shopping bag with gifts for the children. A book of cowboys and policemen and firefighters for

Frank Jr., and a book about birds for Eliza. Eliza was captivated by the birds that came to visit Lizzy and Addie's back garden, and, as a pre-Christmas extravagance, Lizzy had splurged on a carved stone birdbath to attract more. The birdbath had become a prime bird-watching attraction, rivalled only perhaps by the big tree in the front patch of yard.

Eliza's first word had been neither "Mama," nor "Papa," nor "Lizzy," but "bird." She particularly loved any bird sporting color or singing a song. The yellow warblers, the crows with their iridescent black breasts. And the cardinals. The cardinals were an especial favorite because they were both colorful AND musical. It felt to Lizzy as though their songs were never the same from one day to the next. On the cover of the book for Eliza was a dramatic drawing of a male cardinal, his plumage practically on fire against the snow in the artist's rendering. Lizzy smiled. She knew Eliza would love it.

Christmas was well underway when Lizzy and Addie arrived. The house smelled of cinnamon, mulled wine and baking ham, and Frank had even brought in a small fir tree. Essie had festooned it with so much tinsel that some of the branches looked about to give way. There were greens on the mantel, and a brisk fire burning in the fireplace in the front room.

Lizzy personally felt the day was still a little too warm to be wasting wood, but with evening coming, she supposed a fire would be necessary soon enough. And she had to admit that the overall effect was quite festive. Frank had put together a four-sided slatted wooden enclosure, lining it with blankets, for Eliza and Frank Jr. to play in, and he had brought the little enclosure into the front room and placed it by the fire.

Both toddlers seemed entranced by the jumping flames, and they stood, quietly, hands on the rail and heads just clearing the top of the enclosure, transfixed.

They were the very picture of bright-eyed, rosy-cheeked cherubs, discovering Yuletide for the first time. Lizzy leaned in to plant a kiss on the top of Eliza's head, and, after chiding herself for playing favorites, on Frank Jr.'s as well. The solid little bodies felt comfortingly warm from the fire.

It was a perfect Christmas afternoon. Essie was coaxed out of the kitchen and persuaded to have a glass of sherry with her husband and sisters. Gifts were presented, mostly to Eliza and Frank Jr., although Lizzy had bought linen handkerchiefs for both her sisters. They had made tins of cookies in return. Frank Sr. had made it known even before Thanksgiving that no money was to be spent on gifts for him.

As for Frank Jr. and Eliza? They lost interest in the fire when gifts were brought out. Essie had given them each sock puppets, Addie brightly colored rattles, and Lizzy, of course, the books. Both children were quickly absorbed in their new toys. Eliza especially was practically hypnotized by her book of birds. Lizzy held her as she sat, entranced, tracing the outlines of the cardinal on the cover with her finger. Lizzy was fairly certain she could hear Eliza talking softly to herself, repeating "bird," over and over again. Lizzy decided she'd teach her "cardinal" a little later. She had no doubt that Eliza would master it instantly.

There was suddenly a small outburst from Essie. "Goodness me," she said. "I almost forgot. Something special for you, Lizzy." She reached behind the davenport and pulled out a package, wrapped in brown paper and twine.

"We agreed," Lizzy said sternly. "Anything more is too much. And I don't have anything more for you."

"I know," Essie said, smiling. "Just open it."

Lizzy pulled the twine and carefully unfolded the brown paper. She let out a little gasp and felt her eyes well up.

"You mustn't cry," Essie said gently. "I know I've not always been the most accommodating these last few months. I'm sorry for that. And I know it must be hard for you to leave Eliza here. This is just so you can have a little bit of her with you too."

Inside the paper was a small, stiff card, adorned with a black and white image. A photographic print. It was Eliza. The photo must have been taken soon after she managed to sit up on her own. She was focusing intently on a ball of yarn that someone must have thought would be a good distraction to keep her still. The strategy had worked. The photographer had captured her look of concentration, her furrowed brow and slightly pursed lips, and Lizzy was amazed at how the photographer seemed to have brought out Eliza's essence and captured it on film. All of Essie's probing questions and ill-tempered comments were instantly forgotten. Lizzy didn't know whether to clutch the photograph or embrace her sister. She did both.

"I don't know how to thank you," she said, wiping her eyes a little with the back of her hand. "When did you manage this?"

"Right after you started your course studies, in September," Essie said. "It was easy enough. You were out a lot of the day, and then, well, you moved into your house, so it wasn't too hard to arrange it so as to surprise you. We'd been wanting to get a portrait done of Frank Jr., and might as well do them both, we thought."

A pause. "Well," she added, "I think I need to attend to the dinner, otherwise there won't be any." As far as Essie was concerned, the moment was over. She rose from the sofa and made her way back to the kitchen. She was not the most sentimental of beings, Lizzy was not shy to say. But Lizzy thought there must be some heart in there somewhere.

"Did you know about this?" she called after Addie as Addie went back to the kitchen to help with the dinner. Addie just waved her hand, as if to say, "Oh you," and disappeared into the back of the house to help Essie make the biscuits. Lizzy and Frank sat together in the front room for a while, watching the children play, Lizzy still clutching the photograph tightly to her chest.

Lizzy and Addie walked back to their own little house on Elm Street soon after the dinner was finished and cleaned up. Frank Sr., not taking no for an answer, walked them back. Pleasantly exhausted from the festivities, Lizzy put the photo on their own mantel and climbed the stairs to bed. She was sound asleep in what seemed like an instant.

So for a brief moment, the loud banging at the front door confused her. It felt like she had just closed her eyes; was it morning already? It was still dark. She took a moment to get her bearings and realized it wasn't just banging. She could hear Frank Sr. yelling for her to open the door. Her heart sank. *What kind of emergency could this be?*

She and Addie almost collided with each other at the top of the stairs, but Lizzy made it down first. She fumbled with the lock, opening the door to find Frank Sr. there looking terrified.

"It's Frank Jr.," he said. "And Eliza. Both of them. Can you come?"

Of course she could. She tried to tell Addie she wouldn't be needed, go back to sleep, but Addie, stubborn as usual, simply ignored her. They quickly dressed and almost ran the few blocks back to Essie and Frank's house.

They arrived to find Essie ineffectually trying to comfort first one child, then the other. Both children were hot, so very hot, to the touch. Lizzy needed to take only a brief look to know what the trouble was, and she could have kicked herself for not seeing it sooner. Although it wouldn't have mattered if she had, she knew. Those rosy cheeks and bright eyes were not the result of Christmas and the warm fire. No. Those were the telltale markers of fever. Scarlet fever, it looked like to Lizzy. She knew from her training, and also from long-ago experience with Mrs. Jensen, that there was not much to be done, except hope for the best and try to keep the fever down with cool compresses. And pray. There was always that. Worth a try, anyway.

CHAPTER SIXTEEN

GWEN

> *[Its] devotion to family make[s] this a highly desirable bird.*
>
> *Cardinals,* S. Tekiela, p. 5.

Now–Charlottesville, Virginia & Wayland, Massachusetts

A thunderstorm crashed through in the predawn and woke Gwen up just as the light in her bedroom turned to grey. She listened to the rain patter on the windows for a while, and then she fell back to sleep, crossing her fingers for cooler weather to move in. When her alarm woke her for real at eight, she was pleasantly surprised. She ran to the window and peeked out. The sky was a deep azure blue, and when she pushed up the sash, a brisk breeze blew in. It was wonderful. She wondered if she might even be able to give the A/C a rest, at least for the morning.

Taking her coffee out into the back garden, she scrutinized the geraniums, wondering again whose responsibility they were. *Well, no need to worry today,* she thought. *Last night's storm should have perked them up.* And yes, they did look a little fresher than before. She poked around a little near the back door and found a small aluminum watering can hiding in the shrubs. She looked at it appraisingly, and then shook her head. *Later,* she thought. *I'm off duty today.* No housekeeping tasks, no calls from Cindy, ESPECIALLY no calls from Robert. Not even the library. It could all wait.

What DO I want to do? she asked herself.

She picked up her phone and tapped the icon for Rob.

And so, a few hours later, she found herself in the Mustang, on the road to Charlottesville. It was early enough on a Friday so that all the weekend warriors traveling from somewhere to somewhere else had not yet started out, and the traffic was reassuringly light. Rob had seemed genuinely excited at the prospect of seeing her.

In fact, he even hinted at the possibility that there was someone he might like her to meet. Rob had rarely brought anyone home. Gwen wondered sometimes if maybe the example of her and Robert's less-than-ideal marriage had soured him on relationships. She'd never asked, and he'd never volunteered, but she suspected. And she felt a little sad about that. Anyway, she hoped she was right. That there might be someone for her to meet.

As she listened to her phone's GPS app take her through a series of increasingly unfamiliar and rural roads, she was reminded that she had only been to visit Rob once before, and that had been some years back, when he first started lecturing at the university. She and Robert had driven down to help Rob get settled. It was Rob's first real place, and he'd been so excited. She and Robert had been okay then, in her memory of the visit, anyway. Not amazing, but at least still okay. *Was it five years ago?* she asked herself. *A little more?* Pre-Melissa, anyway. *No sense dwelling on all this now,* she scolded herself gently.

And putting thoughts of Robert and Melissa out of her head, she found herself hearing the app telling her she had arrived at her destination. The little house seemed to Gwen even more rustic than she remembered—not much more than a cabin, really, set back off a gravel road. *But it's not me living in it,* she reminded herself. Rob had converted the attic into a tiny but comfortable sleeping loft, where she could stay the night. It would be fine.

And in fact, there was someone for Gwen to meet. Her name was Lucy, and Gwen liked her immediately. She had joined the faculty as a lecturer just this past spring, hired mid-semester to take the place of an associate professor going on leave, and she had been asked to stay on for at least another academic year.

Over Rob's roast chicken and a nice Chardonnay Gwen had contributed, Gwen tried her best to squeeze out any morsels of information. Where had Lucy been before? Did she like it here in Charlottesville? Did she want to try to stay on?

Gwen noticed a quick glance between Lucy and Rob, after which Lucy stammered a little and answered with a vague observation on the byzantine complexities of faculty politics. Gwen decided that perhaps her parent-question-asking privileges had been stretched to their limits, and she let it go. Lucy was lovely, and Rob seemed happier and more content than she'd seen him in some time. That was enough.

Lucy didn't stay long after dinner. Rob walked her out to her car to say goodbye, and Gwen wandered out to the little deck off the kitchen. Rob had at some point invested in a couple of Adirondack chairs, and Gwen poured herself a little more wine and went to sit outside and enjoy the cool air. The weather had held. The humidity was gone, at least for the time being. There were shadows darting in and out of the trees, and it took Gwen a few moments to realize they were bats. She smiled. They could have as many of the mosquitos as they wanted. Rob came back from seeing Lucy off and sat down in the chair beside her.

"It feels so odd," Gwen commented, "having you host me. Makes me feel like you've gone and grown up."

Rob smiled. "That happened a while back, Mom," he said. "You must have missed it."

Gwen had a sudden rush of self-pity. It was as though Rob had reminded her that everyone was moving on. Her ex-husband was starting a new family, and her son had grown up when she turned away for a moment. She was just . . . well, what was she doing? She didn't have a good answer. They sat in silence for a while.

"So," Rob asked, eventually. "What's up with this Richmond caper?"

Gwen took a moment to gather her thoughts and push self-pity aside. "You know? Honestly? I'm not sure yet. I guess I just feel like I need to know more. As though there are some things in our family history that I never knew. It was that box you brought down from the attic that started it, remember? And there was the invitation to the nursing school, which led me to the collection at the University of Richmond, and I guess at each step I just find more questions. The photo of my aunt and the soldier. The poems in the keepsake box.

"Did I tell you?" she added. "I found my aunt's house. It's actually for sale. The current owner even gave me a private tour. It's as though time just stopped there. The little garden in the back looks the same, and there's even a window seat under the front window, where I think I sat with Aunt Elizabeth, and we watched the day go by."

And the birds, she thought. *We watched the birds.* Gwen wondered again what had happened to the book with the cardinal on the front cover.

"Anyway, it's kind of incredible to be going through all of Aunt Elizabeth's papers. She was pretty faithful about making journal entries, at least for a while. They make for fascinating reading. Although of course there are some gaps," she observed.

Rob looked up at that. "So many mysteries," he said. Gwen couldn't quite tell if he was teasing or not.

"Actually," she said, quite seriously, "there are. It feels a little intrusive, somehow, reading through her journals. As though I'm eavesdropping on her entire life. But there are some things that aren't explained, and some things that I'm having trouble processing."

Rob raised an eyebrow.

"Okay. There's this," she continued. "Grandpa never, ever mentioned he had a sister, but, unless Aunt Elizabeth was just making things up in her journals, he did. A twin sister. Named Eliza. Aunt Elizabeth seems to have adored her."

"Well?" Rob asked. "What happened?"

"That's just it," Gwen said. "I can't figure it out. One minute Aunt Elizabeth is in France, making these cryptic entries about being in love and writing about 'SB,' who I guess must be a person, and then eleven months later she and Aunt Addie have somehow made their way back to Richmond, not even Wytheville, and are living with their sister and their sister's husband, and their twin babies. That's a lot of life-changing events to go through with absolutely no commentary, especially when I can already tell that her style was to mention almost anything novel that might have happened in a given day. Seriously, right down to whether there was pie or not in the canteen that evening. Plus, whoever this Eliza was, my dad–your grandpa–absolutely never mentioned her. Not once. She could have been locked up somewhere in an attic for all I know. I guess I just can't let it go. I feel like there's something I'm missing somewhere, something that would help all this make sense, and I feel like it's somewhere in Richmond. In her papers, maybe."

Or in the house, she thought suddenly, the rush of realization almost taking her breath away. But she quickly pushed that thought away as ridiculous. None of her family had lived in that house for over forty years.

"Anyway," she continued, "I wouldn't have known about any of this if I hadn't decided to come down for the Mason-Hall ceremony for Aunt Elizabeth. And, you know? I'm glad I did. I feel like that ceremony has been leading me a little bit down a rabbit hole, but I don't have anywhere else I need to be, so I thought I'd stay for a while and see what else I can find in Aunt Elizabeth's papers. I mean, especially now. If my dad had a sister at some point, I guess I'd like to know about it."

Rob was quiet for a second or two, taking it in. "A mystery, indeed," he said, all hint of teasing gone. "I guess maybe I get my interest in history from you after all," he said, gently.

Gwen laughed a little. "Maybe so," she said. "But don't worry. I won't be driving out to interfere with your social life every other day. And speaking of which," she added, "Lucy is just lovely."

"Oh, Mom," Rob said, suddenly focused on swatting a mosquito. "You always say that." Then he smiled. "Although I happen to think so too."

Gwen could sense the subject being gently but firmly closed. No matter. She roused herself from the chair, kissed the top of Rob's head, and said goodnight. There would be plenty of time to learn more about Lucy in the morning.

Except that when morning came, there wasn't any time at all. Gwen woke to find a message from Cindy on her phone, plus three messages and a voicemail from Robert. It was clear that she probably needed to be back in Massachusetts fairly quickly. There was a buyer for the house, and Robert felt very strongly that Gwen was not moving as fast on this development as she should be. His last text message was positively whiny.

Although of course Gwen wanted to keep things amicable, she had to admit that she was finding a small satisfaction in making him wait. Plus, she could truthfully say she'd had no idea. Cindy hadn't texted her until just this morning, just as Robert's messages were all coming in. She was in the clear. No intent to get under his skin on her part. Just because she enjoyed getting under his skin didn't mean she'd planned it.

Rob had made coffee, for which she was grateful. She didn't linger, though.

"Did he text you too, to see if I was here?" she asked.

Rob just raised an eyebrow again.

"One place I DON'T want to be," he said, "is in the middle. Like Switzerland, I am firmly neutral."

Gwen sighed in exasperation. "Well," she said, "it looks like my 'Richmond caper,' as you called it, will be on pause for a little while. I guess I'm heading back north to deal with the house sale. But I think I'm going to come back here when it's done." As she said it, she realized she meant it. "I feel like there are some loose ends here that need closure."

Gwen grabbed her overnight case from the hallway and rolled it out to her car. Rob walked out with her.

"If you do end up extending your Richmond caper," he said, "it would be nice to have you be nearer. Massachusetts is a long drive."

That was the closest he had ever come to saying he missed her, and she was suddenly a little teary. She gave him a quick hug, making sure he couldn't see her eyes, which she was afraid might be suddenly suspiciously watery.

She'd drive back to Richmond today, pack up, and start the drive back to Wayland maybe even this afternoon. But Monday morning she'd be ready. To do whatever needed to be done.

Gwen pulled into her Wayland driveway around 5 p.m. on Sunday afternoon, after driving for the better part of two days. The front bringing in the crisp air presaging the arrival of fall had made its way up the coast, making it one of those New England days where the sky is so blue, and the air so clean it makes you think the coming winter might almost be a fair price to pay.

Gwen extricated herself from the car and stretched. All was reassuringly as she had left it, although the front lawn did seem to be signaling that maybe her gardening crew was not keeping up with things. The big maple in front was on fire with color, but also, if the lawn was any indication, at least halfway through losing its leaves. She made a mental note. First item on the list, check up on the gardeners.

And then she remembered. That was Robert's job.

And with the thought of Robert, Gwen was hit with an unexpected wave of sadness. To the point where, standing right there on the front walk, she had to set her suitcase down and take a breath. It was as though all the excitement of her Richmond adventure had suddenly drained out of her. And here she was. Right back where she had started. Empty. About to be both divorced and homeless.

Well, she told herself, *we're being a little dramatic.* Divorced, yes. Homeless? Not really. There were plenty of options. She could travel. She could rent an Airbnb somewhere she'd always wanted to live, go somewhere exotic and exciting.

Or she could go back to Richmond.

And with that last thought, she felt a little better. Of course she could go back to Richmond. She'd already told Rob she would, if only to address the "loose ends."

And Jack . . . *Damn.* She swore to herself. She was supposed to meet him in the library tomorrow. It had all seemed very casual Thursday night, and she wasn't sure if he'd even remember they were supposed to meet. Was it (and she hesitated to even think it, because it felt so high school) a date? She didn't know, and she had no way to get in touch with him. She wasn't even sure she remembered his last name . . . Summer-something? Maybe she could look it up online? *God,* she thought, shaking her head at herself. *I am out of practice.* In the meantime, she girded her loins against memories, made her way up the walk, and unlocked the front door.

The house was the same as she had left it, but also, somehow, not. As though all the life had just picked up sticks and gone, with only a tidy arrangement of furniture left behind. And it was definitely tidy–Cindy had made sure of that in order to be able to show it. Rugs vacuumed, fresh flowers on the dining room table, nothing out of place. In a way, that made the house feel even emptier.

Gwen wandered into the kitchen, idly opened the refrigerator door, and saw that Cindy had made sure there were a few things, like milk and eggs, that could easily function as pretty much any meal she chose. Gwen added another item to her mental "to-do" list–thank Cindy–but she really wasn't hungry. She noticed Cindy had also left a nice bottle of wine chilling invitingly in the refrigerator door, and she poured herself a glass to take out to the back patio. Late afternoon and already heading into dusk. The days were getting shorter.

She had taken an actual paper pad out to the patio with her, in order to start jotting down all the many odds and ends that needed to be addressed before "close house sale" could be fully checked off the list as completed. But as she looked at the blank page in front of her, she felt herself shut down for the day. There'll be time for that tomorrow morning, she told herself. She just couldn't quite face it. She sipped her wine and watched the sun dip below the trees at the bottom of the yard.

And then, just like that, a wholly un-moving-related thought popped into her head. "SB's" identity. Of course. Why hadn't she thought of it earlier? It was the serious young man in the photo. Lieutenant Joseph Flynn. *He* was SB, and *he* was the one she was in love with. It had to be. There was nothing of sentimentality in the journals. The only time Elizabeth strayed from the most earthbound of observations was that one entry. And there were no other photos or memorabilia that Gwen had come across in any of the materials she'd looked through. A moment of emotion, and a single photo to memorialize it.

She didn't know how it could be confirmed, but she just knew she was right. It was as though she had found the final piece missing from a very old jig-saw puzzle. Only why did Aunt Elizabeth call him "SB" in her journals? Another mystery to be solved? Well, solving one was enough for this evening. She shivered with a little thrill of accomplishment. What else could she put together?

The next few weeks went by quickly. Although she had been dreading this final step, she was relieved to find that it wasn't as hard to sort through her remaining possessions as she'd been afraid it might be. As she had reassured Rob, she and Robert had already negotiated who was to take custody of what. And with each item packed up, relocated, donated or sold, she felt lighter. As though she was gaining freedom, one moving box at a time. Plus, she had fished the manila envelope out from under the back seat of her car and finally paged through the documents to see where notarized signatures might be required. She had to admit that she had been just a little delinquent in getting the papers signed. Well, no matter. It was done now. Another item crossed off.

The sale was set to close in mid-October, but by the end of September there was not much more to be done. The house was empty and clean. A sweet young family was buying the house, but as much as she sincerely wished them well, she had no desire to be there to hand over the keys. They reminded her too much of her own beginnings there, so many years ago. Had they really been in love, she and Robert? It had seemed so, and she guessed that was enough. Regardless, she didn't want reminders of the past. She wished the couple luck but felt no need for conversation. She would leave them a note. That would be plenty.

Cindy was getting worried about Gwen's lack of concrete plans for her future, Gwen could tell. Cindy had asked several pointed questions about Rob's place and how big it was, was Gwen seriously considering living on a beach somewhere with her share of the house sale proceeds, did she want to stay with Cindy for a few days now that the house was pretty much empty?

In truth, after Gwen's initial bout of self-pity when she arrived back in Massachusetts, the thought of having absolutely no commitments and no constraints had become intoxicating. She had taken Cindy up on her offer of a place to stay, especially as the last of the furniture made its way out the door and the house emptied out. But at night, in Cindy's comfortably appointed spare room, exhausted from a day of packing things up, she would lie awake for a few moments, savoring all the choices spread out before her. She could go pretty much anywhere she chose!

But the thing she wanted to do most of all? That she hadn't even confessed to Cindy, because it seemed so, well, unimaginative? She was going to go back to Richmond. Just like she'd told Rob. She couldn't explain it, even to herself. But it felt like something was waiting there for her. Some piece of her past, maybe even some direction for her future. Prosaic? Perhaps. But that's where she felt pulled to go.

She didn't even let herself think about Jack. In all the commotion of finalizing the house sale, dealing with Robert, and moving out, she hadn't followed through on her plan to look him up. Would he have missed her? They barely knew each other. They'd shared an impromptu lunch, a couple of strolls, a dinner. Hardly a commitment. Maybe she'd bump back into him again at the library. It had all been very casual, hadn't it?

The evening before she was set to drive back to Richmond, she stopped by the house one last time. It was already dusk, the outside lights were off, and the windows were dark. Cindy was trying to be thrifty with the power, she suspected. Still, it felt a bit gloomy and, well, almost unwelcoming as she made her way up the front walk and let herself in. She still had her key.

It was eerily quiet inside. Her footsteps echoed on the wood floors, and she felt a chill raise goose bumps up her arms. *A window open somewhere?* she wondered. She walked through the downstairs rooms, looking for it, but everything was closed up tight in the living room, family room, dining room. There was that loose casement in the sunroom where the breakfast table was, she remembered, and she walked back to check things out. But all seemed nicely locked down there as well. Nothing to see. She found herself standing in the kitchen, waiting for a flood of nostalgia, but it didn't come. The house gave her nothing back.

She walked back through to the front door. No reason to go upstairs, she decided. There was nothing more she needed to see. As she pulled open the front door to leave, though, a slamming noise startled her. Her breath caught, and her heart thudded for a couple of beats. *There are no intruders,* she scolded herself. *Just you. And that casement in the sunroom that you're obviously still having trouble latching.* She caught her breath and waited for her heartbeat to slow.

Just to be on the safe side, she walked back through the house one last time to the sunroom. And the casement was indeed the culprit, swinging and banging in the gentle evening breeze. How had she missed it? She slammed it shut this time, muttering to herself. "You're not terrifying anyone else tonight," she said aloud, latching the casement with some force.

And as she turned to walk back out through the house to the front door for truly the last time, she felt as though her old house, the house in which she had spent so many years, raised her child, loved and then lost her husband, was telling her, in no uncertain terms, that there was nothing more for her here. Goosebumps still prickling, she couldn't have agreed more. She pulled the front door shut behind her and reminded herself to leave her key with Cindy before taking off the next morning.

CHAPTER SEVENTEEN

LIZZY

> **A CALCULUS**
> *There are two cribs.*
> *Two soft bears.*
> *Two of everything.*
> *Except.*
> —Elizabeth Porter, undated

Fall & Winter 1919-1920–Richmond, Virginia

Lizzy lost track of the days.

Was it Christmas? Or New Year's? Or just some other random midnight when Frank had frantically knocked on her door? She felt as though she hadn't been back in her own bed in days.

And she hadn't, really. Essie and Addie fussed up and down the stairs, bringing cold compresses, extra blankets. Lizzy had moved a mattress into Eliza and Frank Jr.'s room, dozing on and off only when they did. The fevers waxed, waned, waxed again. Lizzy tried to spoon feed each of them a little broth, water when they would take it. But both babies, listless and hot with fever, turned their heads and pushed the spoon away. Lizzy herself was almost catatonic with fatigue.

Finally, one morning, Lizzy woke up to find Frank Jr. with eyes open and alert, wailing with spirit, this time not from pain, but from hunger. Lizzy called down to Essie to make him something, porridge perhaps. She leaned over his crib and stroked his damp hair. His cheeks were rosy, but not so extravagantly as before. The rash was peeling. *Better,* she thought. *So much better.* Then, her guard down because of the progress she'd seen with Frank Jr., she turned to check Eliza. Perhaps her fever had broken as well? She reached down to tame the little curl that always seemed ready to droop down and meet Eliza's eyelashes.

Lizzy didn't really remember much after that.

When she found herself again, she was lying on Essie and Frank's bed. Addie had pulled up a chair and was sitting next to her, holding her hand. The room was quiet and dark, shades pulled. Lizzy could hear low murmuring coming from downstairs. She tried to sit up, but Addie shushed her.

"You've had a shock," Addie whispered. "Why don't you just lie here for a bit and gather your strength?"

Shock? thought Lizzy. Shock. She remembered pallor, where before the color was too high. She remembered skin cold to the touch, like marble. She remembered eyes not quite shut, not responding. Then she remembered everything. And for the first time in a long time, maybe even since those nights in the attic so long ago, she started to cry. Anger? Grief? The shattering of her world? It didn't matter. She couldn't stop.

It was April before they could all make it back to Wytheville. There was the weather, of course. It had been unusually cold that winter. There is, one might argue, never a good time for setting headstones, but winter, with frozen ground and freezing rain, would be anyone's last choice.

And there was also Lizzy. Addie was the only one who could elicit any response from her. She refused even to make eye contact with either Essie or Frank, and any question was answered in monosyllables. Frank Jr. she ignored entirely. Somehow, she continued to attend her courses at the University of Richmond, but it was as though she needed all her strength just to get up in the morning, go to whatever class was required, and make her way home. She had no energy left over for anything more than the most basic of human interaction. For several weeks after Eliza's death, any question about "arrangements" was met with silence and a blank stare. Lizzy was simply too numb to respond.

Essie finally took matters into her own hands. It was, after all, to have been her child who died. It had already fallen to her to deal with the undertaker and plan the details for taking the tiny body back to Wytheville for burial. It wouldn't do to wait too long for the memorial service itself.

One mid-afternoon, early in March, Essie walked over to Lizzy and Addie's house for tea and a chat. "We have to finish this," she said, gently but firmly, to Lizzy. Lizzy lifted her head and looked at Essie for the first time since Christmas afternoon. "After Easter?" Essie asked. Lizzy nodded.

Easter was early that year. On the very day after, Lizzy, her sisters and Frank started out for Wytheville. Frank Jr. came too, excited into good behavior by the opportunity to ride the train. Although Frank Jr. had some trouble with his "Rs," Addie was able to coax him out of self-consciousness and into a train song of their own devising, with Addie singing and Frank Jr. repeating and clapping with joy. The mundane family chatter flowed over Lizzy like a cold stream. She spent most of the train ride from Richmond to Roanoke in a seat by herself, with her gaze fixed on the picture window in the carriage, as if daring anyone to intrude on her field of vision.

In truth, had someone asked her what she was thinking, and had she felt the inclination to answer honestly, she would have had to say that her mind was almost blank. And it took a herculean effort, all her strength, to keep that blank slate intact. She felt as though, if she let anyone, anything in, she would just explode, shattering into tiny little shards of sadness.

She had made this journey so many times. When she left home for Mason-Hall. When she returned from the war. When she and Addie had left Wytheville, not even two years ago. And now she was making it again. She had only just turned twenty-five years old. She knew she was being melodramatic, but it felt to her as though now, traveling west to bury her child, she had lived enough of life.

Essie had arranged for Mr. Johnny to meet them at Roanoke and take them on to the church. Lizzy couldn't decide if seeing him was painful or comforting, although at least he presented quite a distraction, it turned out. Since Addie and Lizzy had left, Mr. Johnny had acquired an automobile, which he had proudly parked right in front of the station. A shiny new Ford, Model-T. Instead of hours in the trap, the trip from Roanoke would be only about two hours, maybe three, he told them proudly.

Lizzy had to admit that the automobile, at least, had caught her attention, if only briefly. Although then it reminded her of driving, which reminded her of France, which made her think of Lieutenant Flynn, who, well, wasn't worth dwelling on. They all squeezed in, with Frank riding in the front with Mr. Johnny. Lizzy spent the trip with her face turned toward the dusty automobile window. Early April, and everything was already green. Was spring always this early? She couldn't remember. It was pretty, though.

It was late afternoon by the time they arrived at the church, and the reverend was waiting for them by the front door. They walked together to the back where the little cemetery was. Like everything else, it was just the same as when she had seen it last. *You haven't been gone that long,* Lizzy noted sharply to herself. *What were you expecting?* Lizzy didn't know. She guessed she had been subconsciously expecting everything to show itself a little frayed with the passage of time, just as she was. It was a shock, that was all, to see everything basically unchanged.

Well, not quite everything. In the back of the cemetery, Lizzy immediately noticed the freshly dug plot, marked with a simple wooden cross. It was closer to Mama's grave than to Papa's, and Lizzy felt a brief moment of satisfaction. Not much sense being near Papa—useless in death as well as in life, no doubt. At least the headstones Lizzy had promised herself she would arrange for her parents were in place. She was grateful to the reverend for completing that task.

The reverend didn't speak for long, but even so, by the time the brief service was over, and Eliza's tiny immortal soul had been commended to the Lord, the sun was low and losing strength. It was far too late in the day to begin the return journey to Richmond, and the reverend was happy to let them know that he had already alerted several of his parishioners to be ready for guests. As they all walked out together, Lizzy hung back from the others and took the reverend's arm.

"I want to thank you," she said, "for taking care of my parents' headstones and making sure they were put in place. I am so very grateful."

The reverend replied that it was no trouble at all, and had he mentioned how much he appreciated Lizzy being so prompt with the monthly installments necessary to reimburse him for the cost? Lizzy nodded.

"As you can see, we will now need another headstone. For Eliza. If it's not too much of an imposition, I would like to trust you again with the arrangements," Lizzy continued.

The reverend looked at her quizzically for just a moment. "Of course," he answered graciously. "But is that not something that the parents themselves would like to oversee?"

Lizzy shook her head. "They are quite distraught and have asked me to take care of this," she said, firmly. "I assume it will be the same price as the markers for my parents? I have the funds here with me right now." And with that she rummaged through her purse to find the envelope with eight one-dollar bills carefully placed inside. "There is a little extra, just in case there are any unanticipated charges. If there are funds left over, please accept them as a donation from our family to your community."

The reverend accepted the envelope and bowed his head a little in gratitude. "Have the parents determined what they'd like chiseled on the headstone?" he asked.

Lizzy nodded her head toward the envelope. "It's all there," she said.

CHAPTER EIGHTEEN

GWEN

Birdbaths are essential . . .

Cardinals, S. Tekiela, p. 33.

Now–Wayland, Massachusetts &
Richmond, Virginia

The next morning, the first of October, was grey and damp. It was definitely not as festive a start to Gwen's journey as she might have liked. But she had made her plan, and she was going to stick to it. Even if she was starting to second guess her whole "Richmond caper" (although calling it that made her think of Rob, and thinking of Rob, at least, made her smile). No, the weather absolutely wasn't helping, and the prospect of a day and a half drive to Richmond, in a steady drizzle, was losing some of its appeal. At least she had been able to book the same Airbnb she'd been in before, so she wouldn't have to re-familiarize herself with another living situation. That made it feel a little like going home.

Home, she thought. It did feel like going home, somehow. And not just because of the Airbnb. It just felt like Richmond was where she was supposed to be. She thought of the library and smiled. The answers would be there. She was sure.

And she did love to drive.

It took Gwen a day and a half to get back to Richmond. She drove into the little alley behind the Airbnb around midday on Thursday, unloaded her car, and decided to walk to Arnaud's for a late lunch. She'd been sitting in a car for two days straight, and she needed a stretch. The walk would do her good.

And, of course, there was the possibility of Jack. She didn't want to admit to herself that he might be another reason to make the trip. She felt guilty about not getting in touch with him to let him know where she'd been, but opening that conversation just seemed out of her reach while she was in Wayland. There was too much back in Massachusetts to clean up, both physically and emotionally.

And once again, solitary lunch finished and without really knowing how she got there, she found herself in front of the little house at 24 Elm. It was still looking unmistakably down at the heels, still a little afraid to show its face in front of its much grander neighbors. The elm in the front yard was beginning to change color, reminding her that fall was coming to Virginia just as it had already shown itself up in Massachusetts.

She had thrown a sweater on before starting on her walk, and she pulled it tighter. Odd, she thought, to feel the beginnings of a chill begin to seep under and around the heat of the October afternoon, but there it was. It was a much more subtle sign of the changing seasons than she had ever experienced in Massachusetts. She found herself kind of liking it.

The "For Sale" sign was still there, a little more askew than it had been even a few weeks ago. Gwen looked at it for a moment, resisting the urge to straighten it. She had an idea.

"I'm calling you first because I know you'll be able to help me think of all the reasons this is a dumb thing to do," Gwen said, holding her phone in one hand and trying to clear a clean space off the crumbling retaining wall with the other so she could sit for a few minutes. "So, all the reasons it would be a ridiculous idea to move down here. And buy this house. I'm texting you a picture of it. Go."

Rob, at the other end of the line, was, for one of the few times in his life, at a loss for words. After a few moments of silence, though, he came out with a quite unexpected reply.

"Honestly, Mom? I hate to disappoint you, but it doesn't sound that dumb." He paused for a second, and she heard the swoop of her photo arriving in his phone. "The house is kinda cute. A little old, but, well, cute." He sounded a little surprised at her good taste. "I don't even hate the idea that you'd be closer to me. I mean, financially it probably isn't a bad idea, right? Cost of living is probably lower here than Massachusetts? And there's no reason anymore that you need to be in Massachusetts, is there? The only scary thing, and it's not necessarily dumb, is that you'd kind of be starting a new life. But maybe that wouldn't be such a bad thing."

Not such a bad thing. She was reminded of his desire to remain, like Switzerland, stubbornly neutral. Rob had told her early on that he had no desire to play intermediary between his parents. He loved them both, and he felt it was important to maintain a relationship with them both. And that was the end of that. No reporting on goings on, no spying on one parent to give ammunition to the other. Fair enough.

Gwen wondered, though, if he knew about his new half-sibling-to-be. If he didn't already know, he would surely know soon. Dad having a new baby was not the kind of thing that would stay a secret for long. Or maybe he did know, and this was his way of telling Gwen to let go and move on.

Not such a bad thing. That was probably as close to an unqualified approval as Gwen was going to get. She had a sudden vivid memory of their dinner together, when he had first said he wouldn't mind having her closer. She started to wonder a little about Lucy, and whether that relationship was becoming something more serious.

"Just a small point, though. I mean, have you thought about what you'd actually, like, do? Once you've bought the house?"

Gwen laughed. "The only thing I can think of is the library!" she said, laughing louder. "After all the time I've spent there, I think I'm pretty much an expert, at least in the Special Collections Room."

"Hmm," Rob said. Which was his code for, I don't know if you're joking or serious. And Gwen realized that she wasn't one hundred percent sure either. They said their goodbyes, but Gwen continued to think. It had just popped into her head, but suddenly it felt like an almost reasonable idea. She thought for a while, wondering if Ms. Hamilton needed any help, perhaps even just a volunteer. She'd have to find something, though, that was certain. She sat a little longer on the retaining wall, enjoying the quiet.

She couldn't be sure, but she thought she saw a flash of red up in the high branches of the elm.

It was peaceful in the shade of the little house, and she thought she'd stay for a while, at least until the sun set. The sharp light was in her eyes, though, and so she had a hard time making out the figure she thought she saw making its way down the sidewalk. She couldn't decide if she hoped it was Jack or whether she was too embarrassed to meet him, given that she had kind of just disappeared.

She was relieved to see, as she shaded her eyes from the sun, that it was indeed Jack, and that he was smiling. She started to explain, so sorry to just vanish, Massachusetts, soon-to-be ex-husband, divorce papers, etc., but he didn't seem to be really listening. He sat down beside her on the retaining wall.

"If I'm being honest, I was a little worried I'd been ghosted," he said. "Wasn't sure exactly why. But I hoped not. I'm glad you're back. I was hoping you would be." He took her hand, and Gwen felt a little shock of something. Attraction? Again, it felt a lot like high school. But oddly enough, that was ok.

Gwen smiled, suddenly happy for no reason she could quite come up with. "I have a crazy question," she said. "About your house," she added. "I might want to buy it."

He looked at her for a moment, then nodded as if it was something he'd been expecting all along.

"Who do I get in touch with?" she asked. Jack was quiet for a second or two, and then inclined his head toward the sign. She followed his glance. Only then did she notice, in small print at the bottom of the sign, hiding beneath the large "For Sale" lettering, a line now increasingly hard to read because of the tilted angle of the sign and the bright angle of the sun. "By Owner," it read.

"Huh," she said. "For sale by you?"

"None other," he replied. "I was going to give it a shot, anyway. If I couldn't manage it, I figured there'd be plenty of agents getting in touch with me to tell me what I'm doing wrong and how much I could pay them to fix it. It's been a little slow," he added. "No takers yet. Except, maybe, now . . . you?" It was a question.

Gwen nodded. *Yes.*

Still holding hands, they sat together in silence for a while, the sun sinking lower. "Do you want to go inside and look at anything again?" he asked.

"I don't need to right now," she said.

They were quiet for a while. Then Jack took a deep breath. "Remember when I said I wasn't stalking you?" he asked. "When you walked by the house, and I told you I was putting it on the market? The day I ran after you to give you your card back?"

Gwen nodded, curious now.

"Well, that might not have been exactly accurate. I'd seen you before. At least, I think it was you. You were just turning the corner from Campbell onto Elm. I was walking over to get a couple of things my mom forgot to pack up and take with her, and I saw you. I had this weird feeling that you might have been heading toward the house, but then I turned away for a second, and you were gone.

"When I saw you again the next day, I wasn't sure at first if it was you, but then, when I ran after you after Arnaud's, well, I was pretty sure. Not sure if this qualifies as stalking," he said tentatively, clearly hoping for reassurance, "but I just felt like I needed to come clean. I'm glad you want the house. It feels like a good match. Like you belong here."

Gwen wasn't sure how she should feel, but Jack's confession that he'd seen her before didn't feel sinister. It just reinforced her sense that the house felt right, somehow. Was this part of the pull she'd felt drawing her down to Richmond? She didn't know, and she didn't want to analyze things right now. The Massachusetts house, and the divorce, and the soon-to-be ex-husband with the soon-to-be new baby all started to fade into the background. She and Jack sat together in companiable silence. She leaned into him a little. He didn't move away.

She realized with a bit of a start that she was feeling a sudden urge to kiss him, and she wondered briefly if he felt the same. She didn't have to wonder for long. His lips were on hers—almost chaste. But not quite.

The next few weeks flew by for Gwen. Early mornings were spent attending to whatever paperwork might have come up relating to 24 Elm Street. Then, more often than not, a late morning excursion to the library. She was still trying to determine if any of the boxes of Aunt Elizabeth's papers might hold the missing journal entries from 1918, but so far, she had found nothing. And the journals themselves were numbered sequentially. There were no volumes missing.

There were some curiosities, though. Eliza, for instance. Aunt Elizabeth's entries picked back up in the late fall of 1918, and there were many entries from late 1918 through late 1919 about the twins and their milestones. Teething, crawling and walking, even Eliza's first word. "Bird," apparently, to Aunt Elizabeth's clear delight according to her journal entries. Aunt Elizabeth definitely thought it extraordinary that Eliza had not chosen the unimaginative approach of managing "Papa" or "Mama" as her first utterance.

Gwen almost felt she sensed a bit of personal pride in Aunt Elizabeth's journal entries—as though Aunt Elizabeth herself were responsible for Eliza's clear superiority over her brother. *Silly,* Gwen thought. *But kind of charming too.*

Then, oddly, just after Christmas of 1919, all mention of Eliza just stopped. In fact, the journal entries seemed to pause almost entirely for a while. Not quite as abruptly and completely as they did from January 1918 through to the following fall, but, well, almost. The entries picked back up in late spring, but at that point there was little mention of Frank Jr. and none at all of Eliza. It was as though she had never existed. Gwen asked herself, for the umpteenth time, why had her father never mentioned once that he had had a sister? She could come up with no good reason at all.

As the fall inched on toward November and the holidays, she continued to read through the boxes of material that had taken up a permanent position on her table. Ms. Hamilton frequently reassured her that there were few demands for table space in the Special Collections Room, and even fewer demands for her aunt's papers. So Gwen, taking up residence at her table nearest the collections desk, started to feel like a sort of permanent visitor. Oxymoron, of course, but it made her feel like she belonged there, at least a little.

It didn't hurt that Jack also seemed to be there more often than not. She realized she was starting to take note of his schedule, which she knew was hopelessly schoolgirl behavior. Nevertheless, if she thought he was typically there on a certain day at a certain time, she found herself a little down if for some reason he didn't show up. She knew this was silly, but, fortunately, she had no BFF to confess it to. *How old are you, anyway?* she scolded herself. Her self didn't answer. *Too old for a crush.* Maybe. Maybe not.

As she continued to read, though, she found herself wrestling with a certain disappointment. She hated to admit it, but her first impressions proved right. The material from the later years just wasn't that interesting, which seemed to be a terrible thing to say about her aunt, who was clearly one of the most accomplished women of her era. There was plenty to be proud of. Her aunt had graduated from what was then the University of Richmond's public health program, and she had gone on to seed rural health clinics from one end of the state to the other.

As the years ticked by, though, the journal entries became less and less frequent, and more clinical than personal. There were certainly no more poem drafts scrawled at the bottom of pages. Gwen was left with long technical articles in medical journals to wade through, and try as she might, she was just not that interested. Clearly her aunt had continued writing poetry—the manuscript in her keepsake box was proof of that. But because the draft poems were no longer appearing in her journals, there was no easy way to look for life events that might have inspired them.

If the attraction of her aunt's papers was beginning to wane, at least she had her own excitement to keep her attention. The closing date on the little house on 24 Elm Street was set for the fifteenth of December. *An early Christmas present,* she thought, happily. She walked by the house often, and it seemed to her to be standing a little taller and looking a little more self-confident now that Gwen was to be the new owner.

Although perhaps "new" was the wrong word. "Restored" was perhaps the better choice. Because one rainy afternoon while she was going through yet another clinical article, about scarlet fever this time, Jack came over to her table with a sheaf of computer print-outs in hand. She was grateful for the distraction.

"Remember we were wondering," he began, "if maybe my family might have bought the house from yours, back in the day?"

Gwen nodded. Of course she remembered. She wondered for a brief moment why she hadn't pursued it. Too many other things to worry about, she guessed. It didn't matter. Jack seemed to have an answer.

"I had to do some title research for the house sale," Jack said. "As I suspected, there are plenty of databases to choose from these days for this kind of research. So," he continued. "In 1973, Thomas A. and Jane F. Sommerall, my parents, bought the property at 24 Elm Street from something called the Estate of the Misses Porter. Porter, wasn't that your aunt's family name?"

Gwen nodded. It was indeed. Miss Elizabeth and Miss Adelaide Porter. And Essie, of course, although Essie was an O'Neil by marriage and had passed that name down to Frank Jr. and then, of course to Gwen herself. Jack's family had bought the house from her family. No wonder she had had this sense that she was coming home.

The fifteenth of December dawned cool and bright. Although the sun sliced sharply through the lace curtains of the bedroom, Gwen could tell that, outside, it was definitely chilly. Did it feel a bit like Christmas? Gwen had always thought that Christmas pretty much belonged to New England, but this particular morning seemed to be nudging her toward greater geographic inclusivity. She stretched luxuriously in her bed, waking up slowly and confused for a brief moment as to why she had set her alarm for what looked to be practically sunrise. And then she remembered.

Today, the little house on 24 Elm Street would be hers! She could hardly believe it!

All luxurious stretching summarily abandoned, she jumped out of bed, pulled on a robe and practically ran into the kitchen to get the coffeemaker going. She had a few more weeks reserved at the Airbnb just to give herself some leeway, but she hoped she'd be able to move in for real before Christmas.

One of the very attractive things about a "for sale by owner" transaction is that there is a great deal of flexibility. Jack had been working on clearing out his family's belongings since they had agreed on the offer, and he had already told her that there was no need for her to wait for closing to start moving in. In his mind, the house already belonged to her. But Gwen felt it was important to observe the rules. She had moved a few things over—some boxes from the Wayland house, a flamboyantly petal-pink sofa she'd found at a secondhand store that looked almost the same vintage as the house itself, a new coffeemaker (very important).

There was no rush to furnish the rest of the house. She had already decided she wanted to take her time in picking out just the right pieces. Bringing in her Massachusetts furniture would just make the little house seem like a living mausoleum of her life with Robert. She wanted to start again. A clean slate. She poured herself a cup of coffee and pulled her robe tighter, shivering a little. From the chill or from excitement? She couldn't tell.

By 9:00 a.m., she was beginning to wonder why in the world she had gotten herself so excited so early in the morning. There was literally nothing to do.

Anything that needed to be signed had been attended to. Nothing needed to be brought to the new house except a few odds and ends and her suitcase, and that was packed.

Gwen suddenly remembered–the box that had started this entire journey. The box containing Aunt Elizabeth's life. For a brief panicked moment, Gwen couldn't quite remember where it was. Had she put it in the car? No. Silly. Of course not. It was in the bedroom, in a corner out of the way. She had meant to put it next to her suitcase. Well, she could certainly organize that now.

And there it was, noticeably the worse for wear from its journeys over the last few weeks, in a corner tucked away behind a nightstand. She put it on top of the suitcase and began rolling them out together. The tattered box chose that precise moment to give way entirely, spilling its contents on the floor.

Damn, Gwen swore to herself. Crumbling pages were scattered everywhere. Well, there was nothing left to do but try to resurrect the box and gather the contents back in order as best she could. At least she was well-prepared with packing tape to help the box regain some of its integrity.

Yes, she thought. *Here's all the correspondence.* The commendation from President Nixon. The certificates. The photo of her aunt and the serious young Lieutenant Flynn in the wheelchair.

The manila envelope, though. It had spilled all its papers onto the floor. Gwen looked at it sadly. *I'll never get it back in the right order,* she thought. Nevertheless, with a sigh, she got down on the floor to start picking up the pages.

Then she realized that the last two pages, which had appeared to be blank, were in fact merely turned facing backwards. As though perhaps they were never meant to be part of the manuscript. As though they were being kept in the envelope for safekeeping, a record of what had been sent. One was the table of contents, with a title!

Pieces of Thoughts.

Gwen immediately recognized the phrase from one of the early journal entries. She'd liked it when she ran across it in the journal entry, and she was glad to see her aunt must have liked it too. And she had a sudden thought. *The poem about the cribs and the one about the darkness.* She checked the table of contents. Those two were not listed. Gwen wondered yet again how they had nevertheless wound up, by themselves, in the bottom of the keepsake box. She was starting to think she'd never know.

The other page, though, elicited a small gasp. It was a letter. To a publisher in New York. But not from Aunt Elizabeth.

From Aunt Adelaide.

She was reaching out to a Mr. Hawthorne, of Hawthorne Press, to see if there might be any interest in the manuscript. If there had been a response, it was not in the keepsake box.

Gwen thought for a moment, then went to find her laptop. She typed in "Hawthorne Press." It had been out of business for some years, but while it was still going it had been what used to be called a vanity press. The sisters would have had to pay to have Aunt Elizabeth's poetry published. Gwen wondered if Aunt Adelaide had understood. There was no further correspondence attached to the poems.

Gwen wondered again why the two best poems, the one about the cribs and the disturbing one about darkness, had never made it into the manuscript. And why was it Aunt Adelaide who was sending the poems off, not Aunt Elizabeth herself?

Gwen couldn't shake a sense of unfulfilled promise. In spite of her aunt's many accomplishments, it seemed to Gwen that, in the end, her aunt's life had come to be summarized by a slim manuscript of poetry submitted for publication (possibly unbeknownst to her) in a volume that no one would ever see.

Her thoughts returned to the poem about the dark. Did Aunt Elizabeth escape? Gwen had an unsettling feeling that, however hard her aunt had tried to move on, that darkness was always there. Out of sight, but inexorable. Never more than a couple of steps behind. Gwen sat for some time, thinking about escaping one's past and the economics of poetry publishing.

A little after 1 p.m., Gwen's phone rang again. It was Jack, and he was happy to report that the title was recorded and the sale complete. The little house at 24 Elm Street was hers. She couldn't have been more excited if he told her she had just won the $500 million Powerball. The few things left in the Airbnb were already loaded into her car, and everything was tidied up. She took one last look around. Nothing left to pack. She pulled the front door closed behind her and went to retrieve her car from the alley around the back. She found herself smiling at finally actually driving from the Airbnb to a destination that was basically around the corner. But there was a reason, of course. She could put the car in her own alley, behind her own house. She could hardly wait.

The house gave off an almost tangible air of happy expectation when she pulled up. She pulled the car into the alley (her alley!) and walked back around to the front. The first time she entered as the new owner, she wanted to make it official. She wanted to walk right in the front door. And so, she did.

She spent the afternoon setting a few things up in the kitchen, making a quick trip to the corner market, making sure there were sheets and blankets on the mattress upstairs, towels in the bathroom, and making lists of the kinds of things she'd need to shop for in the coming days. For a moment, she felt a pang of regret for not taking a few more things from the Wayland house, but the pang was short lived. She had made the right decision. She emphatically did not want to bring any baggage—real or metaphysical—with her.

Early dusk was falling when she decided she'd done enough for a first day. The setting sun was at the perfect angle to illuminate the front living room, and the fading light seemed somehow to highlight the sofa she'd chosen, she realized with happy surprise. She hadn't planned it. She'd chosen the sofa just because she liked it. And she had no one else to answer to, so if she wanted a pink sofa, she could make that happen.

As the sun continued to set, though, she realized that another thing she hadn't planned for was, well, nightfall. There was an overhead light in the kitchen, but nothing else in the house, she didn't think. She was pretty sure she had packed away a pair of candlesticks and some candles in one of the few boxes she'd brought along from Wayland, and she decided maybe she'd better see if she could unearth them. It was getting dark.

Thankfully, the bottle of wine she had purchased was easily accessible in the refrigerator, and the corkscrew had been one of the first things she unpacked. She was just starting to rummage through one of the kitchen boxes, mentally calculating the odds of finding candlesticks, candles AND matches, all together, when the doorbell rang. It startled her. Who even knew she was here?

Jack, of course. She opened the door to find him there, a large bouquet of red roses in one hand and a tote bag in the other.

"Congratulations," he said. "I feel like the house is in good hands."

The flowers were beautiful, and Gwen was instantly reminded of Christmas songs having to do with roses. They were her first official Christmas decoration, she decided. She took them from him and started walking back toward the kitchen.

"I hope you thought to bring a vase," she called back to him. "I'm not sure I can dig one out yet."

He followed her to the kitchen. "One step ahead of you," he said, putting the tote bag on the counter. "Actually, a couple of steps." And he took out a vase, a bottle of Champagne, and glasses. "Have you been here all afternoon?" he asked.

She nodded yes. "You didn't by any chance happen to bring candles?" she said, not really expecting an affirmative. "It seems like one thing I definitely forgot to plan for was nighttime. Except for that overhead in the kitchen, I think all the light I have is from my phone."

"In fact," Jack said, making his way back to the front door, "I do have something that might help." He disappeared out the front door for a few seconds, and Gwen heard some rustling from the shrubbery. Then something caught her eye, and she gasped with pleasure and surprise. Every small bit of greenery was draped with tiny white fairy lights. They lit up the front garden, and the light spilled into the bay window and cast a glow into the living room. It was as if the room were filled with starlight.

Jack came back inside, took her hand, and walked her to the back of the house. "There's a little more," he said. Leaning down over the back stoop, he turned a timer switch that was plugged into an outside outlet. And Gwen gasped with surprise again. Because, like the front yard, the entire back garden was draped with as many strands of light as the overgrown greenery could hold. But most important, there, in place of pride in the center of the garden and also glowing with tiny white lights, was the birdbath she remembered from so long ago.

"When did you do this?" she asked, a little overcome. "And where did you find it?"

"Well, as to when, there were quite a few occasions I could count on you being somewhere else. I knew most mornings you'd be in the library, and there'd be no reason for you to drop by. As for where? I had to do a little investigating. I didn't remember it. But my mom did. She and my dad were trying to make more room out back early on, I think, and she just thought it was taking up space that she was thinking of using for a garden. They must not have wanted to sell it, or maybe they did but never got around to it. Anyway, at some point she and Dad hauled it down into the cellar, and it's been there ever since. When I asked her about it, she told me she thought it was still there. And it was. I had a couple of grad students help me move it back up, and, well, Merry Christmas, I guess," he finished a little hesitantly, because he could see that tears were streaming down her face.

"Hey," he said. "The point of this was definitely not to make you cry."

"I know," she said, sniffling, and wondering if she'd remembered to buy tissues at the market. She half-expected to see a bunny hop out from under the fence. "I guess it just feels like another piece of the past, come home."

Jack looked like he wasn't one hundred percent sure what she meant, but also that he wasn't going to ask.

"Maybe it's time for that Champagne?" he asked, tentatively. She sniffed again and smiled through her tears.

"Absolutely," she said, smiling. "It's the perfect time."

They sat together, sipping Champagne on her new pink sofa, as the dusk deepened. Gwen ordered pizza, and they talked a little about easy things—her plans for the house, the course he'd just finished teaching. The front fairy lights twinkled in through the bay window, and the conversation died down. After a little while, when she felt fairly certain she wouldn't start tearing up again, Gwen started to explain why the carved stone birdbath meant so much to her.

"It was my Aunt Elizabeth's, and she loved it," Gwen said. "I only visited once, but, well, I guess a few things still stand out in my memory. Aunt Elizabeth took me out to the back garden to watch the birds and wait for bunnies. There was a little table and chairs just outside the kitchen door, and she and I came out here while all the grown-ups talked inside. There were cardinals. They were so beautiful. And my aunt had a picture book of birds." Gwen trailed off and was quiet for a while.

"Anyway," she said, "my dad was in charge of selling when Aunt Elizabeth passed. He must have decided it would be too much trouble to move, so he left it. I'm amazed it's still here."

They sat quietly for a while longer. Then Jack spoke.

"Look," he said. "I hope this doesn't sound too corny. But I feel like I know you. There's just something . . ." He paused, shook his head, and then, as if thinking well, in for a penny in for a pound, he went on. "I know we only met a few months ago. But . . ."

He didn't finish, because she kissed him. He tasted like Champagne. He kissed her back. And put his arm around her.

"Are we a thing?" Jack asked.

"We might be," Gwen replied softly. They sat in silence for a while, and Gwen was suddenly aware she might be a little tipsy. She decided that she didn't care. At all.

The twenty-fifth of December. Christmas. Gwen warned Rob that she hadn't had time to orchestrate a tree or the dinner, but Rob told her not to worry. And he was as good as his word. Not only did he and Lucy arrive with a fully decorated baby fir, complete with lights and festooned with candy canes, but they also brought with them all the makings for Christmas dinner. After putting aside her initial discomfort at a holiday feast that did not involve some sort of roasted fowl, Gwen decided that a lasagna and apple pie for dessert were her new favorite Christmas menu items. Best Christmas dinner ever, she told Rob and Lucy, and she meant it.

Jack came over in time for dessert. Rob raised his usual eyebrow, clearly (and silently) asking, "New boyfriend?" but kept any actual out-loud comments to himself. Gwen tried to raise an eyebrow of her own that would communicate something like "potential boyfriend, but right now just good friends," but that message seemed a little too complicated for what her eyebrows were able to convey.

She settled with being happy that Jack and Rob seemed to have some acquaintances in common. They quickly launched into a critique of their schools' respective tenure tracks and the rigors of publication, and there seemed to be more than enough to talk about to avoid awkward conversational pauses. She also noted that Lucy hardly drank any wine and wondered if there was any significance to be attached to that. She wondered if it would be acceptable parenting to ask Rob. Probably not, she decided.

Gwen brought everyone out to the back garden after dinner. She had managed to find a tiny patio set that would just fit. She would tolerate no objections—everyone was required to sit outside for a quick nightcap and a little more pie. For once, in Richmond, it was neither hot, nor humid, nor pouring rain, nor uncharacteristically freezing cold. She even had a tiny little propane firepit, which was energetically doing an extremely convincing imitation of a wood fire. The four of them sat together and watched the little gas flames dance. It was a perfect Christmas, and Gwen couldn't have been happier.

"Well, Mom," Rob spoke up. "I think you deserve a toast. You've had the most eventful few months of any of us, I would hazard a guess." Gwen nodded her approval of the raised glasses.

"Good for you for embracing adventure and deciding to attend that Mason-Hall ceremony for your Aunt Elizabeth."

Jack, who had been leaning back in the patio chair with eyes almost closed, suddenly sat up. "Mason-Hall?" he repeated.

Gwen looked at him. "I told you, didn't I?" she asked. "I know I did. All the amazing things she did? My Aunt Elizabeth, who was a nurse in World War I?"

"I don't think you told me where she trained, though," he said. "I would have remembered. Because that's where my grandmother trained. My mom was there this past Labor Day for the distinguished alumnae event. A friend of hers took her—I couldn't go. Too close to school starting. You mean, you were there?"

Gwen could only nod. She had a sudden vivid memory of an older, grey-haired lady in a wheelchair leaving just a few minutes before Gwen had the chance to meet her. Matron had wanted to make introductions, because the lady leaving was the daughter of one of Aunt Elizabeth's best friends, Beatrice Rockford. The photo that Matron had pressed into her hand. Suddenly, Gwen felt as though the little back garden was closing in on her. *Why is my heart racing?* she found herself thinking. She started to feel a little faint.

Too many people, too much conversation, the little propane flames throwing off too much heat. She got up abruptly to start taking things back into the kitchen. Rob followed her, clearly worried that he had inadvertently opened a topic that should have been off limits. He apologized profusely. "I feel like I said something wrong," he said, "although I'm not completely sure what. I had no idea."

"It's fine," Gwen reassured him. "Jack and I just have a connection that neither one of us knew about, and it was unexpected, that's all. It's fine." And she knew it should be fine. Which made it all the more odd that something felt, well, unsettling. She just didn't know why.

Not wanting to drive all the way back to Charlottesville after all the holiday excitement, Rob and Lucy were spending the night in Gwen's newly organized guestroom. Watching them go upstairs together, Gwen wondered briefly about the propriety of a shared bedroom before even an engagement, but in the end, she decided she was being inconveniently old-fashioned. Rob certainly didn't need her thoughts on sleeping arrangements. Jack offered to help finish clearing up, but Rob and Lucy had already worked some kind of domestic magic in the kitchen. It was spotless. There was nothing more to do. Gwen and Jack made their way back to the pink sofa in the living room.

The little Christmas tree Rob and Lucy had brought with them was still blinking in the corner. The remains of Christmas were scattered about–wrapping paper, some stray ribbon, a few deflated glasses of half-finished Champagne. Gwen sat down on the sofa with a sigh.

"I'm sorry about that, back in the garden," she began.

Jack shook his head. "No need for apologies. It took me a little by surprise too." He started gathering up paper and glasses.

"I can clean this up tomorrow," she said. "Really."

"It's not much," he said reassuringly, finding a plastic bag to press into trash-hauling service. "And I can just move some of these boxes out of the way. They're kind of a hazard." Indeed, a couple of the cartons from the move were spilling out of a corner by the bay window.

"I'll probably just put them out in the trash tomorrow," Gwen said. "Please don't fuss."

"Not fussing," he called out, on his way to the back door and out to the alley. Then a pause in his progress, Gwen could hear. "Maybe this one isn't trash?" he called back again.

He came back to the living room, this time with just one box in hand. And Gwen jumped up.

"Not trash!" she said, practically grabbing it out of his hands. "It's Aunt Elizabeth," she said.

He smiled a little crookedly at her, clearly starting to think that there had been too much Christmas cheer.

"Her stuff," she tried to explain. "It's why . . . It's just that it's special. It's her life. I can't just throw it away. That would be like, well, she never existed." Erasure. There it was again. She continued, firmly. "It needs to go in a safe place."

"Well then, I have just the place to recommend," he said. Pushing a few ribbons aside, he knelt down by the cupboard beneath the window seat. "It doesn't look like it would be very big," he said, "but my mom used to keep all kinds of stuff in here. Photos, all our little childhood projects from school, that kind of stuff. It's perfect."

He pulled on the cupboard door, and then swore quietly under his breath. "I thought I had this fixed before the house closed," he said, tugging again.

The cupboard door suddenly gave way, and Jack almost tumbled backward. Gwen ran over to help. "It feels like there's something stuck," she said, reaching in. Jack grunted in agreement.

And there was. Stuck between the side of the cabinet and the hinge was a brittle manila envelope that looked to be very old. Jack looked at it, puzzled.

"I really thought I had all this cleaned up before you took possession," he said. "I'm sure I went through this cabinet."

"Doesn't matter," Gwen said, her curiosity growing. "What is it?"

She sat down on the floor next to him as he gently pulled on whatever was inside.

And then she let out a little exclamation of complete surprise.

"It's my photo," she told him. "Of my Aunt Elizabeth. How is it here?"

Jack shook his head, a little mystified. "No," he said, continuing carefully, "it's my mom's photo of Granddad, from the war. I always wondered why she never framed it and put it out, but she said that Grandma had loved the picture, but never liked that there was someone else in it. I remember I told her she could cut out the part that had Granddad and just put that in a frame, but she said her mom wouldn't do that either, and so, well, that was that. Anyway, that's my granddad. I never knew who the nurse was."

Gwen didn't say anything. She pulled her box of Aunt Elizabeth's things over, rummaged around for a second or two, and found her own copy of the photo. And then it was Jack's turn to exclaim in surprise.

"You have the same," he started, and then shook his head in confusion.

"The nurse is my Aunt Elizabeth," she said. "I didn't know much about the soldier. Until just now."

She placed the two photos together, side by side and looked up at Jack for a moment, when she was suddenly struck by a resemblance. Whoever else was in Jack's family tree was irrelevant. His dark hair, the piercing eyes–looking at him was like looking at a twin of the soldier in the photo. Even though the photo was black and white, Gwen knew now that Lieutenant Flynn's eyes had to have been blue. Jack and his grandfather could have been twins.

Gwen was exhausted. Whatever long past connections were bringing her and Jack together here and now, she didn't feel like she could deal with any more tonight. And Jack seemed to sense that Christmas was over. He finished tidying up, gave her one last hug, and made her promise she'd go get some sleep. After warning her not to forget to lock up, he pulled the front door gently shut behind him.

CHAPTER NINETEEN

LIZZY

> **FIELDS**
> *I think of battlefields*
> *More often than they warrant.*
> *They are in the past*
> *And will remain there*
> *I hope.*
> —Elizabeth Porter, undated

May 1950–Washington, D.C.

Lizzy had not intended to go to the Mason-Hall reunion. It was only after Matron Oakes called with a personal plea that Lizzy reconsidered. She was quite busy, thank you very much, with no need for the distraction of a school reunion. In fact, as she recalled, much of her class had never even graduated. The school apparently decided that their real-world wartime experience was sufficient training for them to receive their certificates, and those had ultimately been mailed out. But their graduation ceremony had been preempted by the war. Lizzy was grateful for her training, but she didn't feel an enormous amount of school loyalty.

Nevertheless, Matron Oakes's plea seemed quite heartfelt. It wasn't just a reunion, in fact, but also a celebration of the seventieth anniversary of the founding of the school. Miss Porter was certainly one of the school's most distinguished graduates, and the school and its staff would be so honored if Miss Porter were able to rearrange her schedule and find a way to attend.

After continuing to equivocate and finally hanging up the phone, Lizzy looked at her calendar and realized that she could, in fact, take a few days to return to the school for the festivities. She wasn't sure why it was so important to Matron that she be there, but there it was. She could take a little time off. Her county rounds were less frequent these days, and although she was trying to finish an article, well, she was always trying to finish an article. It would be waiting for her on her return, of that much she was certain. She thought of asking Addie to come along, just for company, but age had only increased Addie's natural proclivity to stay home, as far away from any spotlight (even one by association only) as she could manage. She knew Addie would say no.

Never mind. She would go by herself; it would be an adventure. She had always loved being behind the wheel. And she had to admit she enjoyed any opportunity to take her Lincoln out for a spin. She'd bought it used, a few years back. A splurge, to be sure, but her only one. She had to admit that Ford had certainly come a long way since the crank starters of the ambulances back in France.

And anyway, it was May. As lovely a month as ever there is in any given year in the South. Winter thoroughly chased away, and summer only just beginning to consider flexing its muscles. As Lizzy drove up the county roads leading north, she rolled the car windows down and welcomed the warm breeze that blew through her hair. She hadn't been back to Mason-Hall, since, well, if she was remembering correctly, since leaving the school to ship out to Europe. So long ago.

She shook her head. So many memories. It would be easy to lose herself in them. She did not intend to.

As Lizzy drove into the city, she couldn't help but be reminded of her first arrival. Everything had seemed outsize. The stately broad boulevards. The trolley that had seemed to Lizzy nothing short of magical. The beautiful trees lining the walkways. And the school itself. It had seemed to occupy an entire city block. She had felt overwhelmed, and very small. The city had seemed to her then to be impossibly shiny and new.

The school still occupied a city block, its presence still imposing. Everything else, however, had shrunk and dulled. Was it just that she was older? The trolley cars looked dirty, and the boulevards seemed less graciously broad, no longer as welcoming. She remembered feeling intimidation bordering on terror as Bea had guided her out of Union Station and they had made their way together to the school. This time, her biggest challenge was finding a side street on which to safely park her car.

Lizzy made it to the check-in desk just in time for the opening reception, with barely enough time to leave her suitcase in one of the dorm rooms that had been pressed into service as weekend lodging for returning alumnae. A quick check in the bathroom mirror showed her to be fairly windblown from the drive, but (she hoped) still recognizable by her classmates.

A mimeographed schedule of events had been left on her bed, and she checked it to find that the reception was being held in the canteen. Lizzy could walk to it blindfolded. As she rounded a familiar corner, though, a sudden flood of memories took her so instantly and completely by surprise that she had to stop and lean against the wall for a moment. Memories of meals together, triumphs and secrets shared, momentous (at the time) tragedies consoled. *Bea,* she thought. *I wonder if Bea is here.* She had simply assumed that it would be too far to travel for Bea, but now that she had arrived and seen the fairly impressive schedule of events, she wondered if Bea might have made the journey after all.

Lizzy had stuffed the schedule into her handbag, and she fished it out to see if, by chance, there was information about the attendees as well as the various events. There was not. Just a listing of events she'd already read through: cocktail reception at 6 p.m., gala dinner at 7 p.m., and then, tomorrow, the "Past, Present and Future" presentation that Matron Oakes had so wanted her to be there for. Well, here she was. Cocktail reception first. She suddenly felt as though she was preparing for battle.

She was not proud of herself. Bea had written several letters over the years. There were, of course, the letters Lizzy had received while still in France, asking if Lizzy might have access to information about Lieutenant Flynn. Lizzy had not known how to reply to those. No mail had reached her on her journey home, of course. And nothing arrived for her in Wytheville while she waited, heavily pregnant, to give birth. But she had asked Mr. Johnny, on their last trip out of Wytheville, to forward mail to her sister Essie's house in Richmond. And a few letters from Bea did finally arrive, including a wedding announcement and then, a few years later, a birth announcement. A girl, Jane. Lizzy sent notes of congratulations. But as the years went on, Lizzy knew less and less how to respond, so she just–didn't. Silence became a habit, hard to break.

Lizzy took a moment to collect herself. Of course Bea was just as likely to be here as she was. And what if she came accompanied? With her husband? Lieutenant Flynn? Why wouldn't he accompany her? Lizzy prided herself on being pragmatic, analytical, and smarter than average. She found it hard to believe she hadn't really thought this through.

Well, there was nothing for it now but to go to the opening reception and meet head-on whatever–or whoever–was waiting there for her. She took a deep breath and made her way briskly down the hall.

Matron Oakes was standing at the open doors and smiling, an enthusiastic receiving line of one.

Lizzy had barely managed to finish giving her name when Matron grasped her hand. "So glad you're able to be here," she said. "Of course we haven't met. But I've heard so much about you and your work. We have a lovely presentation and celebration planned for tomorrow. And I do believe there are several members of your class in attendance! I was just talking to Anna Mae Harrison. I believe you and she were part of the program at the same time?"

Lizzy nodded, pretending to remember, while in truth she had no recollection whatsoever of anyone named Anna Mae. She did, however, see an unmistakably familiar figure across the room. Tiny. Giving off an aura of competent energy even while standing still. It could only be Bea. Matron saw the glance.

"Oh, yes, of course," she continued. "Beatrice Rockford, I think? Weren't you and she also here together during the war years?" Another attendee came up behind Lizzy to shake Matron's hand, and Matron's attention drifted away.

Lizzy made her way into the room, suddenly feeling very obviously alone. She found herself wishing that she had tried to persuade Addie to attend. At least then she would have had someone to talk to. She set out for the refreshments table, making her way carefully around tidy clumps of people, all chatting happily amongst themselves and seeming to have set up invisible but nonetheless impenetrable barriers to anyone else trying to join in. Lizzy recognized not a single face, other than Bea's, and she didn't feel quite up to approaching Bea. Not just yet.

The refreshments table was disappointing. Punch bowls of what looked like watery lemonade and iced tea, and canapés that looked as though they had been laid out just a touch too long ago. Lizzy was trying to decide which of the canapé choices looked the least likely to require the services of one of the nursing school's graduates, when she sensed someone coming up behind her.

"I think I might be able to improve on the beverage situation, at the very least," said a voice in her ear. A voice she recognized immediately. It could have been thirty years or thirty seconds ago, and it wouldn't have mattered. At least she wasn't going to have to attend each event wondering, searching the crowd. Joe was here. Lizzy froze. She was afraid to turn and look.

"Here. This should help." A punch cup, and then the flash of a silver flask. She caught the aroma of Tennessee whiskey. How many years had it been? Since she had left France. At least thirty years. More than thirty, in fact. She didn't want to count. With some effort, she found her voice.

"That is most chivalrous of you," she said, her voice a little squeakier than she would have wished. She downed the tiny little cup of punch in one swallow, poured herself a second glass. Joe enhanced it as he had the first one. *Small sips,* she told herself sternly. *This is for your nerves only. We are not going to make a spectacle of ourselves.* The second cup was downed in two swallows. She waved the flask away as she poured herself a last cup of unadulterated lemon punch. She was going to try to get through this without any more liquid courage.

"You're here with Bea," she stated more than asked. He nodded.

"And you?" he asked. "Here with...?" He looked around, as if expecting Lizzy's escort to appear at her side.

She shook her head no. "I could have pressed my sister into service, but she hates events like these," she said. "I only decided to come at the last minute," she added, instantly mortified by the non sequitur. *Why in the world would that matter at all?* she asked herself furiously. If she could have surreptitiously kicked herself, she would have.

Joe didn't seem to view it as a non sequitur, though. In fact, he nodded, as though this explained a lot. "That's why," he said. "Why you're not on the list."

Lizzy looked at him curiously. "List?" she said.

"The attending alumnae list," he said, pulling a mimeograph out of his pocket. "They sent it out a few weeks back."

Clearly Lizzy should have signed up earlier. It would have been extremely helpful to have had the list.

"I guess people like to know for these reunion events who they might run into," Joe continued.

Indeed, thought Lizzy. *And I've run into you.*

They stood at the table together, making mindless small talk. Lizzy would think about this encounter many times in the years to come, and she always marveled at the ability people apparently have to chat about absolute nonsense when topics of towering interpersonal importance are staring them in the face. After a few minutes, though, Joe cleared his throat and turned that piercing blue-eyed gaze on Lizzy. Just as he had all those years ago in France.

"You know," he said, "I think Bea was checking that list because she wasn't sure if she wanted to see you or not," he said. "She got sad after a while that she never heard more back from you."

Lizzy's first reaction was, essentially, *whose fault was that? What could I have possibly replied?* But another part of her had to admit that she understood. What kind of friend would go completely and utterly silent, for year after year? The kind of friend who is torn between feeling she has done nothing wrong, but who is on the other hand utterly full of regret about a hideous betrayal. That she wasn't even aware was a betrayal until it was too late. What was there to say?

"She doesn't know," Joe said. Lizzy nodded again. "I'm sorry," he added. "You just, you left so fast. There didn't seem to be any way for me to find you.

"Anyway, I got sent back home too. And once I started feeling better, Bea and I . . . ." He didn't finish the sentence. He didn't have to. "Anyway, here we are, I guess." He reached into his jacket pocket again, pulling out a photo this time. "I don't know if you might have heard somehow," he said, a touch of pride coloring his tone. "Our little girl. Jane."

Lizzy looked at the photo, searching for resemblance. She had her father's dark hair. And his eyes. The photo was black and white, and Lizzy didn't want to ask, so she didn't know if they were the same piercing blue shade as Joe's, although she guessed they probably were.

The little girl did look like him. And she could almost feel Bea's industrious energy flowing out of the snapshot. She was hit with a sudden wave of sadness. Why was Bea blessed with a daughter and Lizzy not? Where was the cosmic equity in that? Lizzy wasn't in the habit of shaking her fists at fate, but seeing the photo made her want to shout WHY at the top of her voice. It just wasn't fair.

Nevertheless, it seemed that Joe had kept his and Lizzy's secret, and Lizzy was grateful for that, at least. There was no reason, it seemed, to tell Joe about Eliza. What would be the point? Especially now, after so much time?

Joe poured two cups of the lemonade. "I said I'd bring some back," he said pouring a substantial slug of whiskey into each one. "I think you should come over and say hello."

Lizzy didn't remember much about the rest of the evening. She knew she walked over with Joe to say hi to Bea, she remembered him heartily saying something along the lines of "look who I found."

She remembered Bea turning in surprise, giving her a hug, overflowing with pleasantries. "I had given up on hearing from you," "I'm so glad you were able to come at the last minute," all those nice things people say when they can't think of anything else. Lizzy noted that Bea seemed to know quite a bit about her career. So it seemed possible that if Bea had really wanted to get in touch with her, she might have contacted the offices at Mason-Hall. But she let that go. Again, what would be the point?

The canteen was also the site of the welcome dinner, which had been set up around them while they were chatting. Lizzy wasn't sure she could maintain her cheerful facade much longer, but she knew she had to make it through the meal.

The food seemed to have time-traveled straight from 1916. There was some sort of pallid-looking chicken, a small pile of indeterminate wilted greens, and a stale white roll. Lizzy actually thought she remembered the meal from her days in the program, and she also remembered thinking at the time that the food at Mason-Hall was perfectly adequate. Clearly, she hadn't known any better.

She found herself sitting to Bea's right, with Joe on Bea's left. By the time the food actually arrived, the three of them seemed to have run out of conversation. They ate in what started to feel to Lizzy like an uncomfortable silence. Once she had made a polite effort to eat a respectable amount of what was on her plate, she made her excuses. Fatigue from her long drive, early day tomorrow, whatever else she could think of.

Although everyone's secrets seemed to have been kept, there was a thread of awkwardness running through the conversation, and Lizzy was finding it exhausting. She needed some fresh air to clear her head, and she needed to sleep. She said goodnight to her dinner companions and made a polite exit.

Sleep, yes, but fresh air first. She had forgotten how crowded the canteen could become when full with more people than it was designed for, and tonight was no exception. She found the hallway that led to the ancient stairwell and the front entrance. There were benches outside, she remembered. Cool, stone benches. And perhaps some cool, fresh air. She hoped it was early enough in May that the night breeze wouldn't quite yet be stifling hot.

She sat in the dark, looking at the sky. And she was still absorbed in it when Joe sat down beside her.

"If there's an award for graduate who's done the most, I think you should get it," he said, sincerely. "All that research you've done, those articles, those commendations from the state of Virginia–there's a little description of most of the alumnae in the program for tomorrow, and your entry is definitely the most impressive. I had no idea."

Lizzy just looked at him. She wasn't in a mood to talk about her accomplishments. "You shouldn't be here," Lizzy said, at last. "Bea will wonder where you've gone."

"She's gone back to our room," he said. "It was a long day for her too. I'm outside for a smoke," he offered, by way of explanation.

They sat in silence for a while.

"This reminds me of the boat," Joe said, quietly.

"You disappeared on the boat," she said, tartly. "Some story about Buddy."

"It wasn't a story," he said, a little indignant. "I got Buddy out of trouble, went to look for you, and you were gone." A few more seconds passed. "Our timing has been pretty poor, hasn't it." It wasn't a question.

Lizzy didn't respond. Again, there didn't seem to be much to say. More silence.

"I've always wondered," Joe said finally. "What happened to the Dickens? You left, and I couldn't find it anymore."

Lizzy would have answered, *I took it with me because it was all I thought I had left of you,* but she did not want to begin crying. So she didn't respond.

"I don't feel like I have a right to ask, but I'm going to ask anyway," he said softly. "May I kiss you goodnight?"

She nodded, yes.

He tasted the same. A little like whiskey, a hint of tobacco, just as she remembered. She had thought that after her return to Virginia, her move to Richmond, her loss of Eliza, she would have been immune to tenderness. But that was not the case. She kissed him back, and it was as if no time had passed.

"I love you, you know," he said. "I loved you then, and I love you now."

Somehow, Lizzy got through the next day. As much as she wanted to leave early, it was quickly apparent that she could not. There were several alumnae who were being singled out for some sort of award, and it seemed that Lizzy was one of them. It was to be a surprise, and Lizzy could confirm that she had had no idea whatsoever. It certainly explained Matron's persistence in asking for her attendance. But there was the ceremony, and then the post-ceremony congratulations, and then the closing luncheon. Lizzy felt her face might crack open from smiling so constantly from ten o'clock in the morning onward to past three.

She started making her way back to her room about 3:30 p.m., wondering if she might still be able to make it back to Richmond before it got too late. At least she could give it a try. Her few things were already packed and ready to go, and there remained only some stray toiletries to retrieve from the communal hall bathroom. She picked up her things from the bathroom and walked back to her room.

Just as when she had first arrived, there was an envelope on the bed. Lizzy was curious; Matron had said the award certificate would be mailed out in the coming weeks. She couldn't imagine what else might need to be delivered. The weekend was essentially over; there were no more events requiring mimeographed schedules. The envelope had her name on it, but the handwriting was unfamiliar.

She opened it, took out the contents, and was momentarily confused. It was a photo. An old, sepia-toned photograph. *Who would be sending me a photo,* she thought? And who are those serious-looking young people? She looked closer, and then had to take a breath. The serious-looking young people were none other than herself and Lieutenant Flynn. Joe. As if it were yesterday, she remembered the muddy field, Buddy. The reporter, who was doing a story for *The New York Tribune.* She sat down heavily on the thin mattress. *Joe must have kept it for all these years,* she thought. She fished around in the bottom of the envelope. There was a note.

You should have this, it read. *The photographer sent me two copies. I still have one. I took this with me on the off chance I might see you here. I'm glad I did.* He had signed it, TJ Flynn. She had to think for a moment what the T stood for. Theodore, of course. Teddy and Trish.

And then she wondered if Bea had seen it. She wanted to believe that Bea didn't know about the photo. It would be so much easier that way. But she was forced to admit, if only to herself, that Bea's reticence upon their reunion might have roots in something deeper than bewilderment at losing touch. Joe might think his secret was safe. Lizzy wasn't so sure.

CHAPTER TWENTY

GWEN

[T]he male and female sing beautiful songs and duets . . .

Cardinals, S. Tekiela, p. 15.

Now—Richmond, Virginia

Rob and Lucy left for Charlottesville the day after Christmas, and Gwen kept herself busy as the holiday week wound its way toward New Year's Eve. She had thought that she was bringing basically nothing from her Massachusetts house, so she found it that much more of a mystery that there seemed to be so much to organize, find a place for, and stow away. Jack had made it clear that he was happy to help, but after the discovery that Jack had a photo that was a twin to hers, Gwen felt she needed to take a little time to process the unexpected connection. She told Jack he was very sweet to offer, but there wasn't that much to do. She could get it all straightened out by herself.

Jack seemed to understand, but early in the afternoon of New Year's Eve, Gwen heard a tentative knock on her door. She hadn't exactly developed a wide circle of friends in the short time she'd been in Richmond, so she had a fairly good idea of who it might be. She hadn't come to any life-changing realizations in the time she'd spent alone trying to make order out of chaos in her new home, and the knock on her door made her instantly aware that she was feeling a little lonely. She hadn't even hooked up her TV yet, so she didn't even have twenty-four-hour cable news. The house was very quiet. She felt a sudden longing for company.

She was right, of course. It was Jack at the door. He had no flowers or Champagne in tow this time, but she was surprised at the rush of happiness she felt at seeing him at the door. Had she missed him? Or just companionship in general? It didn't matter. She was done processing, and she wasn't going to analyze anymore. She was just going to invite him in.

"I feel like you've been hiding in here," he said, stepping inside.

"Not hiding, just things to do," she said. "New town, new house, a lot to deal with. Come see the progress I've made," she continued, beckoning him in.

She gave him the grand tour, which made her feel a little silly, since, of course, it had in fact been his house not that long ago. But she was still proud of how she'd been able to make it her own. Most of the boxes were unpacked and disposed of, she'd put up a couple of Ikea bookcases to hold the few books and knick-knacks she'd brought from Massachusetts, and the kitchen was organized and clean. She had considered new paint, at least for the living room, but in the end, she didn't want to take the time. And she was also coming to the conclusion that the old paint wasn't so bad. It was a kind of restful pale green, and it made her new pink sofa pop. No, there was absolutely no reason to repaint right away.

Jack made all the right complimentary noises, but she could sense he was distracted. She offered to make some tea.

"I've been thinking a lot," he called out to her from the living room as she hunted for a tray to bring the tea in. "It was a surprise. That photo. Of my grandfather and your great aunt. I can't quite figure it out."

"I know," Gwen called back, as she rummaged around for teabags. "I haven't been able to come up with anything either. Maybe we need to compare a few more notes on family history?" And with that, with Jack bringing up the photo as if it were the most natural thing in the world, she suddenly knew no awkwardness was necessary. This was just–who they were.

"Okay," he said. "My history is easy. My mom is Jane, maiden name Flynn, married to my dad, Thomas Sommerall."

And Gwen realized that what she had suspected, ever since discovering Jack had the same photo she did, was probably true.

"Maiden name Flynn," she repeated, slowly. "So your granddad was Joseph Flynn, and your grandmother was Beatrice? Who trained at Mason-Hall and was a friend of my aunt's, and who never really liked this photo of your granddad with my aunt, but also wouldn't cut it up?"

Jack thought for a moment, as though pondering a particularly difficult multiple-choice question. "Beatrice Rockford," he confirmed.

Gwen felt a spark of recollection. "Hang on," she said, and ran upstairs. Where had she put it? She'd almost forgotten she had it, the photo that Matron had pressed into her hand at the ceremony. There it was. She'd put the photo in the keepsake box, which was back upstairs and safely stashed in her closet. She ran back downstairs and handed the photo to Jack.

"Is this your grandmother?" she asked.

Jack looked closely, nodded. "She was much younger there than I remember, of course, but, yes. That was my grandmother. Beatrice."

Gwen was silent for a moment, taking in the name. She'd spent the last several months in the Special Collections Room seeing it over and over again. "Beatrice Rockford's name appears all through my Aunt Elizabeth's journals," Gwen said at last. "At least, it does during the time they were at Mason-Hall together. Then there's a gap in the journal entries, and after that Beatrice is hardly mentioned at all."

"So what would have prompted my grandmother to keep that photo of your aunt with my granddad, even though she didn't like it?" Jack wondered aloud.

And what would have prompted my aunt to keep the same photo, Gwen wondered silently to herself. *Love, maybe?* She thought about her aunt, and about Beatrice, her aunt's friend. She thought about the last of her aunt's journal entries, just before they came to an abrupt halt in early 1918. "I think I am in love," it said. No more than that.

Gwen had already concluded with 99% certainty that the likeliest possibility was the handsome Lieutenant Flynn. Love was almost always a good answer in situations like these. Love in all its complications, love even when it was angry and jealous. Certainly it would explain why Aunt Elizabeth had kept the photo.

And from Bea's perspective? Her husband and her friend, inexplicably together and memorialized in sepia? Gwen wondered if Jack's grandfather had ever been called upon to explain the photo. Well, it certainly didn't matter now. In any event, it seemed like a compromise had been reached. The photo was not discarded, nor was it displayed. A truce.

Gwen and Jack drank their tea in silence, each considering the implications of what they had discovered. Aunt Elizabeth, part of Gwen's family, was somehow intertwined with Jack's grandfather. And now she and Jack had managed to connect. Through the little house at 24 Elm Street. It seemed to Gwen as though the little house was giving off a bit of an air of being quite proud of itself.

Gwen couldn't explain it, and she certainly wasn't going to try. Anyone would think she was crazy. But the house seemed almost to breathe a little sigh of relief. That someone was finally on track to figuring things out and putting things right. Back where they should be. Or should have been. Gwen wasn't quite sure, and she was starting to get a little bit of a headache thinking about it. She decided to put thoughts of family connections aside for the time being.

Gwen shook her head and turned to Jack. "Plans for tonight?" she inquired, raising an eyebrow.

"Well," he said, a little sheepishly. "It's never been one of my favorite holidays. I tend to order Chinese, watch the ball drop in some more convenient time zone, and go to bed embarrassingly early."

"That's exactly what I do," Gwen replied.

They spent the rest of the afternoon tidying up odds and ends. They took down the Christmas tree, Jack helped her hook up her TV, and the two of them moved some furniture around just to see if perhaps a different configuration might work better (in the end, of course, things ended up right where they'd started).

The last task was getting a few bulky file boxes out of the way. Financial and legal records of her previous life. She couldn't discard them, but she didn't want them greeting her every morning as she walked down the stairs for breakfast, either. She had originally thought of putting them in the little cellar along the side of the house (where Jack had managed to locate the birdbath), but Jack talked her out of that. The cellar was damp, and Jack was not happy admitting it, but he felt compelled to confess that the occasional rodent might have been seen. Gwen suggested one of the spare bedrooms, but again, space was limited, and why waste it with copies of old financial records and tax returns? Jack offered to put the boxes in the attic, and Gwen gratefully accepted his help.

They pulled the rickety ladder down from the attic and braced it on the second-floor landing. It didn't look very secure to Gwen, but Jack seemed unfazed, and Gwen realized he was undoubtedly accustomed to being the one sent up there to fetch things. She held the ladder for him and manhandled the boxes up.

"There's more up here than there probably should be," Jack called down. "I thought I'd done a better job cleaning all this stuff out."

"Well, what's 'all this stuff'?" Gwen called back.

"I don't know," he replied, his voice a little muffled. "There's an old rug up here. I'm kind of afraid to unroll it to be honest. I guess I better see if there's anything else behind it." She could hear him scuffling around and then thumping his way back to the ladder. She held it steady while he climbed back down.

"It's just a book," he said, "but I have no idea who kept it or why. It doesn't look like anything I remember–" He stopped mid-sentence, because Gwen had grabbed it from him and was hugging it to her chest, dust and all, like a long-lost friend. Jack looked at her inquisitively, hoping for an explanation, but she wasn't sure she trusted her voice to explain. She recognized the book instantly.

"I don't think it's something you'd remember," she finally said, hoping that Jack would think her watering eyes were due to the dust. "It must have been left behind when our family sold the house to yours. It's the bird book. The one I remember looking at with Aunt Elizabeth. Look, here's the cardinal on the cover, in the snow, just like I remember."

And there the cardinal was, its vivid red feathers slightly dusted with what looked like powdered sugar, a half-frozen brook bubbling away under the branch. Gwen could hardly believe it. She held it tight and sat down on the stairs, overcome. It was only then that she realized something was keeping the book from closing fully. She paged through to the end, looking for whatever was keeping the book open. A photo fell out.

It was an old photo, sepia, just like the photo of Aunt Elizabeth and Lieutenant Flynn. The image was of a little girl, no more than about a year old, Gwen guessed. On the back, someone had written "Eliza. Born September 1918. Died December 1919. Beloved daughter. May she rest in peace."

Eliza. Her dad's sister? At least, that's what the journals indicated. The back of the photo was sticky, as though it had been taped to something. And Gwen remembered the back of her copy of the photo of Aunt Elizabeth and Lieutenant Flynn. A faint sticky residue remained there, too. Gwen wondered if the sticky place on the back of Aunt Elizabeth's photo might match the sticky place on the back of Eliza's. And then Gwen started to wonder whose daughter Eliza really was. Because suddenly, she wasn't sure.

The house giving up its secrets, one secret at a time. That's what Gwen decided it felt like, as she looked through the bird book over and over that afternoon. First, of course, the house itself. Still there, exactly as she remembered it, it had been the original lure. Then the birdbath, source of a most vivid memory of her aunt, rediscovered and now restored to its pride of place in the back garden. And now the book. The book that she remembered sharing with Aunt Elizabeth so long ago. To say nothing of the photograph carefully pressed within. She wondered if there were any more treasures left to uncover. Time would tell, she supposed.

In the meantime, she sent Jack back up to the attic with her very best flashlight, but he found nothing else of interest. Just an ancient copy of *A Christmas Carol,* and some dog-eared ladies' magazines that looked as though they should have been tossed long ago. Perhaps some other helper had put it all up there? Gwen's dad would have had the responsibility to do the final cleaning out, and he certainly could have hired someone to help, but Gwen would never know for sure. In any case, there certainly didn't seem to be anything left up there now.

By about 5:30 p.m., Gwen felt like her head was spinning a little, and she was tired of trying to come up with ideas of how the book and the photo might have found their way to the attic. But she did think it was safe to say that Jack's grandfather and her great aunt had meant more to each other than anyone at the time had realized.

Which made her start to think about what Jack might mean to her. She quickly came up with an answer. She liked him. Well, more than liked him, if she was being honest.

Jack offered to go out to pick up dinner. Gwen started tidying up a bit, gathering up the book and the photos that they had been studying, making room for a casual dinner on the coffee table. And the photo of Eliza caught her eye. A thought struck her, and she put the photo side by side with the one of her aunt and Lieutenant Flynn. No need for imagination or for color film. Eliza's eyes and Lieutenant Flynn's eyes were exactly the same. She picked up the photo of Eliza, turned over her copy of the photo of her aunt and Lieutenant Flynn, and gently overlaid the picture of Eliza over the outline of long-ago sticky tape. The picture fit exactly. The pictures had been together for some time before someone split them up.

They were reunited now.

"Hear me out," Gwen said, as she put dumplings on two plates, the TV on mute showing anticipatory clips of the ball falling somewhere to the east, Australia most likely. "Remember I told you that Aunt Elizabeth's journals talked about twins? That my Dad had a twin sister? Who he never, ever, mentioned? I think that was Eliza! Her name is in the journals. And maybe the reason he never mentioned her was because he never knew her.

"Think about it. Let's say you were my Aunt Elizabeth, and you had a child out of wedlock, back in the early 1900s. Wouldn't you try to find a way to preserve everyone's reputation? What better way than to give the child to your sister, in a community where maybe people don't know you well, and suddenly your sister has twins! No one suspects, because the family is new to the city, and no one knows them. But now we know that Eliza died! In December of 1919. My dad wouldn't even have been two years old yet. He would have been too young to remember her, and everyone else would have just decided letting the memory go would be easiest for everyone. Except for Aunt Elizabeth. The memory never faded for her."

Gwen held up the photo of her aunt posing with Lieutenant Flynn in the wheelchair. "This was her photo," she said. "And Eliza's photo, which clearly belongs taped to the back, says 'beloved daughter.' Nothing about a niece. Also," she added almost as an afterthought, "my Dad's birthday was November, not September. Doesn't match the inscription on the back. So, there's that. And then, of course, the poem. It's the only one that made me cry. The one about the crib."

Jack nodded, quietly, taking it in. "OK," he said. "Is there any way to confirm any of this? Because the journals don't cover this time period, right?"

"I'll bet they did," Gwen said, starting to think. "I bet there's something missing somewhere. Because why would she stop and start journaling, just leaving big chunks of time unexamined? It just doesn't seem like something she'd do."

"There is one way to get a little more information, though," Jack offered thoughtfully. "Does your family have a cemetery plot somewhere? Maybe your aunt decided to be a little more honest about things when they were being chiseled in stone for posterity."

They were quiet for a while, the Chinese food cooling in its waxy containers in front of them. Glittering balls continued to drop down the TV screen as each time zone reached the new year. Neither Gwen nor Jack paid them any attention.

"Look," Jack said finally. "I'm sure this is a lot for you to take in. It is for me too. Just, well, all these connections.

It feels like we're fulfilling some crazy destiny by coming together. And I get why you might have started feeling a little claustrophobic at Christmas dinner. In a strange way, it almost feels like we're being pushed to be together." He paused, then continued.

"But honestly? I don't care if something's pushing us. I've felt something for you from the moment I saw you at the library." He smiled. "Truthfully? Maybe even before, when I saw you walking down Elm Street past the house. I guess maybe I was stalking you after all," he said, sheepishly. "Just a little." He paused again, then took a deep breath. "I know this sounds crazy, but maybe there's some cosmic second chance going on here. I'm not sure what happened with your aunt and my grandfather. I don't think it worked out for them. But . . . well . . . maybe it could work out for us?"

By way of an answer, she kissed him. It lasted a while.

But then she felt him pull away. "I didn't mean . . ." he stammered a little. Then he continued. "Are you sure about this?" he asked. "I don't want to rush you into anything. I feel like fate, or the cosmos, or whatever, has finally managed to get us together. I don't want to go too fast now. I feel like this is worth waiting for."

"I think we've waited long enough," she said. They kissed again, and she leaned backwards onto the sofa, his mouth on hers and his hand slipping under her shirt to find her breast, leading her to forget completely how inconveniently small the new sofa was. She half slipped off the cushions and narrowly missing hitting her head on the coffee table. Jack apologized profusely, and she burst into laughter.

"If we're going to do this," she said, still giggling, "I have a brand-new bed upstairs. That might require fewer gymnastics."

They went up together.

CHAPTER TWENTY-ONE

LIZZY

> My Dear Mr. Hawthorne—
> I beg your forgiveness for the many delays in send-ing you my sister's manuscript. My sister and I have been suffering from health problems, and we have been much consumed also with the care of our youngest sis-ter, Mrs. Esther O'Neil. To our great sadness, she has recently passed away. Although we continue to grieve her loss, her passing has made it possible for me to turn once more to the preparation of my sister's poetry for publication.
> As you may recall, her poems span the years be-fore, after, and including World War I. She served as a nurse and an ambulance driver. I feel that her poetry truly captures her experiences and will, even to this day, illuminate the horrors of war. The tentative title for the collection is "Pieces of Thoughts."
> I hope to have the package ready to send to you by June at the latest.
> I remain, with best regards,
> Yours very truly,
> Miss Adelaide Porter.
>
> Letter from Miss Adelaide Porter to Mr. Nigel Haw-thorne, Hawthorne Press, April 3, 1970.

October 1972–Richmond, Virginia

Dismantling a life. That's what it felt like to Lizzy. But it had to be done. Her nephew, Frank Jr., had gently but firmly made that clear when he came down to help her last July. Now that Addie and Essie were both gone, there was no reason to keep the house. *Well, she* thought, *I'm the last one standing. So I guess that means I get to be the one to do the final closing out.* Frank Jr. had assured her that the New Vistas home opening up a few blocks away was one of the nicest ones he'd seen. She wasn't sure how encouraging a recommendation that was, but she reluctantly accepted that it was the only choice that made sense right now.

The dining room table was covered with file boxes, papers, assorted books and scholarly journals. The books, especially, felt like her friends. Some were compendiums in which her own articles appeared; some were research references; some, like old friends, were just companions that she liked. No other reason than that.

At least the University of Richmond had accepted her offer to donate her papers. *Thank goodness,* she thought. *I would have hated to throw everything away. And Addie would never have forgiven me. After all the work she did to try to get the poetry published.* Lizzy still felt certain that, if Addie had lived just a few months longer, she would have pulled the manuscript together and sent it off for review. And then who knows what would have happened. *I could have been famous, she* smiled to herself. Doubtful, of course. Not many people reach fame through poetry. Not these days, at least. And certainly not at her age. She sighed, thinking of Addie. It was hard to believe she'd been gone now for more than two years, Essie for three.

Where was that manuscript, anyway? There! she spotted it, all the way over on the other side of the table. Lizzy sighed and rose somewhat stiffly from her chair. She paged carefully through the typed sheets, one poem to a page. What to do with the manuscript was one of the only arguments she and Addie had ever had. Lizzy had never wanted to try for publication. The poems were private, and Lizzy's desire was to keep them that way. Addie thought they were too good to hide away. So they had compromised. Addie could send the manuscript in, but Lizzy would have final say as to which poems would be included. Lizzy only cut two of the poems, but she was quite adamant. They were the most private ones.

Where were they? The two poems? About Papa, and Gwenny? No, silly, not Gwenny. Eliza. The one I wrote just after . . . There it is. And the other one?

Addie had promised. She wouldn't send those two in. But somehow, there they were. At the back. With a table of contents that Lizzy had never seen, and the draft of Addie's letter to Mr. Hawthorne. Had Addie planned to send those two poems anyway? They weren't listed on the table of contents, but maybe Addie had planned to include them later? Lizzy felt herself getting a little angry. She took a deep breath and thought about her blood pressure. *Anger is a waste of energy now,* she chided herself. And anyway, Addie never got beyond the first inquiry letter. A stroke took her, just as she was preparing the letter to re-engage Mr. Hawthorne's interest. Neither the manuscript nor the letter was ever actually sent.

She looked again through the letter to Mr. Hawthorne. Lizzy had never read it very carefully. She had left all that to Addie. So she was surprised, now, to see that Addie had a title for the collection. She liked it. It was how she had explained poetry to Addie so many years ago. *Good for you, Addie,* she thought. *You remembered. Well done.*

What to do with the manuscript? she wondered. *Should it go to the library? Or perhaps Gwenny might like it?* Definitely for Gwenny, she decided. She might enjoy reading the poems someday. She put the manuscript in the little stack of memorabilia she was putting aside for Gwen's keepsake box. Not the two private poems, though. No one should have those. She put them aside. She'd figure out what to do with them later.

Well. She had spent far too much time on this.

Stop daydreaming, she scolded herself. *You have many miles to go before this is done.* The university had told her they would send over a graduate student to help her label everything and pack it up for donation, but she wanted to make sure she knew exactly what was going to be put into the collection. There were one or two things she wanted to pack up for Gwenny and Frank Jr., keepsakes to remember her by. And there were a few other things that she felt might best be destroyed. No need to have everyone start asking questions, certainly not now.

An hour or so later, she was fairly pleased with her progress. One entire sector of the table had been cleared off, and the tabletop was actually visible. She gave herself a mental pat on the back and started in on the next adjacent pile, only to have all headway brought to a sudden stop. It was the picture book, the one for Eliza. The one Gwenny had loved too. With the cardinal on the cover. She and Gwenny had taken the book out to the back garden together, to look for birds visiting the birdbath and to watch for rabbits. Lizzy sat, quietly, for a little while, remembering the afternoon.

She hated getting old. Because it meant she couldn't always remember where she'd put things. *Where was that photo of Eliza?* She started rummaging through piles of already sorted papers, leaving them in even more impressive disarray than they'd been in when she'd begun the task. After about fifteen minutes of recreating chaos, she remembered. Of course. The photo was where she'd put it herself–taped to the back of the one of her and Lieutenant Flynn, together, in France. Now where had THAT one gone? Perhaps in the pile of her personal journals?

With the bird book hugged closely to her chest, she rose carefully from her chair and walked around to the other side of the table, where the volumes of her personal journals, going all the way back to 1916, were stacked. She had a sudden vivid mental image of Addie and Essie, as they had been so long ago, solemnly presenting her with her very first notebook.

"For your journeying," Essie had said. *Well,* she thought. *There was quite a lot of that, wasn't there.*

But seeing the volumes of her personal thoughts brought her back up short to her initial task. Some of the volumes contained entries about events that were entirely too personal to be donated anywhere the public could access them. She would need to go through the journals and make sure nothing inappropriate was in the materials set to go to the library.

Although, she was fairly sure that if she could just find that volume from around 1918 . . . There it was! Volume 5! No one would probably even notice if some of the pages were missing. There were probably some inappropriate entries scattered throughout some of the other volumes as well, she realized, but she didn't want to start going through all the volumes and razoring out more. In any case, there shouldn't be enough entries left to raise anyone's curiosity too terribly high. Removing the last third or so of pages from Volume 5 should do it.

She turned her attention back to the small stack of items neatly collected to go to Frank Jr. and to Gwenny.

Now, where had all that gone? She had meant to put all those keepsakes in the hallway, to be set aside until Frank Jr. came down again to collect them. But good, they were still here, on the floor beside her. Of course they were. Where else would they be? She needed them close by. There might be more to add.

Anyway, back to the photos. The one she was looking for. Of Gwenny. No, not Gwenny. Eliza. Lizzy shook her head. She kept getting confused. But there was a reason for her confusion, she told herself sharply! Because Gwenny and Eliza were so, well, they could have been twins for all the resemblance they shared! "Darn it," she swore aloud, softly. *That photo has to be somewhere in this mess.*

And then, success. There it was. The photo of Lieutenant Flynn. Joe. The photo of Eliza she was looking for was still stuck to the back, as Lizzy had taped it, even though the old, yellowing tape itself had long disintegrated. These couldn't be donated. They were part of her soul. Simple as that. They would go with her to New Vistas.

Terrible name, she thought, not for the first time. Most of the residents would much prefer the memory of old vistas and had little use for new ones. In fact, most of the residents probably couldn't see vistas at all. New or otherwise.

The bird book forgotten, she pulled the smaller photo off the back of the larger print and looked at it more closely, holding it side by side with the photo of Joe. It felt as though, if she looked at them long and hard enough, she could will all of the black and white images back into solid flesh. Joe, who passed away sometime in the 1960s, not long after Bea (Mason-Hall sent out death notices for their graduates, and sometimes for the spouses as well). And Eliza. Most especially Eliza.

Although, truth be told, Lizzy had the inescapable sense, as she looked at Eliza's photo, that Eliza was still here. Because Gwenny was her spitting image. Genetics must be playing a parlor trick, she felt. But it was almost like a miracle. Navigating her way down the family chromosome, Eliza had come back alive in Gwenny.

The phone rang, and she put the photos down. Perhaps it would be that graduate student, calling to let Lizzy know when she might be coming by to start helping organize. She got up to answer the phone and was hit by a wave of dizziness. The heat, she supposed. She refused to believe it could be anything else. She'd turn on the ceiling fans when the young lady arrived to help. In fact, she thought, might as well turn them on now.

Eyes closed and enjoying the sudden rush of moving air, she completely failed to see that the larger photo, the one of Lizzy and Lieutenant Flynn together, fell to the floor, next to the box of keepsakes that Lizzy had been putting together for Gwen. As did the two sheets of paper with the poems that Lizzy had pulled out from the manuscript. A graduate student coming to help organize papers for donation might easily think both the picture and the two poems had been meant for that keepsake box.

That same graduate student might also be forgiven for quickly tucking the photo of an unidentified toddler into the bird book, just to get it out of the way, with perhaps a note made (and quickly forgotten) to ask Miss Porter what should be done with them. Neither the bird book nor the photo of the toddler would seem to be the kind of thing that would be donated to a special collection. In fact, it wouldn't be at all surprising if they ended up as part of a last pile of junk that found itself moved unceremoniously up to the attic, perhaps as part of a final tidy-up, in advance of finally selling 24 Elm after its last resident passed on.

All kinds of odds and ends might find themselves banished that way—a stray copy of *A Christmas Carol*, perhaps; ancient magazines with crumbling pages that had been saved for so long it felt wrong, somehow, to toss them. Frank Jr. himself would find a small box with his name on it carefully stacked in the hall, along with a box of keepsakes that Aunt Elizabeth had told him were meant for Gwen. Her commendation from President Nixon. Her graduation certificates. And, unintentionally, the picture of her standing with Lieutenant Flynn.

There would have been no reason for Frank Jr. to think there was anything more anywhere else in the house. Not the bird book, not the picture of Eliza. Not the Dickens, not the magazines. They were important only to Lizzy. No one else. No questions would have been asked.

And certainly no one would have asked about missing journal pages. Any poems scribbled in among the journal entries had already been copied and given to Addie. There was no trace at all left of the journal pages themselves. Because Lizzy took them out to the back garden and burned them.

CHAPTER TWENTY-TWO

GWEN

> *"Cardinal" comes from the Latin word "cardo" which means "hinge or door." So the bird was literally named as a representation of a door between the spirit world and the earth.*
>
> "When a Cardinal Appears," B. Lecat, bonnielecatdesigns.com, November 3, 2018.

Now–Home

Gwen had hoped that February in Virginia might be a little less depressing than February in Massachusetts. She was disappointed to find that this was not the case. In fact, she had to admit, Virginia might almost have been worse. Because at least in Massachusetts there was the pillowy beauty of snow. The pale sun, sparkling on tree branches laced with ice. Virginia was just, well, grey and rainy. Too cold for a sweater, too warm for just a winter coat. Definitely an outerwear conundrum.

Nevertheless, Gwen was excited. It was Saturday, the first day of a long weekend, and they were driving out to visit a cemetery in Wytheville. Gwen had to admit that it sounded a little odd for a holiday excursion, but she had actually been looking forward to it for some time. Jack had finally convinced her to do a little research on "Find a Grave," and she had found that several members of her family, going back to the late

1800s at least, had been buried there. Her dad had never mentioned the Wytheville church, making it clear that he wanted to be laid to rest with Gwen's mom in the tiny cemetery in western Massachusetts behind the church her mom had grown up in. And Aunt Elizabeth had made it clear in her will that she did not wish for any extravagant send-off. She wished to be cremated, and her ashes interred in the small columbarium annexed to the Richmond church she'd begun attending late in life.

However, Gwen's grandparents, Essie and Frank, Gwen discovered, were buried in Wytheville. And also her great-grandparents—Aunt Elizabeth's, Aunt Addie's, and Aunt Essie's parents. Gwen had searched on "Find A Grave" for Eliza O'Neil, but there were no matches. Jack had finally suggested they just go out to the graveyard to see what they might find.

"Cremation wasn't a thing back then," he said, "so I have to believe she's buried somewhere. Might as well start where we know there's a connection."

And so, they found themselves in the car, driving through the soggy Virginia countryside. Even soggy, though, Gwen had to admit, grudgingly, that there was a hint of spring. If she squinted her eyes up tight, it almost looked like some of the trees might be sprouting a faint tinge of green. You wouldn't see THAT in Massachusetts in February, that was for certain.

They stopped a couple of times, once for gas and again for coffee, so the trip took even longer than they had estimated. Gwen had tentatively planned on stopping in Charlottesville to see Rob and spending the night there before driving back to Richmond on Sunday, so they wouldn't have such a long drive ahead of them for the return. Also, Gwen was very curious to see if there had been any change in Lucy's condition. Rob hadn't said anything, but, well, if Gwen's suspicions were correct and there was a bump, Lucy wouldn't be able to hide it by now. Perhaps wedding bells might be under consideration? Gwen knew that Rob and Lucy's business was none of hers, but–she could always hope.

But first things first. As they drove along the main county road heading west, Gwen wondered if things had really changed much in the hundred or so years since her Aunt Elizabeth had lived there. There were fences and farms, with properties spaced so far apart that there would have been no illusion whatsoever of neighbors. There was still the occasional horse enjoying an afternoon graze in the field, but not much other sign of life. It was hard to imagine any kind of community. Gwen found herself understanding why her Aunt Elizabeth was obsessed with leaving.

Gwen had called ahead to the reverend, but he had told her that if all they wished to do was to visit the cemetery, there was no need for an appointment. He would leave the gate open, and they were welcome to walk around the back and stay as long as they liked. "The back door is never locked," he added, a bit conspiratorially. "So, should you need to come inside and use the facilities, please feel welcome." After a four-hour drive, Gwen found that reassuring.

They parked in the small pull-off just to the side of the church, and Gwen unfolded herself from the car. It felt good to stretch her legs. Jack took her hand, and they followed the little walkway around to the back. The gate was unlatched, just as the reverend had said.

"I wish we had a map," she said, standing at the entrance and looking at the headstones. There were more than she expected.

"It's not that bad," Jack reassured her. "Here. I'll start on this side, you start on the other, and we'll meet in the middle."

Gwen nodded in agreement. They started off.

Some of the headstones were quite hard to read, and Gwen decided that if those were so old that the writing had literally weathered away, they were unlikely to be from the right time period. And the new ones, with the lettering still crisp and clean, were likely to be too recent. She walked on. She didn't consider herself in the least bit religious, but she was surprised by how peaceful the place was. She found herself wondering if they had plots left. And then she shook her head. *Reverie over,* she told herself. *That's not what we're here for.*

Jack called out. "What was the last name again?" he asked.

"O'Neil," she called back. "Frank and Esther O'Neil. They'd be near Essie's parents, family name Porter. And Eliza should be near Frank and Esther. Eliza O'Neil, if she really was my dad's sister."

"You should come look at this," Jack called back. "I think I have Frank and Esther. And there's an Eliza, but the last name isn't right."

Gwen found herself walking quickly through the grass. It didn't seem proper to run. Jack was right. There were the headstones for Frank and Esther, and for Esther's parents. And then, off to the side, was a small headstone, only a tiny bit weathered. There were two carefully carved angels adorning the lettering, and Gwen found herself thinking how much that must have increased the cost. She looked closer for a better look at the name.

"Eliza Porter Flynn," the stone read. "September 9, 1918 - December 29, 1919."

"No wonder we couldn't find it," Jack said, quietly. It's my mom's name—my granddad's name. I wouldn't have guessed that. Although I suppose it makes sense, my granddad and your great aunt, and then my granddad and my grandmother, right? It kind of makes my head spin a little."

Gwen nodded her agreement. She'd been right. Eliza wasn't Frank and Essie's daughter. Whatever charade was being enacted in life, in death she was the daughter of Elizabeth Porter and Joseph Flynn. Gwen needed no more confirmation than that.

Gwen had a sudden thought. The poem about the two cribs, the two stuffed bears. It must be about Eliza's death. It couldn't have been clearer. She wondered if she'd ever find the genesis of the scary poem about darkness. She doubted it. The inspiration for that one would remain well hidden, she suspected.

Gwen was glad she had alerted Rob that they would be spending the night in Charlottesville. Although it wasn't that late, only mid-afternoon, Gwen had to admit she did not feel up to the drive all the way back to Richmond.

The anemic February sun was already considering twilight, and the afternoon had turned decidedly chilly, any hint of spring long since departed. Gwen found herself hoping for a fire and one of Rob's comforting pasta creations. She was grateful that Jack had offered to drive, and she found herself reaching across the center console to take his hand. He squeezed her hand back. Such a small gesture, but it almost brought tears to her eyes. She wasn't sure why she was so emotional. Maybe just more discoveries today than she had expected. She felt entirely wrung out.

The motel Gwen had booked was not too far from Rob's house, and she was glad she had thought ahead to make the reservation. It somehow felt entirely too soon to ask her son to accommodate both her and Jack in his own house, even if they were becoming a "thing," as Jack had so romantically put it. It was one thing to have a new state, a new house, and a new boyfriend (boyfriend! She wondered if people over fifty actually used that term!), but it was entirely another to deal with sleeping arrangements in her son's house.

When they arrived, the house was cozy and warm, and she felt instantly better the moment she stepped inside. The fire crackling away in the small fireplace was enthusiastically taking the February chill off the room, and something fabulous was clearly being assembled in the kitchen, because the smell of garlic and butter was intoxicating.

She was happy to see that Lucy was joining them for dinner. Trying to be subtle, she surreptitiously scrutinized Lucy for signs of a kind of condition that might discourage alcohol consumption, but Lucy was wearing a loose tunic top that would have disguised any condition up to quadruplets. Although perhaps the fashion choice was itself an indication? *Well, I can be patient,* she thought. If Lucy was pregnant, that was the kind of secret that couldn't be kept forever.

Rob scurried around the living room, tidying up a bit and making excuses for a mess that Gwen honestly couldn't see, except for a few piles of newspapers scattered about. She busied herself gathering them up and started back to the kitchen, looking for the recycling bin.

"Not those!" Rob called out in mock panic. "Mom! Seriously! Those are the crosswords I haven't finished. You know better than to clear my newspapers away!"

He was half joking, half serious. Gwen brought her stack back, carefully setting it back by the chair she'd taken them from.

"Of course I do," she said, contrite. "Although I'm surprised to see you're this far behind," she teased.

"I save them for Lucy," he replied. "We do them together." They exchanged a glance that was so intimate Gwen had to look away.

She went back to the kitchen to pour herself and Jack glasses of wine. Rob already had his, and, as Gwen had noticed at Christmas, Lucy was still not drinking. More evidence! And potentially more excitement for the day. Gwen wasn't sure she could handle any more surprises until after dinner.

Rob, of course, was quite curious as to what Gwen had found at the cemetery, and Gwen answered his questions by showing him the picture of the headstone that she'd taken on her phone. He looked at it intently, quietly, then gave her the phone back.

"So this was your dad's sister, do you think?" he asked.

"I think it's who everyone decided would be my dad's sister," Gwen said. "But I don't think that's who she really was."

Rob nodded. "She was Aunt Elizabeth's daughter, wasn't she." It wasn't a question.

Gwen nodded. "It's kind of a long story," she said. She looked at Jack, as if to ask how much should be shared. He smiled, shrugged.

"The past is what it is," he said. "There's no changing it now."

So, over dinner, Gwen and Jack told Rob and Lucy what they'd discovered. That Aunt Elizabeth had had a daughter. Almost certainly with Jack's grandfather, Joe Flynn. That the daughter had died. That Aunt Elizabeth had never married. That Joe and Beatrice Rockford had married and had a daughter, Jane—Jack's mother. That Gwen and Jack had known none of this until Gwen arrived in Richmond to look at the collection in the library and learn more about her great aunt. And that they would probably never have put all the pieces together if Gwen hadn't purchased the little house at 24 Elm.

"In fact," Gwen said, "it was kind of the house that brought us together."

Rob looked skeptical, but he didn't argue. He wasn't a big believer in serendipity, Gwen knew. She hadn't been a big believer in serendipity either. Right up until now.

After dinner, they sat down again by the fire, finishing the wine. Looking at the pile of newspapers next to Rob's chair, Gwen, thinking it might be a parlor game all could happily play, asked if maybe they could pool their mental resources and finish up some of the puzzles.

Rob allowed as that might be a welcome closure. "A couple of the puzzles are just missing one or two clues," he said, a little sheepishly.

"In fact," he said, "here's one that has both of us stumped. 'Disney Dawn.' I think it must be related to one of those Disney princess movies, but my knowledge of Disney princesses has been pretty spotty up to now. Lucy and I might have to work on that over the next few months."

Gwen let out a little gasp of delight. "I knew it!" she said, getting up to give Rob and Lucy both hugs. "You must already know, then—a little girl?"

Rob and Lucy nodded together. And suddenly, all talk was of the baby-to-be, when she was due, how Lucy was feeling, how excited everyone was.

The princess clue was quite forgotten. Until, lying awake that night in the motel room, Gwen had a sudden thought. She poked Jack, who grumbled a little in response.

"Aurora," she whispered.

"What are you talking about?" he asked, groggily.

"Aurora," she whispered again, sitting up. "That's the answer for the Disney Dawn." She waited, expectant. Jack was infuriatingly silent.

"Aurora! AKA, Sleeping Beauty! The crossword answer made me think of it. *That* was Aunt Elizabeth's code for Lieutenant Flynn. While he was unconscious for all that time."

Jack sat up, rubbed his eyes. "Why would she have used a princess abbreviation as a nickname for an unconscious male soldier?" he asked, in the patient tone he might have used to negotiate with an unreasonable toddler.

"Because, first, it was efficient. Easy to write quickly. And second, as far as she was concerned, he was beautiful," she said, thoughtfully. "It would have been as simple as that. I doubt she thought much about the gender inconsistencies." She lay back down and snuggled against him.

"You know," she continued, "you look so much like him."

"You've told me," he said, taking her in his arms.

Later, as she was drifting off to sleep, a thought came to her. She was instantly awake, as excited as she'd been in a long time. What are you actually going to do? Rob had asked her. Well, she had the glimmer of a plan. Better than volunteering at the library, although, she realized happily, one hardly precluded the other. She whispered again. "What do you know about . . . publishing?" she asked him.

He rolled over and opened his eyes, shook himself awake. "Seriously?" he asked. "Publishing? You want to talk about tenure now? It's pretty much the middle of the night. But I mean, okay."

She kissed him. "That's not the kind of publishing I meant," she said. "I was thinking more, well, poetry. But it can wait until morning."

Silence for a beat or two. Then, she couldn't help herself. She took a breath, as if to speak again. There were plans to make! He put his fingers on her lips. "I'm sure whatever it is, it's a great idea. But it can wait until morning," he echoed her.

She lay awake for a little while, thinking. She thought he'd probably gone to sleep. So she almost missed what came out as a whisper.

"I think I love you."

She closed her eyes again and snuggled up against him. "I think I love you too," she said.

Her aunt's poems had waited this long. They could wait a few hours longer.

And so. What is a house, really? A carefully arranged, but thoroughly inanimate construction of concrete and plaster. It has no awareness. It can't have an opinion on, much less act to rectify, missed chances and mismatches. It cannot keep secrets or reveal them. It cannot do these things. Of course not.

Wishful thinking.

ACKNOWLEDGMENTS

A HUGE "thank you" to JuLee Brand, who took me seriously at the Tucson Festival of Books! This book would not have come to fruition without her!

And heartfelt thanks to all who encouraged me to keep writing–Louise, who read every draft and had so many insightful suggestions; James, who kept gently nudging me about my progress and who offered thoughtful and always kind comments; Olivia, who reassured me that Gen Z would be interested in reading the finished product; John, who helped Gwen come alive; Jennifer and Nancy, who were enthusiastic and encouraging; and Laurie, who told me it was exactly the kind of book she would read.

And the most thanks of all– to Mark. You have always been my biggest fan, and you never let me give up. Love always.

Journeying Home is Ms. Nydam's debut novel. An English major at Yale (magna cum laude with distinction), Ms. Nydam won the Yale Schoenberg Prize for writing. She continued her education at Georgetown University Law Center, where she was Managing Editor of the Law Journal, earning a J.D. (magna cum laude) and practicing law for several years. She and her husband have lived all over the United States as well as in Thailand, where their twin boys were born. She can still speak enough Thai to be quite a hit among the staff at Thai restaurants! Ms. Nydam is also a singer, with several solo albums and performances at Jazz at Lincoln Center and the Sydney Opera House to her credit. In her spare time, she loves cycling, skiing and working on her acoustic guitar skills.

emilysaxenydam.com